Praise for

GRACE INTERRUPTED

"Hyzy has another hit on her hands."

—*Lesa's Book Critiques*

"A most intriguing and engaging read."

—*Once Upon a Romance*

"Hyzy will keep you guessing until the end and never disappoints."
—AnnArbor.com

GRACE UNDER PRESSURE

"Hyzy creates the well-researched and believable estate of Marshfield Manor, part mansion and part museum . . . Well-drawn characters like busybody secretary Frances, handsome landscape architect Jack, and stalking wannabe PI Ronny are supported by lively subplots, laying series groundwork to rival Marshfield Manor's own elaborate structure." —*Publishers Weekly* (starred review)

"A strong, intelligent, and sensitive sleuth . . . Each page will bring a new surprise . . . A must-read for this summer!" —*The Romance Readers Connection*

"Julie Hyzy's fans have grown to love Ollie Paras, the White House chef. They're going to be equally impressed with Grace Wheaton, a young, competent woman taking over a job she loves. Hyzy is skilled at creating unique series characters. Readers will love Grace."

—*Chicago Sun-Times*

contin

"Exciting and delicious! Full of heart-racing thrills and mouthwatering food, this is a total sensual delight."

—Linda Palmer, author of *Kiss of Death*

"A compulsively readable whodunit full of juicy behind-the-Oval Office details, flavorful characters, and a satisfying side dish of red herrings—not to mention twenty pages of easy-to-cook recipes fit for the leader of the free world."

—*Publishers Weekly*

Praise for the novels of Julie Hyzy

"Deliciously exciting."

—Nancy Fairbanks

"A well-constructed plot, interesting characters, and plenty of Chicago lore . . . A truly pleasurable cozy."

—Annette Meyers

"[A] solid, entertaining mystery that proves her to be a promising talent with a gift for winning characters and involving plots . . . Likely to appeal to readers of traditional mysteries as well as those who enjoy stories with a slightly harder edge."

—*Chicago Sun-Times*

"The fast-paced plot builds to a spine-chilling ending."

—*Publishers Weekly*

"A nicely balanced combination of detective work and high-wire adventure."

—*Kirkus Reviews*

"Riveting . . . A twisty, absorbing, headline-current case. First rate."

—Carolyn Hart

"A well-crafted narrative, gentle tension, and a feisty, earthbound heroine mark this refreshingly different mystery debut."

—*Library Journal*

GRACE
AMONG THIEVES

JULIE HYZY

BERKLEY PRIME CRIME, NEW YORK

THE BERKLEY PUBLISHING GROUP
Published by the Penguin Group
Penguin Group (USA) Inc.
375 Hudson Street, New York, New York 10014, USA

Penguin Group (Canada), 90 Eglinton Avenue East, Suite 700, Toronto, Ontario M4P 2Y3, Canada
(a division of Pearson Penguin Canada Inc.) • Penguin Books Ltd., 80 Strand, London WC2R 0RL,
England • Penguin Group Ireland, 25 St. Stephen's Green, Dublin 2, Ireland (a division of Penguin
Books Ltd.) • Penguin Group (Australia), 250 Camberwell Road, Camberwell, Victoria 3124, Australia
(a division of Pearson Australia Group Pty. Ltd.) • Penguin Books India Pvt. Ltd., 11 Community
Centre, Panchsheel Park, New Delhi—110 017, India • Penguin Group (NZ), 67 Apollo Drive,
Rosedale, Auckland 0632, New Zealand (a division of Pearson New Zealand Ltd.) • Penguin Books
(South Africa) (Pty.) Ltd., 24 Sturdee Avenue, Rosebank, Johannesburg 2196, South Africa

Penguin Books Ltd., Registered Offices: 80 Strand, London WC2R 0RL, England

This is a work of fiction. Names, characters, places, and incidents either are the product of the author's
imagination or are used fictitiously, and any resemblance to actual persons, living or dead, business
establishments, events, or locales is entirely coincidental. The publisher does not have any control over
and does not assume any responsibility for author or third-party websites or their content.

GRACE AMONG THIEVES

A Berkley Prime Crime Book / published by arrangement with the author

PUBLISHING HISTORY
Berkley Prime Crime mass-market edition / June 2012

Copyright © 2012 by Julie Hyzy.
Cover illustration by Kimberly Schamber.
Cover design by Rita Frangie.
Interior text design by Laura K. Corless.

ISBN: 978-0-425-25139-3

BERKLEY® PRIME CRIME
Berkley Prime Crime Books are published by The Berkley Publishing Group,
a division of Penguin Group (USA) Inc.,
375 Hudson Street, New York, New York 10014.
BERKLEY® PRIME CRIME and the PRIME CRIME logo are trademarks of
Penguin Group (USA) Inc.

PRINTED IN THE UNITED STATES OF AMERICA

10 9 8 7 6 5 4 3 2 1

ALWAYS LEARNING   **PEARSON**

To the descendants of Joe Dutz,
Chicago circa 1930,
wherever you are

Acknowledgments

I so enjoy writing Grace's adventures and am grateful to readers who e-mail me about her adventures with Frances, Bennett, and Jack. I cherish every message, Tweet, and Facebook comment I receive. Thank you for welcoming the Manor House gang so enthusiastically into the world of cozy mysteries. I hope to continue Grace's stories for a long time.

Bringing Marshfield Manor to life is made possible through the efforts of my terrific editor, Emily Rapoport, and all the wonderful people at Berkley Prime Crime who provide amazing and cheerful support. Sincere thanks to my agent, Paige Wheeler, who's always on top of things and who remembers to keeps in touch with me far better than I do with her.

Speaking of keeping on top of things, a big shout-out to my publicist, Dana Kaye. Talk about enthusiasm and energy! Thanks, Dana, for all you do for Grace and Ollie. You're the best!

I have the most wonderful family in the world, and if it weren't for Curt, Robyn, Sara, and Biz, I would be nowhere at all. I love you guys, so much. Thank you for putting up with Mom's weird quirks. A very special thanks to Biz for allowing me to borrow a first name for a villain. I'll be the first to admit that my character is nowhere near as cool as hers.

Chapter I

BENNETT CALLED TO ME FROM ACROSS THE
second floor's central hall, "Gracie, we need to talk."

When I'd first started working here, Bennett saying,
"We need to talk," would throw me into a panic, but back
then his pronouncements were usually accompanied by dis-
approving scowls.

He was wearing a stern expression now, and I had a feeling I knew what had put it there. I waited next to a long line
of green velvet cordons and gripped one of its brass up-
rights as he strode across the room. I hoped I was wrong.

Bennett Marshfield, the septuagenarian owner of pala-
tial Marshfield Manor, was one of very few I allowed to call
me Gracie. I'd become extraordinarily fond of him and he
of me in the months I'd worked here. Although Bennett and
I had suffered a rocky start, he now treated me less like
hired help and more like a favorite niece. Fit and healthy as
a man twenty years younger, he narrowed his eyes as he
joined me. "Where are you off to?"

"Corbin Shaw is waiting for me in the banquet hall," I

said. "Would you like to come along?" I gestured toward the first floor, although Bennett clearly didn't need to be reminded where his banquet hall was. Born and raised in this grand home, he knew its secrets better than anyone.

Tucked into the North Carolina mountains, Marshfield Manor served as a major tourist attraction. It was, in fact, the crowning jewel of tiny Emberstowne. As curator and manager of the estate, I was living my dream. Despite a few bumps along the way, I woke up every morning delighted and awed to be part of Marshfield's magnificent history.

"I most certainly do," he said. "There were camera crews in the back staircase last week. Do I need to remind Corbin that my rooms are off-limits? Didn't you make that clear?"

"I did, absolutely," I said. "Your suite will not be filmed. Nor will any of our administrative offices or security stations. I allowed them access to a couple of staircases to make it easier to keep their equipment out of sight."

Bennett grimaced, clearly unconvinced, so I continued to assure him. "Corbin may be the director but we're paying the bills. I've explained the rules. Of course, if you want to make certain he understands—"

"I trust you. I would, however, like to impress upon him personally how much leeway we've granted."

I had a feeling Corbin knew exactly how much of a coup this gig was, but Bennett's presence never hurt. With his shining white hair, ramrod straight stature, and piercing blue eyes, the owner of the estate cut an imposing figure.

"Then let's go talk to him," I said, ever hopeful to avoid the touchy subject I guessed was on Bennett's mind.

He made a sharp left. "Let's go this way." Pointing to an alcove behind another set of velvet ropes, he added, "Short-cut."

Unlocking the rope's brass claw, he allowed me to pass and then secured it behind us. This late in the day meant fewer tourists on the premises and we managed to sneak through without being seen. Cutting through restricted areas in front of guests risked encouraging bold souls to follow suit simply to see what might happen. Too often, nothing did. Despite our chief's best efforts, security was lacking at Marshfield Manor.

Bennett led me through a dark interior passage that opened to the banquet hall's dazzling upper gallery. This stone walkway—about six feet wide—lined the room's perimeter one level up from the expansive dining room floor. The walkway itself was off-limits to guests, but those below who chanced a glance upward were rewarded with a colorful collection of oversized portraits and antique tapestries. Soaring gothic windows framed the masterpieces, their bright illumination casting an ethereal glow into the mosaic ceiling above.

Walking past one of my favorite tapestries—a vivid French-crafted piece depicting neither religious figures nor classic hunting scenes, but rather a family frolicking in a colorful garden—Bennett turned to me. "This is one of the best spots in the house," he said. A moment later he sighed. "I wish . . ."

He didn't finish and I didn't have to ask. As much as Bennett took pleasure in sharing his home with the hundreds of thousands of guests who visited each year, I knew he longed for more. Above all else, Bennett wanted family. He yearned for evenings of conversation and laughter, for discussions of ideas, but what he settled for was providing a lovely destination for strangers who tramped through daily, marveling at his considerable wealth.

Years ago, after two marriages and no children of his own, Bennett had taken stock of his life and, ultimately, decided to bequeath his entire estate to the City of Emberstowne as a permanent tourist attraction. Although the actual transfer wouldn't take place until Bennett's death, he refused to leave future strategies to the town's well-meaning bureaucrats. He set out to make his vision a reality during his lifetime by establishing Marshfield's pattern for success while he still retained control.

By all accounts he'd succeeded fabulously, and for years the mansion's popularity grew. Recently, however, due to changes in the world at large and also to a level of stagnation here at the estate, tourism had fallen off slightly. Bennett came to realize he needed help to update his vision to twenty-first-century standards.

In every other respect a shrewd businessman, Bennett had been late to the technology party. As he became aware of how quickly things threatened to spiral downward if he didn't make an effort to keep up, he sought help. Under his direction, I was brought in, as was our head of security, Terrence Carr. Daily tours of Marshfield Manor had become a staple of Emberstowne, and now, under our management, protections were being put into place. It was a slow process, but we were finally making headway.

Terrence and I answered to Bennett and he answered to no one but himself. We all benefited from the fact that businesses in Emberstowne bent over backward to keep its wealthiest citizen happy. After all, Bennett reserved the right to change his will at any time.

One of the most popular stops on the mansion's tours was this banquet hall. Nearly two-thirds the size of a football field, this majestic room featured nearly identical walk-in fireplaces facing one another like linebackers in opposing end zones. As Bennett and I strolled along the high walkway, I glanced up at the mosaic ceiling. Hundreds of white flowers burst forth from a cerulean background, framed in shining twenty-two-carat gold tile. Soaring three stories above the main level—one floor above where we walked right now—this mosaic always took my breath away, especially this close. I reached upward, longing to touch, but even from here it was too far above me.

Bennett made a noise of disgust, bringing me back to earth. I followed his angry gaze. Below us, in the far corner of the banquet room, Corbin Shaw stood with his fingers laced across the top of his head, oblivious to our presence. Undoubtedly planning the next morning's shoot, he rotated in place, surveying the glorious surroundings, his concentration evident by his intense squint and pursed lips. The director's presence wasn't causing Bennett's reaction.

Hillary Singletary's was.

Bennett's stepdaughter had sauntered into the room to stand behind Corbin. Unaware of us watching from above, she finger-combed her blonde bob and smoothed her tight skirt before stepping forward to tap Corbin on the shoulder.

He turned. We couldn't see his expression, but his hands came down from his head and he took a quick step backward—the kind of reaction you'd expect from an individual encountering a rabid dog. Hillary's movements were more feline; I could almost hear her purr as her words carried upward, "Corbin, how delightful to see you again."

"Right there is what I wanted to talk about," Bennett said, keeping his voice low.

"The filming?" I feigned misunderstanding, still working hard to avoid any discussion of Hillary. "You know we're right on schedule. Corbin believes he can have the first shipment of DVDs to us within three months." I spoke quickly, eager to keep Bennett engaged. This DVD project was my baby. We'd contracted to have Marshfield Manor digitally immortalized; not just for posterity's sake, but to produce the DVDs en masse to sell in our gift shop for happy visitors to take home and remember their trip.

The souvenirs we currently offered were pathetic. Our tiny gift shop had been an afterthought by my predecessor, carved into a small corner of the mansion only after guests began demanding keepsake items for purchase. Featuring a few high-quality pieces made by Emberstowne artisans and a small assortment of mugs and key chains, the store cried out to be relocated into a bigger space and stocked with more enticing goodies. That was another of my many plans for the future. One step at a time.

"Not the filming," Bennett said, crashing my hopes to avoid the subject. "Hillary."

I glanced down again. Bennett's forty-six-year-old step-daughter, whose sole ambition seemed to be to convince the world she hadn't yet seen thirty-five, smiled as she eased closer to Corbin. With a lovely, if tightly preserved face, and a petite, well-maintained figure, Hillary was—on paper, at least—a catch. That is, until she opened her mouth and her personality spewed forth.

Even from our vantage point I could spot the glint in her eyes and the flirtatious pitch of her hip. "Is that why she's back?" I asked quietly. "She intends to be part of the DVD, doesn't she? I haven't had a chance to talk with her since she arrived." Truth was, I'd gone out of my way to avoid talking with the woman.

I'd heard, from my nosy assistant, Frances, that Bennett's stepdaughter had returned because she'd been dumped yet again, and I wasn't in the mood for another one of Hillary's "woe is me" sagas. Although I'd had my own share of romantic disappointments in recent years, I wasn't interested in a pity party. It wouldn't do either of us any good.

Time and again, suitors fawned over her, eager to pamper, eager to please. Then, when they discovered that she wasn't heir to the Marshfield billions it was *hasta la vista*, baby. Rather than count her blessings for being rid of leeches, Hillary harped at Bennett, urging him to change his will and leave Marshfield to her.

Why she would want a husband who only loved her for her money was beyond me.

Below us, she laughed delicately and found reason to touch Corbin on his hand, his arm, his shoulder. Best of all, she didn't notice us watching her little performance.

She took a predatory step closer and Corbin again

stepped back. He swung a pained, guilty look all around, as though expecting a surveillance camera to capture this little tableau.

Instead he found us. Was that relief on his face? Or panic?

Bennett waved. Corbin blushed, raising a hand in return greeting. Spotting us watching, Hillary's animated expression fell flat.

"I suppose we should get down there," I said.

Bennett gave a snort. "Let her squirm. She's embarrassed now, and she should be. She's getting too old for such silliness. I should have clamped down harder on her when she was younger . . ."

He let the thought hang, but I knew what he was thinking. He'd often lamented the fact that his second wife had shunted him aside when it came to parenting. I knew he regretted not being a stronger influence on Hillary's life.

"All I am to her now is a bank account," he said.

"She respects you. In fact, I think she's a little afraid of you, too."

He gave a sad smile. "That's something, I suppose." He rested his arms on the gallery railing—an elegantly carved waist-high wall of stone—and folded his hands. Extending his two index fingers in Hillary's direction, he said, "I want to thank you for your discretion, but I also want you to know that I'm fully aware."

I leaned on the railing next to him, the walkie-talkie in my skirt pocket making a muffled thump against the low wall. "You lost me. Aware of what?"

"Don't play dumb." His gaze swept the room, neatly avoiding eye contact. "You know I'm talking about the recent thefts."

"Ah," I said. Several items of great value had gone missing: a jewel-encrusted brush, mirror, and comb set from Bennett's mother's former dressing room; two signed first-edition books from the main library; and a small gold picture frame. What bothered me most was that the frame had held a photo of Bennett as a toddler. That was the real crime. A piece of Bennett's history was gone. Probably forever.

He went on, "I'm painfully aware that our losses began shortly after Hillary came to visit. And yet you haven't mentioned your suspicions."

"I never—"

"You never said anything," he finished. "But you thought it." He glanced at me sideways, eyebrow raised. "Didn't you?"

My turn to squirm.

"Stop trying to come up with a politically correct response, Gracie."

I smiled. "You know me too well."

"Hillary's financial troubles are getting worse," he went on, "and it would be just like her to 'borrow' an item or two and think nothing of it."

I'd been afraid of that, but I couldn't help trying to put a Pollyanna spin on this difficult situation. "Corbin and his crew have been here as long as Hillary has. They started filming the interior shots the same day she arrived."

"There's one major difference." I knew what it was, but I let him continue. "Terrence has had security accompanying the film crew every step of the way." His voice rose as he threw his hand outward. "As opposed to Hillary, who has the run of the place."

She must have heard her name because her attention snapped back up to us, her eyes narrowing. I waved again, in a "We'll be there in a moment" gesture.

After the most recent item went missing, Terrence and I had decided to limit filming to non-visitor hours. Corbin hadn't been thrilled, but we hadn't suffered any losses under the new schedule. I hesitated to mention this because Hillary had been a constant presence throughout the process. When the timing shifted to six in the morning, Hillary stopped hanging around the film crew. And the thefts had ceased.

I waited, but Bennett didn't seem at all ready to leave his perch.

I studied his profile. "What else is bothering you?"

The lines in his face tightened. "It's not only the stealing," he said. "Yes, I'm upset about that, and yes, I want it stopped. But the truth is, I can afford these losses. What I can't abide is the fact that she can do this to me. When she wants money, she calls me Daddy, and when my back is turned, she steals."

"You're assuming she's guilty."

He didn't turn. "Who else could it be?"

"I'll do my best to find out." Patting his arm, I straightened. "Let's get down there."

He still didn't budge. "There's something else I wanted to talk about."

Uh-oh. I returned to leaning on the railing. "About Hillary?"

Bennett inhaled deeply through his nose. "About Jack."

My stomach dropped and I felt my face flush. "Our landscape architect?"

Again Bennett shot me a sideways glance. "No need to be coy with me. He's far more to you than simply a consultant." He shifted to look me straight in the eye. "At least he *was.* He hasn't been around much lately. In fact, Davey tells me that Jack—"

"Speaking of Davey, how is he working out?"

"Bringing him on was a good decision," Bennett said, graciously allowing the change of subject. "Most of my other assistants are getting up there in years. They don't have the energy to get things done the way Davey does." Warming to the topic, his face relaxed. "In some ways, he's become my own personal concierge. Good for me because then I'm not overtaxing my aging butlers. Good for him because the job changes by the minute. He's actually very adept at organization."

"Your other assistants don't resent him?"

"On the contrary, they're relieved. They prefer keeping to what they know: serving meals, tidying rooms, and ensuring my clothing is clean and pressed. They don't like to surf the Internet, investigate e-readers, or set up a new DVR." Bennett gave a low chuckle. "And up until a few weeks ago, I didn't know what half of those contraptions were. Thanks to Davey, I not only understand them, I enjoy them. Davey is a godsend," he said. "But we were talking about Jack."

"No," I said gently, "*you* were talking about Jack."

"Ah. Is that your polite way of telling the old man to keep his nose out of your business?" He asked it with a smile but I could tell I'd hurt his feelings.

"Not at all." The last thing I wanted to do was wound Bennett. "Truth is, there's nothing to tell. I mean, you're right. I did think that we . . . I mean, I originally believed that . . ." I struggled to put into words what I'd thought— what I'd been so sure of. How differently things seemed to be working out.

I tried again. "Jack has practically disappeared from my life since . . ." I shook my head. "I mean, he stops in at my office now and then, but . . ." Words failed me. "I can't blame him," I finally blurted. "I had a lot to do with hurting his family."

"The hurt was there. It was not your fault." This time Bennett patted my arm. "Because of you they can finally face the truth and begin to heal. Give Jack time."

I forced a laugh to lighten the mood. "Well that's easy enough to do. It's not like I have men lining up to ask me out."

"That's because you spend all your time here. You need a vacation."

I smiled. "I haven't been employed here long enough."

"Well then, maybe you should take a working trip. I'm overdue for an excursion myself. There are always treasures to be uncovered in distant lands, right?" He straightened.

"That's it! An ideal solution. When this filming is over and Corbin packs up, let's talk about a trip overseas."

"You and I? Together?"

"As long as you wouldn't be embarrassed to be seen in the company of an old man."

"Old man? Who else are you intending to invite along?"

He smirked at my flattery but seemed energized by the idea. "Wonderful. We'll make plans. I think it's what we both need. There's been far too much trouble around here lately. And *you* need to meet an eligible bachelor or two."

"You just advised me to give Jack time."

He shrugged. "Nothing wrong with a little competition. Makes the win even sweeter."

"I don't know, Bennett—"

He held a finger to his lips, letting me know the subject was closed for now. "Let's go down," he said, "before Hillary steals anything else."

Chapter 2

"CORBIN!" BENNETT'S VOICE BOOMED AND echoed in the cavernous space as we made our way to the far side of the banquet hall. "How is the project going?"

"Right on schedule." Corbin raised both fists in the air, and grinned widely. "Couldn't be better."

I liked Corbin, but it had taken me a while to get used to that wacky smile of his. I'd come to realize that despite the fact that all his front teeth showed at once—stretching his face far more tightly than it was meant to—his expression of glee wasn't as forced as it first appeared. A personal quirk. Part of his charm.

And charming he was. A bundle of energy, the sixty-three-year-old director sported gray hair, which fell to his collar, and a small diamond stud in one ear.

Bennett wore a deadpan expression. "I see you've met my stepdaughter."

"Oh, Daddy." Hillary sidled up to grip his arm. "Corbin and I are good friends. You know that. I told you how excited I am to be working with him. And since he's been here we've gotten to know each other *very* well."

Corbin raised a hand, as though to correct her, then changed his mind and ran it through his hair. "Really, Ms. Singletary, we've only talked a few times . . ."

Still holding Bennett's arm with one hand, she raised the index finger of the other and wagged it at Corbin. "Silly boy. You know to call me Hillary."

She waited for acknowledgment, but he kept mum.

Thrown off by this, Hillary's coquettish demeanor disintegrated. An over-the-hill girly performance like the one she'd attempted required an audience. Without one, Hillary resembled an awkward teen trying to fit in. Not quite the youthful glow she was going for. In an obvious attempt to regain control, she widened her perfect smile and pulled Bennett closer, still addressing Corbin. "You need to understand that Papa Bennett can be forgetful sometimes. It's a good thing I'm here to remind him." She used both hands to squeeze Bennett's arm. "Isn't it, Daddy?"

"I don't forget nearly as much as you wish I would." Bennett extricated himself from her grasp and stepped closer to Corbin. Towering over the director, he arched an eyebrow. "You are respecting boundaries here at Marshfield." It wasn't a question. And from the rumbling timbre of Bennett's voice, it was clear he wasn't referring only to his rooms.

"Of course," Corbin stammered.

I felt sorry for the man. Seeking to break the tension, I cleared my throat. "What's next?" I asked. "That is, what's on the agenda for tomorrow?"

Gratitude washed across his face. "As I was just about to tell Ms. Singletary . . ." I noted how he inched away even farther from her. Chalk one up for Corbin. "Our next segment will feature the antiques we identified for inclusion in the DVD. Thank you, Ms. Wheaton, for the historical material you provided. We'll be focusing on these, recording voiceover performances of your write-ups. And if there's time, we'll get started on our final segment of filming: the main rooms and your personal message, Mr. Marshfield."

"I'd like to come tomorrow," I said.

Hillary looked aghast. "To do what?"

This was the part I'd been looking most forward to. I wanted to hear how all the information I'd provided would sound when brought to life by professional actors. "I'm particularly interested in seeing how the history is handled." To Corbin, I said, "It may be helpful for me to be here in case there are any questions. That is, if you don't mind."

"Mind? That's wonderful. Having you available to share your expertise will be of invaluable service. Thank you."

Hillary frowned. To Corbin, she said, "You know, I've done modeling work in the past. I'd be a great spokesperson. I'd be happy to help."

"Ah . . ." Corbin bit his lower lip. "We hired talent to do voiceovers. Male."

Hillary wasn't about to let a chance at stardom slip through her fingers. "Don't you think it would be so much warmer, so much more inviting, to have an actual family member hosting the program?"

"Unfortunately, we already have an actor to narrate. He's done much of the overview and we're more than halfway through the project." Corbin's gaze shifted from me to Bennett and back to me again, clearly looking for support. "Remember the plan I presented? The contract you signed? Switching gears now, this far into filming, would be a nightmare."

Corbin's pain was evident. As was Bennett's amusement. He must have taken pity on the director, however, because he ended the man's misery with a swift proclamation. "You will continue as planned. No changes at this late stage."

"But, Daddy—"

"Let the man mind his job. And you mind yours." Bennett affected a thoughtful look, tapping fingers to his fore-head. "Ah, that forgetfulness you mentioned earlier. Remind me, Hillary, what exactly is it you do for a living?"

She bit the insides of her cheeks, deepening her mario-nette lines. All of a sudden she looked every inch her real age. "I'm going through a difficult time right now. A little sympathy would be nice." She flung a hand out toward Corbin. "Not to mention a chance to help promote our beautiful home. I'm just trying to help."

Bennett was spared having to reply by the unmistakable sound of a crowd approaching: late-day visitors, probably a tour group. Amid shuffling and murmured conversation, I heard a considerate but commanding voice urging people to keep moving.

Corbin excused himself. "Much to do before we return." To me, he said, "See you tomorrow." As he departed I real-ized I'd forgotten to ask about accommodations for his crew. I knew there had been a mix-up. I'd have to remember to ask him about it next time I saw him.

At that moment about forty tourists, ranging in age from twenty to seventy-five, came around the corner a moment later. They shuffled forward, their attention rapt on their guide, John Kitts. I'd met John a couple of times. Nice man. Tall, late fifties, with gray hair turning white at the crown, he had a ruddy complexion and a warm smile.

Employed by a big-name travel company, John led weeklong tours of the mid-Atlantic region, most of which involved a day trip here to Marshfield. Articulate, efficient, and kind, he was good-looking in an older man sort of way.

I knew John liked to bring his new group in for a sneak peek on the afternoon before the official visit, and I stepped aside as he walked backward toward us, describing the ban-quet room and talking a little bit about Marshfield's annual Christmas display which, he promised, would be worth a future trip.

"The last time children celebrated Christmas here at Marshfield Manor was when the current owner, Bennett Marshfield, was a boy." At that he glanced back, smiling when he saw me. I watched surprise come over his features when he spotted Bennett next to me.

He raised an eyebrow in question. I nudged Bennett and quietly asked, "Is it okay if he points you out?"

Bennett gave a resigned shrug. I turned back to John and nodded.

"This is our lucky day," he said with a sweeping gesture. "May I present the owner of Marshfield Manor, Bennett Marshfield."

"Good afternoon," Bennett said to the crowd. As much as he preferred anonymity among strangers, he seemed to brighten as the small crowd reacted with awe.

Amid their murmured acknowledgments, John went on, "And, next to him, the woman who keeps the mansion running smoothly, Grace Wheaton. Under her guidance, the Marshfield experience has been getting better every day."

I blushed, but didn't have time to respond. Hillary edged past me and addressed John, even as she kept her eyes on the audience, slipping into performance mode as easily as she might don a neck scarf. "I hate to correct you in front of all these nice people, but you are mistaken on one count at least. I was a child here for many Christmases. Not all that long ago."

Not that long ago? I waited for Hillary's nose to sprout like Pinocchio's, but it remained pert and cute and small.

John coughed. "Of course. Everyone, allow me to present Hillary Singletary, Mr. Marshfield's niece."

"Daughter," Hillary said.

"Stepdaughter," Bennett corrected.

"My mistake." John handled the moment with a hint of a smile and I wondered if he'd intentionally misidentified her. "As I mentioned earlier, Mr. Marshfield has generously opened his doors to the public to share his treasures with all of us. While I possess extensive knowledge of the manor's history, no one is better versed in it than Mr. Marshfield here." He smiled encouragingly at Bennett. "Would you be so kind as to regale us with a story about the banquets your father hosted back in the day?"

Bennett glanced over to me. I gave a "Why not?" shrug.

"If you insist, I'll share one of my particular favorites." He cleared his throat and began. "When I was twelve, my father invited Judy Garland to stay with us for a few days." He waited for the crowds' collective "oohs" to die down before continuing. "This was the year before my aunt Charlotte died. She'd been an enormous fan of *The Wizard of Oz* . . ."

I'd heard many Marshfield family stories, including this one. Overwhelmed with excitement about Judy Garland's upcoming visit, Charlotte had hired a well-known pianist and invited fifty of her closest friends and their children to attend. The plan was to coax Judy into entertaining the guests with a medley of show tunes. At the very last minute, the famous woman's assistant called to cancel the visit. Judy's little daughter had apparently come down with a bug, one that she'd most generously shared with her mom. Judy developed a bad case of laryngitis. She sent her sincere regrets.

Charlotte didn't cancel. Instead, she convinced the pianist to accompany guests as they stood up and sang for the crowd. One ten-year-old girl, Sally, utterly unable to carry a tune, belted out a thoroughly unpleasant rendition of "Over the Rainbow." Her joy and exuberance, however, were contagious and she finished to thunderous applause.

That wasn't all she'd won. At the tender age of twelve, Bennett fell in love. The two youngsters became inseparable. As soon as she turned eighteen, he married her.

Bennett embellished, keeping our guests enthralled, but I tuned him out. Not because I didn't enjoy hearing him tell the tale, but because I'd noticed that someone else had tuned him out, too. The disinterested guest was a tiny woman with white-blonde shoulder-length hair. She had turned her back to the group and was inching ever farther away. A moment later, she disappeared behind the crowd. I casually circled around, intent on keeping her in sight.

Another tourist noticed me watching her. Standing toward the back of the small gathering, he was at least six feet tall, with dark hair in what my mom used to call the perfect haircut for a man: short and parted on the side, with neatly trimmed sideburns. He gave me a quizzical, though not unfriendly glance. I read it as him asking if I needed help. I raised a hand in thanks, holding him off, and he returned his attention to Bennett's talk.

The petite woman had snaked her way back along the tour route. Behind the banquet hall was the Music Room, a round, high-ceilinged space that jutted out to the north from the main structure. Designed for maximum acoustical pleasure, I wondered how much better young Sally's song might have sounded had she performed in here. Of course, that might have made it worse.

In either case, I had a feeling I knew where my quarry was headed. Our docents fielded many questions every day. One of them was, "Where does that door lead?" always accompanied by a curious finger point.

Just inside the Music Room's entrance, a door had been built into its wall, matching so perfectly as to render it almost undetectable, save for the narrow gap that defined its perimeter and a small lever mechanism that released it to swing open. Maps we handed out at the start of each tour made no mention of the small area built between this room and the banquet hall. There wasn't much in there of value, but rules were rules.

I turned the corner in time to catch the woman slipping past the velvet ropes, headed directly for that door. John's was the last tour that had been allowed in and docents assigned to this area had apparently taken off once the group had ambled past. This meant that there was no one around to catch her in the act. Except me.

She didn't look from side to side, didn't pause. Without missing a beat, she pinpointed the lever mechanism and pulled at the door.

I called out, "What are you doing?"

With a yelp, she turned. I expected her to blush and apologize. Mostly, I expected her to retreat. She didn't. Instead she yanked the door wide and stepped through.

Chapter 3

I SHOUTED TO HER, "STOP!"

Catching someone overstepping was one thing. This woman's outright disregard for boundaries and of authority—mine—was altogether different. I started after her, dragging my walkie-talkie up as I ducked around the nearest cordon's brass post. I called for security. "Music Room," I said into the device. "We've got a jumper."

Anyone who stepped off the prescribed path of the tour was termed a "line-jumper," or "jumper" for short. Although we mostly dealt with curious children, adults occasionally needed to be herded, too, and they were always worse. Kids lost awareness of boundaries when they stepped out of line. Adult jumpers, on the other hand, believed the rules didn't apply to them.

The dispatcher acknowledged my request and I shoved the device back into my pocket.

What if? My pulse quickened at the thought. *What if this is one of our thieves?*

"Hey, you, stop," I shouted again.

The woman disappeared from sight. Windowless, the tiny area was dark, and I heard her stumble. I hit the light switch and caught her scrambling to stand up. She turned to face me, eyes panicked and wide, darting back and forth as though looking for escape. But the only way out was through me. About five feet wide by ten feet deep, with a low ceiling that made me duck, it was more accurately termed a closet than a room. Warren Marshfield, Sr., had it installed as a convenient hiding place for his family's Christmas gifts when the house was built. With the tree and celebrations taking place in the adjacent banquet hall, it was the perfect alcove for his happy stash. As his children grew, however, the room wasn't needed, and these days it remained empty and quiet.

"You can't get away," I said. "I've called security."

"Why did you do that?"

Her question was neither arrogant nor confrontational. From the look on her face and the plaintive tone of her voice, I got the impression she truly couldn't fathom why I'd felt the need to call for help.

"You're trespassing," I said. "Or hadn't you noticed?"

She perched a fist on her hip. I couldn't tell if her reddening cheeks indicated embarrassment or anger, but she struggled visibly to compose her features. A few years younger than me, she was youthful enough to affect that "Yeah, so?" attitude teenagers often strike when confronted with an uncomfortable situation. For being in her mid- to late twenties, she wore a stylistically odd combination: elasticized hot-pink sweatpants over scuffed white gym shoes. On top, she wore a lace vanilla blouse with plunging neckline and gold hoop earrings the size and shape of pears.

Streetwalker top, mall-walker bottom, I thought.

"Please don't get me into trouble. I didn't mean any harm. I was just curious. And I have . . . a problem."

"I've noticed."

"Not like that. When I get something into my head I have to do it."

"That's not much of an excuse."

"No, you don't understand. If an idea pops into my head, like 'Touch the railing with your right hand,' I have to do it. Or like 'Start up the stairs with your left foot.' Stuff like that."

"And if you don't do the thing that pops into your head? Then what happens?"

She wrinkled her nose. "Something bad, probably."

"But it never has?"

"I don't know. I never *don't* do it."

"Sounds like OCD." When she didn't agree, I added, "Obsessive-compulsive disorder."

She shrugged. "I guess."

I heard the comforting sounds of people running. Several people.

"Come on," I said, wiggling my fingers. "Let's go."

She gave a last look around, then touched two walls with two fingers each, making sure they hit at the same moment. "Okay. I really didn't mean any harm. I had to see what was in here. And, like now, I had to touch it."

"Or something bad would happen?"

She gave an uncomfortable laugh. "Sounds ridiculous when you say it. But it's real to me."

I waved my hand to shoo her out the door in front of me. My plan was to keep an eye on her for as long as I needed to, but five uniformed guards surrounded us, relieving me of the duty the moment we emerged from the room.

Our chief of security, Terrence Carr, stepped forward. Muscular and handsome, he could easily be the old Old Spice Guy's doppelgänger. "What's the problem?"

"Everything's under control," I said. "But I believe we need to escort this guest off the property."

"No," she cried, grabbing my arm. "Don't do that. Please don't kick me out. I didn't do anything. I didn't even touch anything. Except for the walls, I mean."

I eased out of her grasp. "This woman left her group and snuck into one of our off-limits areas."

Terrence stepped forward. "Let's see some ID."

"You won't kick me out, right?" she asked even as she dug into her purse. "I'm part of a group. They've got to be wondering where I am."

"Maybe you should have stayed with them," he said.

She kept her mouth shut and presented her driver's license.

Terrence squinted at the laminated card. "Your name rhymes," he said. "Lenore Honore."

A flash of anger. "It's pronounced ON-or-ay. Lenore ON-or-ay."

Terrence nodded acknowledgment. "Well, Ms. ON-or-ay, looks like you've overstayed your welcome."

From behind me, a booming voice. "Lenore!"

We all turned. John Kitts stood with his arms akimbo. "What are you doing now?" To me, he asked, "What happened? Why is security here?"

His tour group clustered around him, their faces bright with interest. I noted that Bennett and Hillary weren't among the curious onlookers and decided they must have given up on my return. A sixtyish woman who looked as though she'd spent fifty-nine of those years in the sun, wagged a finger at Lenore. "Listen, missy, I told you to watch yourself. You've been a thorn in my side all day." To John, "I told you she'd be trouble. But you didn't listen."

Terrence must have experienced the immediate claustrophobia I had the moment the throng surrounded us because he held his arms out, pressing them to back up. "Everything is under control," he said. "Let's not get excited."

"Don't use that tone with me, young man," the woman said. "I have a right to be angry."

Terrence didn't respond. Still holding tight to Lenore's ID, he murmured to his guards to keep an eye on the situation, then stepped a few feet away and pulled up his cell phone. I knew what he was doing: a quick call to the Emberstowne Police Department to find out if little Lenore had a record. We'd suffered too many losses over the past few days to let any transgression slide.

While Terrence was busy, John questioned Lenore, asking why she hadn't stayed with the group. His tone was measured, even calm, but the tendons in his neck stood out in sharp relief.

I scanned the group, seeking out the handsome man who'd caught my eye earlier. He was near the back, looking skeptical. Like a person who wanted to know more before he cast the first stone. When he noticed me watching him, he held up a hand in greeting and gave a rueful smile. I wondered if he and Lenore were traveling together. He was a bit older than she was but that didn't necessarily mean anything. Of course, if they were together, why wasn't he stepping up to defend her?

John continued his mild rant at Lenore while doing his best to prevent others in the group from drawing and quartering their wayward companion. Lenore was oblivious to their wrath, growing more confused by the moment.

The sixty-something woman who'd complained earlier took a menacing step toward John and pointed to the girl. "Because of her, we're going to be late for the show, aren't we? They aren't going to hold the curtain for us, are they?"

John tried to speak but she jumped right back in.

"We paid to see this show. It's one of the things I was especially looking forward to and we should get to see the whole thing, not have to wait for intermission to be seated. So what are you going to do about it? We're supposed to be back at the bus"—she tapped at her watch, a giant black-banded monstrosity with a face the size of silver dollar— "five minutes from now. We'll never make it."

"Marlene, let me . . ." he began.

"Does it look like this is going to be settled in five minutes? You told us we would only have a half hour to change and be back out the door. Why did you squeeze in this extra visit this afternoon, John? We're coming back tomorrow.

That is, if Lenore hasn't ruined it for all of us. Maybe they don't want us back now. Do you?" This last part was addressed to me, but I let John handle her.

He did his best to manage the group's uncertainties. "We may have a little more leeway than I admitted. Let me handle it. Why don't you all start back for the bus now, and I'll join you shortly."

"With or without her?" Marlene asked.

"Let me worry about that. Head back now. All of you. Do you remember where the bus is parked?"

"Of course we do," Marlene snapped. "We're not children."

She stormed out. The rest of the group followed. A few cast sympathetic glances at Lenore as they tramped after their outspoken comrade.

As soon as they were out of earshot, Lenore asked, "Can I sit down?"

The guards exchanged a look. "Yeah, sure," one said. He spoke into his microphone, letting Terrence know we were changing locations, before escorting Lenore to the front vestibule, where we maintained benches for visitors' use.

I sidled up to John. "That was one unhappy lady."

"Lenore?"

"No," I said, surprised. "The ranting woman."

"Oh, she's okay," he said softly. "I had her on another trip. Really sweet person, assuming you don't step out of line."

"Like Lenore did?"

He rolled his eyes. "I understand Marlene's frustration. We've been touring Emberstowne all day. We had a tasting at your friends' wine shop by the way. Excellent, as always. We also watched a glass-blowing exhibit, and made about five additional stops. Lenore has been late getting back to the bus every single time."

"Ouch."

"These people want their money's worth. They want to

have all the experiences promised in the colorful and exciting brochure they received when they signed up. You get a problem child like Lenore in the group and it throws everything off. Marlene's just blowing steam. By the time she gets to the bus, she'll settle. She knows I won't let the group down."

"What about getting to the theater on time?"

He smiled. "I have a little pull with the management. Plus, I always build in more time than needed. A tour guide's dirty little trick."

"Good for you."

"I'll be glad when I can drop Lenore off at her final destination."

"When is that?"

"Seven more days. Long days. This past one has been tough. Lenore is clearly the most challenging guest I've encountered in twenty-four years of giving tours."

"That's saying something."

He glanced at his watch. "The sooner we wrap this up, the better. Where did your security chief go?"

Just as he said that, Terrence returned. John and I joined the group of guards surrounding Lenore; I couldn't help but notice that the look on Terrence's face was more sad than stern. He handed Lenore her driver's license. "Okay, Ms. Honore, you're free to go."

She clutched the ID to her chest. "Really? Oh, thank you. I knew you were a nice person."

"Nice has nothing to do with it."

John heaved a huge sigh of relief, then addressed Terrence. "We're scheduled to come back here for the full tour tomorrow. Is that going to be a problem?"

Terrence considered it. "I'm not inclined to allow Ms. Honore back inside Marshfield."

Lenore's mouth dropped open. Her expression slid from happiness to gloom in the time it took me to blink.

"That is," Terrence continued, "unless she promises not to step out of line again."

She lit up. "I do. I promise."

"And no touching."

"No touching," she said.

"I mean it." Terrence pulled out a set of handcuffs. "You see these? You touch anything at all and we'll wrap them around your wrists and haul you out."

"Yes, sir," she said, nodding vigorously.

I hoped for her sake that nothing would "pop into her head" tomorrow that she'd feel compelled to do.

To John, Terrence said, "You may want to consider making it a rule that no one walks away from the group alone. Institute the buddy system or something. Do whatever works for you as long as you make sure she's never out of the group's sight."

After a couple more reminders, John led Lenore away. Terrence and I walked them to the front door, where a shuttle waited to take them to the parking lot.

"You let her off easy," I said the minute they were gone.

"Rodriguez vouched for her."

I could barely contain my surprise. Rodriguez was one of the town's two detectives. Middle-aged and more eager for retirement than to make his mark on the world, his patience been stretched thin by two recent murders here at Marshfield. I liked the man and appreciated his style far more than that of his younger partner, the edgy, hyper-suspicious Flynn. Rodriguez giving Lenore a pass was good enough for me, but I had to ask, "She doesn't have a record, I take it?"

"Not a criminal one, at least. But before I could even spell her name, Rodriguez knew who I was talking about."

"I don't understand."

"Seems our Ms. On-or-ay"—he strung out the pronunciation—"arrived in Emberstowne a couple of nights ago and got lost walking back to the hotel where she was staying."

"Pretty hard to get lost in Emberstowne."

"Tell me about it. Anyway, she ran into your good friend Ronny Tooney, who made sure she was safe."

"And this involves Rodriguez how?"

Terrence rubbed his eyes. "People are weird."

I waited.

Fingers still massaging his eyebrows, he sighed. "You know Tooney is about as welcome at the P.D. as rats are in a restaurant, right? Well, it seems that the lovely lady in question managed to get drunk out of her skull. In her impaired state, she couldn't find her way back to her hotel and wandered around Emberstowne until Tooney noticed her. He couldn't be sure she had her hotel name right, so he took her to the police and let them deal with her."

"Seriously?"

"The guy may be a pest, but he's not stupid. You ask me, he was afraid the girl might turn around and blame him for some indecency. The man was covering his . . ."

"Tracks?"

"Yeah," he said with a grin. "Exactly the word I was about to use. Anyway, while she slept it off at the station, Rodriguez ran her name. She may have over-imbibed, but her record is as clean as my momma's kitchen floor on Sunday."

I laughed.

He continued, "When Lenore woke up the next morning, it was like she hadn't been drunk at all. No hangover. She ate everything the cops put in front of her. And she talked. A lot. They couldn't get her back to her hotel fast enough. Rodriguez says he feels sorry for the lady. He even went as far to declare that if she's a criminal, he'll hire Ronny Tooney as his personal assistant."

"Whoa."

"Which is why I let her go. But I'm holding John responsible for her. He knows that."

"He's got his hands full."

Terrence grinned again. "You couldn't pay me to take on that man's job."

Chapter 4

WHEN I MADE IT BACK TO MY OFFICE, FRANCES was waiting for me. Wearing a peach polyester shell and coordinating plaid slacks, she stood in front of her desk, arms folded across her ample bosom. She tapped her sensibly shod foot impatiently against the golden oak floor and glared at me like a cranky principal about to hand out a tardy. The tiny pink note she held between two fingers completed the image to perfection. "And what was all the fuss about?" she demanded, pointing toward the first floor.

"Wow," I said. "That was fast, even for you. You need to let me in on your secret."

Unappreciative as usual of my humor, she sniffed. "The Mister stopped by. Told me to tell you that he was headed back up to his rooms. He also said to tell you that as soon as the fuss started, Hillary took off like a shot." Frances's eyes narrowed. "The Mister thinks she's behind all these thefts, doesn't he?"

I didn't answer. Hillary's innocence or guilt would be proved by facts, not by gossiping behind her back. Pointing to the pink slip of paper Frances held, I asked, "Is that for me?"

She extended her arm, presenting it high, near my face. "Some woman you know who works at the Kane Estate in California. She called. Sounded important."

"Nadia?" I said, grabbing the note to read it. Not much information. Her name, number, and Frances's scribbled, "CALL ASAP."

I must have frowned because my assistant was quick to pounce. "I know you *prefer* e-mails instead of notes written on paper, but like I told you before, we've got a crate of these 'While You Were Out' forms, and if we don't use them they'll go into the garbage. Is that what you want, for me to waste the Mister's money?"

I counted to five silently as she ranted, reminding myself that Frances protected Bennett as though it were her solemn duty. What she didn't understand is that I shared that responsibility. My assistant was doing her job the best way she knew how. I only wished she'd learn to converse rather than confront.

"This note is fine," I said. "Did Nadia tell you what it was about?"

"If she had, don't you think I would have written it down?"

I made my way to my office, tapping the paper thoughtfully. Nadia and I had met years ago, when I was a grad student and she a tenured professor. Despite the age gap, we'd forged an enduring friendship and shared a love of all things historical. She'd retired from teaching last year and had taken an assistant curator position on the West Coast in one of the finest homes in the country: the Kane Estate. She and I kept in touch via e-mail and snail mail because Nadia refused to own a cell phone, claiming that at her age she didn't need to be available every minute of every day. In her mid-eighties, the woman was fit, spry, and perennially cheerful. She was as opposite Frances as a person could get. It was very odd for Nadia to call, and I wondered what was up.

I sat at my desk and picked up the phone, talking to myself. "I hope she's okay."

Frances shouted from the other room. "She sounded fine."

I put the receiver down, got up, and went to the doorway that separated our offices. "Thanks," I said to my assistant. Then I shut the door.

Back at my desk, I dialed Nadia at work. She answered on the first ring.

"Grace," she said, with such joy in her voice I was immediately warmed. "I'm glad you got back to me so quickly."

"It's great to hear from you." Nadia's voice was strong, her tone upbeat. Relief surged over me. "But I have to tell you, I was a little concerned when I read the message. It says to call you back ASAP."

"Then your assistant did her job," she said. "What a charming woman. She asked me all about you and how you and I knew each other."

I closed my eyes and shook my head. "Did she?"

"It sounds as though you've had your share of trouble at Marshfield over the past few months. I remember you e-mailing some of the story, but I didn't realize how close you'd come to getting hurt."

"Frances exaggerates."

"I'm not so sure about that. She seemed genuinely concerned for your safety."

"Well . . ." I was about to launch into an accurate description of Frances, but stopped myself before getting the first negative word out. Why spoil Nadia's happy impression? No good would come of that. "She's certainly efficient."

"That's wonderful to hear. I'm so pleased to know that you're working with other good souls. People can make or break a job, you know."

Before I could respond, she switched gears. When she spoke again, her tone was serious.

"I'm sorry to bring more trouble your way, Grace, and I sincerely hope it turns out to be nothing . . ."

I sat up, pressing the phone tighter to my ear. With Nadia in California and me in North Carolina, I couldn't imagine what trouble might be brewing. Unless . . .

"My sister hasn't been in touch with you?" I asked, feeling oddly breathless. "Last I heard she was out West. Please tell me she hasn't hit you up for a loan."

Nadia put my fears to rest immediately. "No, honey. Don't worry. It's not about Liza."

"Thank goodness."

My sister was currently missing in action, but fears about her returning to wreak havoc on my life never drifted far enough from my mind to give me peace. I longed for the day when I could relax completely, but I knew my sister too well to believe she would ever stay out of my life for good. My only hope was that it would be years, not months, before I heard from her again. Maybe by then I'd be strong enough to forgive her. Despite the fact that I was better off without my former fiancé, Eric, the memory of their dual duplicity still made my throat catch. Sisters didn't do that to one another—at least not sisters who cared.

Nadia had been shuffling papers. "Here it is," she said, although I couldn't see what it was she referred to. "I made a few notes so I wouldn't forget the details."

"I'm listening."

"First of all, everything I'm about to share is strictly confidential. We're working with the authorities and carefully monitoring how much information will be released to the media when the story eventually breaks."

"This sounds serious."

"It is. Grace, we've been robbed. Three items of great historical significance, not to mention considerable worth, are gone. A few smaller pieces have been taken as well."

I sucked in a breath. "What's missing?"

"I wish I could tell you, but I'm under strict orders not to share more than absolutely necessary." Her voice lowered. "It seems there have been other thefts at other historical sites like ours over the past couple of years. I can tell you this much: They have a specific MO. That's the term for 'modus operandi,'" she added helpfully. I knew that, but let her continue. "They snatched the smaller pieces early on. The theory is that's how they start. Kind of a practice. A dry run."

"What did you do when the first pieces went missing?"

"We began an investigation, of course, but that's where it gets interesting," she said. "Their timing was perfect— too perfect to be coincidental. They stole the first few items mere days before we'd scheduled a giant fund-raiser."

"I don't understand."

"Kane supports many worthwhile charities but we rarely host them on-site. Insurance concerns, you understand. This time, however, we'd planned a gala fund-raiser to benefit at-risk teens. We not only opened our doors to four hundred generous donors, we invited thirty disadvantaged teens as well."

I still wasn't getting it, but Nadia hadn't finished explaining.

"The three major pieces we lost?" she continued. "They disappeared during the event."

"Oh, no."

"Oh, yes. The thieves started a small fire during the party. You can imagine the chaos and fear that caused. Fortunately, no lives were lost. What's important to note is that the disturbance provided a diversion. While guests and security scrambled to prevent a major disaster, the thieves made their move. Two people were injured, including one of our security guards. He's hospitalized with a gunshot wound."

"Is he okay?"

"Doctors say he will be. But he couldn't identify the gunman. He said it happened too fast."

"That's terrible, Nadia," I said.

"Initially, the police wanted to interrogate the kids, thinking they were behind the theft. Poor people are always the easiest targets, aren't they? Thankfully, before that public relations nightmare got started, we realized that this had been a strategic strike."

"How so?"

"The three stolen pieces were all from the same dynas— oh, I'm getting too specific. Let's just say they were all from the same region, the same century. We had acquired them from different sources at different times and we'd received the final piece in the collection the week before. Although they were housed in the same general area, they were not grouped together. In fact, whoever stole these passed up several other valuable pieces nearby. The thieves knew what they wanted. Probably for a collector who isn't picky about provenance."

I'd heard of fencing operations like these. They usually targeted museums, though they tended to do so infrequently, both because security measures were improving by the minute, and because one successful haul provided plenty to live on while strategizing the next hit. I sat back, stunned, "I'm so sorry to hear this. Do you have any leads?"

"Not much. And what little we have I can't share. What I am allowed to tell you is that the authorities believe the thieves took advantage of the fund-raiser to cover for their big heist. In a situation like that there's always some confusion, a few mishaps, and hundreds of unfamiliar faces. We think they blended in, grabbed what they wanted, and were out before we knew anything was missing."

"Wow," I said, because there wasn't much else to say. "What prompted you to call me about this?"

"I remember you telling me about the company you

hired to film a DVD of Marshfield. We hired a crew to tape the fund-raiser."

I got a sudden sick twist in my gut. "Who did you use?"

"I'm not allowed to say. Legal mumbo-jumbo. But if you tell me who you're using . . ."

I gripped the receiver tighter to my ear and gave her the name of Corbin Shaw's group.

She gave a sigh of relief. "Not the same company. You may be safe."

I felt a tiny wash of relief.

"Understand, honey," she went on, "there's no positive proof the film crew has done anything wrong. But I remembered what you'd told me and I thought it worth a phone call. They were here during the fund-raiser. For all we know, the thieves simply waited for our guard to be down before they pounced. If so, you may want to keep your eyes open, and talk to your security chief about tightening things up. Just until the film crew is gone. And then—"

"We are missing items," I admitted. "A few. Nothing major."

"When?"

"Since the film crew has been here."

"What's missing?"

I named the items, thinking that if Nadia hadn't gotten in touch, we might have been poised to lose even more. "We've kept close tabs on the crew," I said, even more glad that I'd agreed to come in early the next morning to oversee the project. "We've limited filming to hours when the mansion is closed to visitors."

"Be careful. Like I said, we had a couple of people injured. These thieves are ruthless. With all that's gone on with Marshfield lately, I was worried you may have enough chaos in your midst to attract the thieves' attention."

The last thing Marshfield Manor needed right now was another tragedy. Despite the fact that the two murders here in recent months were helping attendance rather than hindering it, our goal was to draw seekers of beauty and lovers of history rather than morbid gawkers who wanted to see where bodies had been found.

At least this time we had forewarning. "Thanks, Nadia," I said. "You have to know how much I appreciate this."

After we hung up, I called Terrence. "Hey," I said, "got a minute?"

BOOTSIE SAT IN MY LAP AS I READ THE NEWS-paper at our kitchen table. The house was quiet, save for her gentle purrs thrumming softly against the inside of my left arm. The little tuxedo kitten had become part of the family from the moment she'd joined us, and I had to admit that I was secretly pleased she'd attached herself most firmly to me.

My roommates, Bruce and Scott, were busy at Amethyst Cellars, their wine shop in town. Because we were at the beginning of Emberstowne's high season, I didn't expect either of them home before ten and it was just past eight now. I'd texted both to let them know that I'd probably be in bed when they got back, so I was surprised when the back door opened and Bruce rushed in.

"Great," he said, "I caught you."

"What are you doing here?"

Bootsie raised her head, looked up at me, then wriggled onto her back, snuggling to make herself more comfortable.

Bruce placed a bottle of wine on the table in front of me. Wrapped in red and clear cellophane twisted at the bottle's neck with ribbons cascading in silvery free fall, it was a lovely presentation. I turned it to read the label: one of their more expensive vintages. But the gift card, the "To-zee, From-zee" as we'd always called them in my family, was blank.

"Who's this for?" I asked.

"That's the thing," he said, sitting across from me. "Mr.

Marshfield's stepdaughter came in this afternoon and picked it out. She didn't give us a name."

"Hillary was in the shop?"

"She came in for a wine tasting. Alone. But she left with at least two phone numbers. That woman works fast."

"I'm still not getting this," I said, pointing to the wine bottle.

"I'm not sure I get it, either. Hillary waited until her two new conquests were gone, then picked out this cabernet. After she paid, she requested gift wrapping. We told her it would be a couple of minutes, but she said she had an appointment and couldn't wait. She knew you were planning to be at Marshfield early tomorrow and asked that we have you bring it." Bruce held his hands up apologetically. "She was out the door before we could stop her."

It would be like Hillary to arrange for me to be her delivery person. "No worries, Bruce. I'll take it."

Bootsie gave a little huff. Indignation on my behalf, possibly? She jumped off my lap and began kneading my plush yellow slippers. That was one of her favorite pastimes. I had to admit I got a kick out of it, too.

"You will?" Bruce asked. "I really hate to impose, but this is a pretty special wine. I'd be happy to deliver it myself, but she said the place would be closed in the morning except for you, her, and the film crew. And that you'd all be there bright and early at six A.M. That's ridiculously early."

"Just what I need. Hillary at six in the morning."

He laughed. "You always have your hands full at Marshfield." He glanced at the clock. "Shouldn't you get to bed? You've got an early call."

"Wait until I tell you the rest." I explained about talking with Nadia then said, "When our items first began disappearing, we switched filming to pre-visitor hours. I don't know what else we can do to prevent what happened at Kane from happening at Marshfield."

Bruce was shaking his head. "Shouldn't you consider rescheduling this DVD filming? At least for the time being?"

"Bennett is completely against that." I didn't mention that was because he was convinced the thefts would stop as soon as Hillary left the premises. "Delaying our filming would put all our plans for expansion behind schedule. Corbin is booked for the next eighteen months. Bennett wants this done as soon as possible. And honestly, I would hate to have to reschedule." I massaged my temples. "What a headache that would be. Especially since we don't even know that there's any connection between the Kane Estate thefts and Marshfield's missing items. Now that we're forewarned, though, we can be prepared."

"If there is any connection, you've already thwarted them by limiting chaos as cover," Bruce said. "You have to feel pretty good about that."

I took another look at the bottle of wine Bruce had brought home. "You said Hillary was flirting up a storm?"

"Like there was no tomorrow."

"Curious."

"Why?" he asked.

"I thought she hated Emberstowne and everyone in it."

He twisted his mouth and shook his head.

"What aren't you telling me?"

"I don't think she hates it here as much as she pretends. I was watching her today at the wine bar. She got this look in her eyes."

"Predatory?" I asked with a smirk.

Bruce didn't laugh. "I'd call it wistful. She seemed to want to fit in but didn't know how. I think she's uncomfortable interacting with others. Unless she's flirting with men"—he pointed to himself—"or antagonizing other women." He pointed to me.

"She flirts with you?"

"All the time; Scott, too. For all the good it'll do her."

Now he did laugh. "That's what I mean, though. She doesn't know how to interact with men except in a sexual way."

"I still don't understand why she's hanging out in town. Something doesn't add up."

"She's not so bad, you know."

I cocked an eyebrow. "Has all that female flirting addled your brain?"

"I feel sorry for her. Sure, she looks all put together, but she has to work at it. Hard. And the cracks are beginning to show. She wants to be happy, but doesn't have a clue how to get there."

I thought about that. "You're pretty insightful."

"Now I know you're exhausted. Say good night, Gracie."

He was right. I stood. "Good night."

Chapter 5

FROM ALMOST THE TIME I'D REALIZED I WAS allergic to Bootsie, she'd shifted her sleep pattern, voluntarily accommodating me as though aware of my discomfort. Instead of sharing my pillow the way she had from the start, she'd taken to making herself comfortable behind my knees, nestling into their crook every night, while I stroked the side of her face until we both fell asleep.

She lifted her head when my alarm went off at four. "Sorry, kiddo," I said, scooching away so as not to disturb her slumber. I needn't have worried. As I tucked my feet into my big yellow slippers, I glanced back. She'd rolled over, sound asleep again. Lucky cat.

Forty minutes after waking, I was out the door. Although nothing required my presence at the filming this morning, I wanted to make certain that the treasures featured today were described accurately. And after Nadia's warning, I didn't want to leave anything to chance.

I parked in my usual place in the underground employee lot, leaving Hillary's bottle of wine there to retrieve later.

Instead of cutting through the mansion I went straight outdoors, making my way around to the front. The early morning air was cool and damp, filling my senses with that gorgeous mossy scent of green, and tickling me as though the dew were settling directly on my skin. Shuffling through the soft underbrush, I breathed deeply. Life was filled with promise and hope. Today was sure to be a good day.

I came up a small rise and turned at the mansion's northeast corner, surprised to see trucks parked outside the giant front doors. They were panel trucks, very similar to the one I'd rented when I moved here from New York. These, however, were solid black rather than bright yellow, and bore no logo whatsoever.

Corbin and his team were assembling outside the front doors when I arrived. Marshfield's outdoor spotlights kept the area bright as day, but the darkness that sheltered the woods beyond gave me a creepy shiver. I heard a wolf howl.

Corbin sipped from a steaming cup as he directed the bustling activity. "Wow, you guys are early," I said as his crew pulled tripods, flash umbrellas, and lighting equipment from the backs of their vans.

"That's why our clients like us," he said. "We show up when we say we will and deliver more than we promise."

About fifteen people dressed in black T-shirts and jeans unloaded equipment with minimal conversation. Intent on their tasks, they gave me no more than a passing glance as they ferried lights and big black boxes trimmed in chrome up to the front door.

"I heard there was a mix-up with your accommodations in Emberstowne. Where are you staying?" I asked.

Corbin scowled. "We *were* staying at the Waltham Arms," he said, "but a union dispute broke a couple days ago. There's no way we're crossing picket lines, so we had to find another place with room enough for the duration. The only place with vacancies was this rinky-dink Oak Tree Hotel. More like motel, if you ask me."

I knew of it. Quite a drop in opulence from the Waltham Arms.

Corbin squinted up at the sky. "They predicted a clear day. I hope it doesn't get too hot in there." He waved a hand in the general direction of the equipment. "I always work up a sweat around those lights. And I have an idea for a few additional outdoor shots. I walked past the garden yesterday. It's magnificent. My compliments to your staff."

"They'll be happy to hear it," I said, thinking that this would give me an excuse to contact Jack. Maybe one of these days, he and I could have a real adult conversation. At this point, I was less interested in pursuing a romantic relationship than I was in setting things right. I wanted us to be friends if we could. If not, I wanted to know why. I deserved that much.

"What's the grimace for?" Corbin asked.

Embarrassed to have my emotions play across my face, I stammered, "I'm sorry. Just something on my mind."

Corbin's bright eyes sparkled in the dim light. "It's a man, isn't it?"

I hoped the flush I felt didn't show. "That obvious?"

"I have two daughters. They're both married now, but I remember that look. I always saw it when their boyfriends messed up and my daughters were trying hard to forgive. Rationalizing, justifying." He shot me that wacky grin. "Am I close?"

I smiled. "Closer than I'd like to admit."

"If you'll indulge an old dad's intrusion, I'll tell you what I told them: Your guy is going to make you frown once in a while. That's life, kiddo. But if there are more frowns than smiles, maybe it's time to take another look around."

"Thanks. I'll keep that in mind."

The dozen or so staffers sipped from steaming paper cups as they went about their work, speaking only when necessary, as though reluctant to dispel the morning's tranquility. Corbin noticed me watching and handed me one of the extra coffees he had nearby.

"Wow," I said, after a quick sip, "this is strong."

"Can you think of a better way to get a group moving this early?"

We talked a little more and then I pointed to the vans. "You don't have any logo on the sides of your vehicles."

"You ever work for a film company?" he asked.

"No."

"Well, let me tell you. The entire world has stars in its eyes. You hang out a filmmaker shingle and every DiCaprio or Streep wannabe comes knocking at the window to ask if they can be an extra, or audition, or whatever. We tell them that it's not up to us—that's the casting director's role."

"Aren't you the casting director?" I asked.

"They don't know that, do they?" He winked. "Seriously, that's why we took our identification off the trucks. We could be anything: movers, laundry service . . ." He got a mischievous look in his eyes. "Shadowy transport for serial killers."

I laughed politely. After two murders on Marshfield property, I didn't find his humor particularly funny. "Let's hope we don't have to worry about that."

"Don't worry. I do extensive background checks before I hire my employees, and most of them have been with me for at least ten years."

"Most?"

He surveyed the area, squinting. "I don't see . . . Oh, there." He gestured with his chin and I followed his gaze. Two men were unloading large silver boxes from the back of one of the vans. "Those guys—a couple of freelancers— they're new to me with this job."

"Freelancers?" I repeated, feeling a little queasy.

"Don't worry. They've worked for other film companies like mine and came with excellent references. I interviewed them both personally. They're good, hard workers. Trustworthy. You could stake your life on that."

I hated when anyone said that. Sure it was just a cliché, but staking one's life, or saying the equivalent of "to die for," always bugged me. Now that I thought about it, that quirk of mine was fairly recent. It had started right after the first Marshfield murder.

I looked at the two men. Neither struck me as appearing overtly evil, nor angelic. Both were of average height, average weight, and without distinguishing features. I'd have to say they were both simply ordinary. "Did either of them work at the Kane Estate recently?"

Corbin didn't recall. "Harry," he called. "Donald Lee."

The two glanced up as Corbin waved them over. They exchanged the briefest of looks, one I took to mean: "Why are you pulling us away from what we need to do?" But both dutifully put down their gear and hustled over.

As he introduced them, they extended their hands and nodded acknowledgment. Up close, Harry Hinton was in his early forties and moved in a loose-limbed way. He was thin, had hollowed eyes and a sallow complexion.

Donald Lee Runge was slightly older and slightly larger, with a receding hairline.

"Ms. Wheaton here was wondering if either of you worked on a film project at the Kane Estate recently."

The two men exchanged another look. "No," Harry said. "Any particular reason?"

"I hoped to borrow ideas from their project to enhance ours." That was a fib, but an innocuous one.

After more small talk, the two men asked if there was anything else I needed. When I said there wasn't, they returned to their duties.

"Harry and Donald seem very capable," I said neutrally.

"He prefers Donald Lee," Corbin said with a shrug.

Weren't serial killers and assassins often identified with middle names? There was that unpleasant thought again. I needed to stop ruminating about murders here at Marshfield. That wasn't what we were known for. Well, at least not until I started working here.

"Something wrong?" Corbin asked.

"No, nothing. Thanks."

Corbin lifted his paper cup in a mock toast. "No time like the present," he said. "It's been nice chatting, but we'd better get started. Feel free to watch. Don't worry about being quiet until we call for silence. Just try to stay off camera."

"That won't be a problem," I said. "The last thing I want to see is my face on the DVD."

He shook his head. "Sorry to tell you, but Bennett specifically requested your presence."

"What?"

Corbin grinned again. "He'll be there with you, so no need to get stage fright."

"Hardly stage fright," I said. "I don't belong. Bennett is the owner, not me."

"He seems to think of you as family."

Though cheered by Corbin's words, I felt it wouldn't be right for me to take a spot that was reserved for family, not unless it was ever proved that Bennett and I were, actually, related. And the chances of that happening were . . . well, weren't.

"I'll talk to him," I said.

Corbin finished his coffee and tossed it into a waste bin they'd brought with them. "Good luck with that."

Inside, Marshfield Manor was quiet as a mausoleum. The overnight spotlights glowed, transforming our every move into a dance of silhouettes along far walls. Gym-shoed footsteps across the marble entryway bounced, creating a cacophony of eerie squeaks. Terrence was already there, dispelling the shadows with each flick of the lights. "Good morning," he said.

He and I worked together to ensure that Corbin's crew had everything they needed, and then we stood back to watch. I was impressed by their conscientiousness as they shifted lighting and navigated around priceless treasures.

Later in the morning, Corbin gestured toward Terrence with his eyes and said, "I know he's keeping a close watch on us all." Our chief of security stood with his back to a nearby wall, arms folded, taking in the entire event. He'd done this every day since filming began, bringing along a dozen additional guards, who formed a rough perimeter around the entourage. No one would be able to sneak anything out under such close scrutiny. I was feeling better by the moment. "Makes me feel like a criminal," Corbin said.

Time flew, and I felt as though I'd taken a crash course in DVD production. I followed the team around, peering over shoulders as crew members gauged lighting, composition, and placement, and marveling at the ease with which the team handled equipment—and talent—as they brought Corbin's visions to life.

After several extended sequences shot in the banquet hall, they called a wrap for the day and the team snapped into teardown action. Within minutes, they were carting equipment out the front door.

In the midst of it all, we heard a woman exclaim, "What's going on?"

Hillary appeared in the doorway. Hands on hips, her feet were spread apart as though expecting to play an intense game of Red Rover. Lasering her gaze at Corbin, her tone switched to plaintive. "Why did you start without me? Corbin, you promised."

When he looked to me for guidance, I sighed. "We talked about this yesterday, Hillary."

Her eyes lit up. Clearly a more appealing scapegoat than Corbin, I bore the brunt of her anger as she wheeled on me. "Oh, I get it," she said, her mouth tugging down at the corners, "you're trying to muscle me aside. You're jealous of the fact that that I'm Papa Bennett's daughter and you're not."

In my head, I silently corrected, "Stepdaughter."

"Let me tell you something about my father," she went on. Again the little *plink* in my head: "Stepfather."

"Family means everything to him," she said, stopping just short of being nose to nose with me. "You may think you're important to him, but he's using you because you're good at your job. Like Abe was."

I knew Bennett had regarded Abe as family, and I watched that recollection dawn across Hillary's face a heartbeat later. "You know what I meant," she said, as though she hadn't undercut her own argument.

"I have your bottle of wine in the car," I said. "Would you like it now, or do you prefer to pick it up later?"

My abrupt change of subject had the anticipated effect. Her perfect little eyebrows arched as her mouth opened like a surprised codfish's. A half second later, however, she'd resumed her prim, injured air. "I appreciate you bringing it in. But I'll pick it up later at your office."

She gave a little nod of acknowledgment, then latched on to Corbin. Physically. Wrapping both hands around his bicep, she practically cooed in his ear, "What exactly do you have in mind for my scenes?"

Chapter 6

MAYBE IT HAD BEEN THE EXTRA-STRONG COF-fee, but after a thoroughly enjoyable and enlightening morning, even Hillary's diatribe couldn't ruin my mood. I retrieved her gift-wrapped wine bottle from my car and practically skipped up the stairs to my office on the third floor of the westernmost wing.

This section of the mansion housed our administrative office and, immediately above, on the fourth floor, Bennett's rooms. Calling his living space "rooms" was a bit of a misnomer. To describe them that way conjured up images of an elderly man living in a barren walkup with only a hot plate to fix his meals.

Bennett's living space could easily have housed a family with eight kids, allowing each member to claim a room of his or her own. In addition to his own master bedroom and adjacent sitting room, he had a dining room that comfortably sat twenty, a library, billiard room, study, gourmet kitchen, butler's room, four full baths, and more miscellaneous guest rooms than he would ever need.

Although I'd visited upstairs often enough, I hadn't actually seen all of the rooms yet and Bennett hadn't seemed inclined to grant me access. I suspected the reason for that. Once, early on, I'd been required to assist in getting him safely to his bedroom. His personal space had been crammed with antiquities and collectibles that Bennett obviously valued but which hadn't yet been catalogued.

Subsequent conversations, coupled with Bennett's need to bid at every auction he found out about, led me to understand that Bennett was a pack rat. A very upscale hoarder. He certainly had the means to collect anything that caught his fancy. The difference between reality-TV hoarders and Bennett, however, was that he had a team of maids who kept his collection sparkling. No mold and mildew. Just lots of expensive stuff.

I sensed he was embarrassed to have had me see evidence of his overindulgence. Either that or he didn't want to scare me off with the workload. I had no doubt it would fall to me to catalogue and inventory his entire stash. I welcomed the challenge and had told him so. Maybe one of these days, when we weren't investigating murders, I'd have time to get to it.

Although we didn't have a murder on our hands right now, we did have the not-so-small problem of missing items. Terrence had already alerted the local police department and I would probably need to talk with Detectives Rodriguez and Flynn soon myself. One of their colleagues, Tank, who had proven to be a valuable ally, had recently returned home to Michigan. Not for the first time did I wish they'd sent Flynn up north instead.

My cranky assistant was at her desk, as always. Her graying hair was piled high on her head and her glasses low on her nose. The crystal eyeglass chain that wrapped around the back of her neck seemed to have been chosen to coordinate with her lilac-colored twinset. Over time, I'd noticed that Frances favored shades of purple. She raised tadpole eyebrows over a baleful glare when I bounded in. "Good morning, Frances," I said. "A gorgeous day, isn't it?"

"How much coffee have you had this morning?"

I ignored that. "I think Corbin got some excellent footage today."

She sent a pointed stare at the clock on her desk. "Are they gone yet?"

"Packed up and disappeared before the first guest stepped foot on the grounds."

"I'm surprised the Mister agreed to this idea."

"I'm not. Marshfield Manor needs to establish its brand. We have one of the most beautiful homes in the world here, and we haven't even begun to showcase it to its fullest potential. Just you wait," I said, "you'll see how this will take off."

She snorted. "You mean like some of the Mister's belongings are taking off? You know they're not growing legs and walking away on their own. Mark my words, bringing all these strangers in and giving them free rein of the house, you're asking for trouble."

"I'll keep that in mind."

"Of course you will." Her scowl punctuated her sarcasm. Changing subjects, she said, "You're going to fall on your face, you know."

Recently my unpleasant assistant had become ever so slightly less so. In fact, on occasion, she'd been almost nice. Which is why I was surprised to have her predicting my downfall again. She hadn't done that for weeks. I thought she'd finally gotten used to me. "Bennett seems pleased by all this," I said, truly puzzled by her pronouncement. "I don't think he's going to fire me because we're filming a DVD."

She huffed and rolled her eyes. "Why you always think the worst of me I'll never know."

Now I was truly lost.

"I'm trying to warn you about crashing. You're too upbeat for someone who's been here since the crack of dawn. The minute you sit down and relax for more than five minutes, you're going to deflate."

"I don't know, Frances," I said, "I'm feeling particularly great today. Maybe it's the weather. Summertime makes me believe anything is possible."

She sniffed. "I thought that was supposed to be spring."

"Maybe I'm simply in a good mood."

Turning her attention to the papers on her desk, she made a face. "So what else is new?"

HOURS LATER, EXCEPT FOR A QUICK VISIT from Hillary who'd stopped in long enough to retrieve her gift-wrapped wine, the afternoon had gotten heavy and quiet. I was loath to admit it, but Frances had been right. I stared out the windows through dry and scratchy eyes, knowing that I ought to get up and move around or risk falling asleep in my seat. The door between our offices was open and when Frances's chair creaked, it roused me from my torpor in time to look busy before she made it across the threshold.

I glanced up, acting surprised to see her, pretending she was interrupting some very important business.

"Looks like I was wrong," she said. "You're still hanging in there."

Giving credit where it was due, I allowed myself a yawn. "No, Frances, you're right on the money. I'm zoning out here."

I could tell she was surprised that I'd admitted she was right. "Maybe you should take off, then." She glanced over at the clock. "There's not much more left to the day and you're not going to get a lot accomplished if you're exhausted."

"That's true enough."

"You start shorting yourself sleep, you're going to get sick."

I didn't have a chance to respond before she eased into the wing chair across from me. Hesitant, yet sly, she regarded me with interest. "Not that it's any of my business . . ."

Immediately my hackles—whatever hackles are—zinged to attention. "What's up, Frances?"

"How is Jack Embers these days?"

This from the queen of gossip. "Why do you ask?"

"Haven't seen him in a while."

I didn't respond, but that didn't stop her.

"He used to come by here all the time and it wasn't to visit me. Back when Abe was in charge, Jack stopped by once a season, if that. Up until the recent"—she shrugged, obviously searching for an appropriate word—"unpleasantness, he used to visit you a couple times a week."

She waited for me to answer.

"Not that he was fooling anyone, I might add. We all knew he was sweet on you. What happened?"

The ultra-sincere look on her face wasn't fooling anyone either. Did she really believe I'd open up to her when it was guaranteed that my love life—or lack thereof—would immediately become fodder for lunchtime entertainment?

I sighed and smiled. "It's funny you should ask . . ."

She scooched forward.

"Because I was about to ask you the same thing," I said. "After that recent 'unpleasantness' you mentioned, whatever happened with you and Hennessey?"

Her eyes narrowed and she sat up straight. "Don't you have more pressing items to concern yourself with?"

"I'm sure we both do."

That shut her up. Thank goodness. I was in no mood to banter. I was about to tell her that I'd take her advice and knock off early, when my walkie-talkie crackled to life. It was Terrence. "Grace, switch channels."

I switched to a secure frequency as I stood up, gesturing for Frances to leave. She didn't budge.

"Terrence? What's up?" I asked, quickly adding, "Frances is with me."

He was out of breath. "Staff passage in the east wing. Red stairwell. Get there as fast as you can."

"Got it," I said.

Frances followed me as I started for the door. "What happened?"

"I guess I'm about to find out."

Chapter 7

I SHOT THROUGH THE DOOR THAT SEPARATED the administrative wing from the public areas, hurrying across the Gathering Hall, noting that attendance was sparse. Owing to the time of day, that wasn't a surprise. I raced to the east wing. The red stairwell was the far one at the end of the hall, on the right.

When the house was designed and servants lived here, high up in the tiny, spartan rooms that lined this end of the mansion's top floors, a very wise, very efficient decision was made to paint each of the four stairway walls a different color, making for quick and easy identification in this end of the home.

I was still at least a hundred feet away from the turnoff to the red stairwell when groups of people came around the corner, heading the opposite direction guided by security guards. Chattering, exclaiming, and throwing glances over their shoulders, they allowed themselves to be shepherded toward the wide, central staircase. Several of the guards shot me questioning looks as I rushed past. I shrugged a reply, just as I heard Niles ask a family to please step down-stairs and await further instructions.

Further instructions for what? I wondered. But I didn't stop to ask.

Making my way past the guest rooms on my right, I slipped under the velvet ropes that cordoned off a long hall. The red staircase was down this way.

I was about to rush in when I heard a shout from behind me. "Hey!"

I turned. Another guard, William, raised his hand. "Sorry, Ms. Wheaton. I didn't recognize you."

"What's going on?" I asked as I gripped the doorknob.

His mouth was set in a grim line. "Best you see for your-self."

Prepared for the worst, I took a deep breath and threw open the stairwell door.

The landing before me was empty. Light from the sky-light above spilled down, illuminating the dust motes that floated overhead. This staircase was one of the larger ones in the home. Shaped like a giant square doughnut, its steps ran along its perimeter, with a square center that opened up to the skylight like a ten-by-ten-foot flue. I'd stepped onto the third-floor landing. There was one flight above me and, because this staircase descended all the way to the sub-basement, four flights below.

Cries and exclamations rose up, echoing through the narrow chamber. Terrence's voice shouted above it all, straining to take command. I took a step forward, gripped the oak rail, and peered over the edge.

A woman lay at the very bottom of the stairwell, motion-less. She was in a position so crooked, with so much blood pooling beneath her, that I had no doubt she was dead.

"Terrence," I called, but my shaking voice was too thin, the din from below too great.

I became aware of the backs of many heads, one level below me, staring down at the limp figure, as I did. Jostling for position, they swarmed the lower stairs, peering down, crying out, pointing.

I'm not coordinated enough to take stairs two at a time going down, but I ran as fast as I could, my breath coming in gasps as I pushed through the gaggle of onlookers. This part of the mansion should have been strictly off-limits. What could have happened to the woman at the bottom? Why all the gawkers? What were they doing in this part of the building? I needed answers. Now.

"Excuse me," I said darting between those jockeying for a better look. Whoever was dead must have fallen. There was no other explanation. I tried to tune in to what people were saying, but I moved too fast and they all seemed as puzzled as I was. "Let me through."

As I started down the final flight of stairs, I spotted Terrence and John, the tour director, on the lowest level. They were as far away from the woman's prone form as possible. Behind them, three doorways opened to maintenance corridors that ran like tentacles under the house. Right now the mouth of each was jammed tight with staff members crowding close to see what had happened.

John's face registered shock as he paced in small circles, his hands in constant movement—frantic, furious, helpless all at once. I looked at the woman again. Young, I thought. When I noticed pink sweatpants, her identification clicked. Lenore. It had to be. The body shape, size, hair: all right.

My gut's instant reaction ground me to a halt as I reached the bottom level. *Oh my god.*

I moved forward gingerly now, giving the death scene a wide berth. I caught Terrence's eye. "What happened?" I asked from behind John.

Still pacing, the tour director massaged his brow with one hand and grabbed at the air with the other, as though searching for answers. "Don't you have sensors on these doors?" he asked. "Shouldn't some alarm have sounded? How could this happen? How in the world . . . ?"

Terrence interrupted. "Grace is here, John."

John turned, but I could tell he wasn't seeing me. It was as though fifty thoughts were careering around in his mind at once, broadcasting fear, horror, and disbelief on his face as each emotion zoomed by.

"Grace." Terrence strove for control. "You stay here with John. Protect this area. I have to get up to find out why this happened. The crime scene is getting trampled."

I grabbed him before he could take off. Pointing to Lenore's motionless body less than fifteen feet away from me, I asked, "Crime scene? This wasn't an accident?"

Terrence's expression tightened. "She was pushed. Another tour member was injured as well. Ambulance is on its way."

He was gone, taking the stairs two at a time before I could press for more details. John had resumed making small circles in the tiny area. I looked up at the skylight, more than five floors above. Bewildered faces stared back amid shouting, pointing, and tears. "Step away," I heard Terrence roar as he ran. "Step away from the railings. Return to the designated tour areas. We will be questioning each of you."

The red walls high above closed in on me as I stood at the very bottom, trying to sort out what little I knew. I did my best to urge John into the nearest hallway. Though I had no idea what the forensic experts would need, the farther we stayed away from Lenore, the better.

The laundry ladies and maintenance guys who'd been drawn from their basement alcoves to peer into the stairwell stared in shock at me, their eyes wide. "Please, folks. Let's not make this worse," I said to them. Spotting a staff member whose name I remembered, I designated her to be the leader. "Get everybody back to work, Monica. We'll let you know more later."

She complied as I pulled John toward one of the doorways. As soon as we were alone, I asked, "What happened?"

"The poor girl." His voice cracked. "I don't know."

Vibrating with agitation, the normally unflappable John was about to lose it. In a soothing voice, I did my best to talk him down, asking, "Terrence said someone else was injured?"

"Yes, yes." Now he gripped his hair with both hands. "One of the other guests, Mark, was shot."

"Shot?" I looked around. No one had said anything about a shooting.

John took a deep breath, clamped his eyes shut for a long moment, then opened them and fought for control. I could barely hear him. "Mark Ellroy. He's part of our tour. He was traveling alone, too, and he and Lenore sat next to each other on the bus, so I thought if I asked him to keep Lenore out of trouble . . ."

This wasn't explaining anything. I raised my voice. "I don't understand."

Noises from above prevented me from asking more. People shuffling, complaining, and crying created an angry din amid guards' shouts urging cooperation. Slowly, the noise dissipated and the scene finally quieted, but all I could think was that forensics would be a nightmare.

"John?" I urged.

John's gaze swept the floor behind me. His eyes tightened and reddened and I knew even before he turned away that he couldn't bear to look at her. Taking his arms, I pulled him around so that I was facing Lenore. Fortunately for me, John was large enough to effectively block the view.

Once settled again, he pursed his lips, then swallowed. "I'm not usually rattled," he said.

"I know."

"She was such a young thing."

"John. I need to know what happened upstairs. Where is this Mark Ellroy?"

"If he doesn't make it . . ." John's lower lids burned red. "These people are my responsibility."

"Take a deep breath. Tell me what you know."

"Yes, of course." He sucked in a deep breath. "You remember yesterday? I promised to keep an eye on Lenore. I did my best. But my job is to provide a worthwhile experience for *all* our guests, not be a babysitter. After I explained to Lenore how important it was that she stay with the group, I thought she got it. I really did."

"Go on."

"She's a—she *was* a sweet girl. Scatterbrained, but sweet. I knew she might forget the rules and Mark was all by himself. Like your security chief suggested—a buddy system. They were singles, traveling alone, and seemed to get along well enough. I thought I might be helping them both, in a way. Lenore didn't seem to mind, so they paired off."

"And someone in the mansion attacked them?"

He nodded, eyes reddening still. "We heard Mark shout and I ran back there to find him on the ground, bleeding. He'd crawled out of the stairwell, looking for help. Just outside the stairs near the Highland Guest Room. You know the one."

I nodded, but none of this was making sense. "What were they doing in the stairwell?"

John was having a hard time keeping himself together. "Lenore had been talking with one of the docents. I think she was interested in a particular piece and had questions. When it was time for the group to move on, I figured she was safe. How much trouble could she get into while talking with one of the staff? So we continued our tour. But because of the buddy system, Mark stayed back with her."

"He told you all this?"

"No. I'm telling you what I remember. Mark was in too much pain to say much. It was the docent who killed her. The guy who worked here." His words caught.

"Oh my god," I said. One of our staff? How could that be? "You saw him? You'd be able to recognize him?"

"I don't know."

"Where is he now?"

"The killer? I don't know."

"The man who was shot. Mark Ellroy?"

"We have a doctor in the group," he answered dully. "A woman. I left her up there with him."

I turned toward Lenore's body. "Did you touch anything around her?"

"I had to find out if she was still alive," John said in monotone and held up two fingers, covered in blood. "I checked. She wasn't."

"Has anyone called the police?"

"Your chief of security." Although John's voice had gone flat, his eyes were wild. I was afraid the man was going into shock.

"Are you sure?"

He shook his head, looking lost.

Monica took that moment to peer out the door again. "Get a chair for this man, would you?" I said.

The look of horror on her face reminded me that not everyone happened upon murder victims as often as I had. "Please," I added, "bring it to the door, I'll take it from here."

She disappeared and in a moment was back with an old metal folding chair that screeched as I opened it. I thanked her then grabbed John by the arm. "Here," I said, placing the chair in the doorway, facing him away from Lenore.

John lowered himself onto the small chair and dropped his head into his hands.

I pulled up my walkie-talkie. "Terrence, are you there?"

Lots of static. No answer.

"Terrence?"

I switched channels. "Security, this is Grace. Has anyone called the police?"

A woman at the other end answered, "On their way."

I glanced upward. Terrence and his team had managed

to drag all the onlookers back from their perches above. The tall, empty stairwell was silent. "Ambulance on its way, too?" I asked.

"Affirmative."

Our security would be stretched to the breaking point so I wouldn't request assistance down here until I absolutely needed it. I was about to sign off, when, in a moment of brilliance, I said, "Get in touch with my assistant, Frances. Have her meet me at the bottom of the red stairwell. Tell her to cut across the main floor, not the second floor. Got it? Come via the main floor or the basement."

"Copy that."

It would take Frances a few minutes to reach my position, but I needed someone I could trust to keep an eye on John until the police arrived. Monica would be a poor choice and I needed to get up to the second floor, where I could be of more use.

In the meantime, I tried to get more information from John. "This has been horrible. I'm so sorry. Is there something I can do for you?"

Sitting seemed to have helped his color return. He blinked, looking upward. "My tour group . . ."

"I'll go up there to check on them as soon as my assistant gets here."

"I'm all right," he said, taking a deep breath. "Nothing like this has ever happened before."

"I understand."

He looked up, his usually bright eyes clouded with sadness.

We fell silent.

Arms folded, I focused on the opposite wall, trying hard to keep from looking at Lenore.

"You've had a rough go of it here at Marshfield these past few months, haven't you?" John asked.

I nodded. I'd been thinking the exact same thing. I hadn't been here a full year yet and this was the third murder on Marshfield property. If I didn't know better, I'd consider myself a jinx.

"I know you need to be upstairs," John said. "Go ahead. Do what you need to do. I'll be okay."

"I'd rather wait for my assistant," I said. "Just in case."

"I'm not a child," he said, his voice gaining strength. "I know not to touch anything. I don't need a babysitter."

"Of course you don't," I said, smoothly, uncrossing my arms and stepping closer. "What else can you tell me about this Lenore? Do you have any idea who might want to harm her?"

John's eyebrows came together. "She hasn't been exactly tight-lipped about the fact that she's recently divorced. I got the impression it was ugly, but I never sensed fear from her. I think she said her husband was cheating. He divorced her."

"That doesn't sound very threatening."

"Unless she wasn't telling the truth." John looked frail all of a sudden. "But I doubt that. If anything, she shared too much. Drove a few of the other group members up a wall."

"Enough to kill her?"

His gaze rolled up to meet mine. "That isn't funny."

"It wasn't meant to be. The police will want to know."

He stared at the floor and bobbed his head. "That's true enough."

"That wouldn't explain the guy in the staff uniform," I said. "He must be an imposter. The fact that he was able to get in without being noticed, though, disturbs me greatly." Instinctively I turned toward Lenore, then wished I hadn't. "Do you think the killer chose her at random?"

"I don't know what to think."

"Can you tell me where you were when you last saw her?"

"The police will want to know that, too, won't they?" He rubbed his face, thinking. "We were outside the Highland

Guest Room and I was giving the little spiel on how the room got its name. That's when the docent—or whoever he was—gestured to Lenore. I saw him. My first thought was that she'd gotten into trouble again, but the guy was smiling, so I ignored them and kept talking. When we moved on down the hall to the next stop, I noticed the guy pointing something out to Lenore. I didn't know what." He stopped, thinking. "Now that I look back, I believe he was pointing toward the stairwell."

"This is all good. Keep a mental picture of the guy. It may be our best lead to catch him."

Though overwhelmed, John pressed on. "I didn't even think twice," he said miserably. "Your staff is friendly. This all looked perfectly normal. Now Lenore is dead. What if Mark doesn't survive? This is all my fault."

I heard a voice cutting through the distant basement chatter, and Frances appeared in one of the far doorways. The annoyance in her expression changed as she swept the area with keen attention. I could tell exactly when her gaze lighted on Lenore. "Oh my," she said bringing a hand to her mouth. Recovering quickly, she asked, "She fell?"

"Pushed," I said. "You know John, the tour guide. Would you please stay here with him until the detectives arrive? They should be here any minute."

"Where are you going?"

"To talk to the man who was shot."

Frances's eyes widened, but she pulled her lips in tightly and gave the briefest of nods.

To John, I said, "I'll get back as soon as I can. I'm very sorry." There wasn't much more to say and he remained silent. I didn't expect he really cared whether I returned or not.

Frances found her voice again as I started away. "How come we never had any murders at Marshfield before you got here?"

I stopped, but didn't turn. "You're slowing down, Frances," I said over my shoulder. "Took you almost thirty seconds to blame me this time."

Halfway out the door, a thought occurred to me. I spun. "Frances," I said. "This could have been a ruse gone wrong."

Understanding registered in her expression. "What do you want me to do?"

"Call Lois. Order an emergency inventory."

"Scope?"

"The entire mansion." I'd been fooled into falling for a ruse once before when a crime had been committed elsewhere in the manor. I wasn't about to let that happen again. "I'll alert Terrence."

I called our head of security on his radio as I ran out. "This may have already occurred to you, but our killer might have another agenda. If he was—"

"I'm on it," he said. "The woman might have seen him steal something and he reacted in fear. Problem is, murder is still murder. But, don't worry, as soon as I heard, I put the house on lockdown. No one gets out without being cleared."

After he signed off I realized he'd said, "As soon as I heard." Which meant that there was a chance our bad guy might have gotten away. I didn't want to think about that.

Before I could get far, I was notified via radio that the police had arrived. An alert front desk staffer had already rushed the paramedics up to the second floor so it fell to me to escort the police to the scene.

Detectives Rodriguez and Flynn had worked the two prior murders here at Marshfield. Rodriguez viewed the world through hooded eyes, analyzing everything with a ponderous demeanor that still drove me crazy sometimes. I'd first judged him slow and plodding, but came to understand that the portly detective absorbed far more than he liked to let on. I trusted him.

That was more than could be said for his young counterpart. Tall, lanky, and impulsive, Flynn leapt to conclusions before ensuring the evidence supported his claims. I supposed their two personalities balanced each other out, but I was disappointed that this mismatched team was the best Emberstowne had to offer.

I met them at the front door, where dozens of visitors had been brought to wait. "This way," I said to the detectives, trying my best to appear unruffled.

My efforts to avoid frightening people were in vain. All the guests I saw looked plenty shaken. Whether these people knew what had happened or were simply alarmed by the fact that armed guards were preventing their departure, I didn't know. Nor could I worry about that right now.

Still trying my best to keep quiet, I asked Rodriguez, "Where to first? The girl who was killed or the man who was shot?"

The detective spoke in a low growl, close to my ear. "What's going on here, Ms. Wheaton? A town like this shouldn't have these kinds of problems."

That was twice in as many minutes that someone had made a point to mention the recent upsurge in murders. Rodriguez hadn't called me out personally the way Frances had, but that didn't mean he wasn't thinking it.

I decided not to answer that as we walked quickly across the main floor.

"I want to talk to the shooting victim," Rodriguez said. "Let's hope he's still alive by the time we get there."

Chapter 8

WITH HIS BACK UP AGAINST THE OAK WALL, the victim sat on the floor, head hanging down. At first I couldn't tell if he was unconscious or not, but the fact that he retained a grip his left shoulder and remained upright was encouraging.

Terrence's staff had managed to clear the immediate area and paramedics were working on the injured man, faces calm, expressions serious. One of them confirmed that the victim's vitals were being transmitted to the local hospital. "You're in good hands, sir," he assured his patient. "Try to keep alert. We need you to stay awake."

Another paramedic, nearer the victim's head, asked about allergies. Yet another set up a saline drip. The woman who had so spiritedly taken Lenore to task yesterday was now crouched on the floor conferring with the paramedics. It dawned on me that she was the doctor in the group who John had mentioned. I'd pegged her as a retired kindergarten teacher. What was her name again? I racked my brain. Marlene.

Marlene spoke in a crisp tone, asking questions, issuing directives.

"Oh," I said, startled, when the man on the floor looked up. Spotting me, he tried to straighten, and I could tell he was trying to place who I was. Just then, however, Marlene lifted the man's arm to examine his wound, causing him to stiffen and wince.

I winced, too. So much blood from one bullet hole. The victim clenched his eyes and turned away.

"You know him?" Rodriguez asked from over my shoulder.

"Not really," I answered. "He was part of the tour group that came through here yesterday when we had that altercation. I remember seeing him. The tour guide says his name is Mark Ellroy."

The man on the floor focused mad, dark eyes on me now. He tried to get up but the paramedics held him down. "Lenore," he asked, voice cracking. "No one will tell me anything. Is she all right?"

I turned to Rodriguez. "He doesn't know."

Whispering served only to stir the man's agitation.

"Oh no," he gasped, his gaze frantically bouncing between my face and Rodriguez's, "she's not okay, is she?"

The concern in his expression gripped me. I had no words of consolation, but I was moved with pity. "I'm so sorry," I began, realizing by the widening of his eyes that that was probably the worst way to begin. "Can you tell us what happened?"

Flynn, who up until now had been mostly silent, gave a grunt of displeasure. "Since when are you in charge of questioning witnesses?" he demanded under his breath.

Rodriguez had placed a restraining hand on my arm. His voice was gentle. "Let us handle this. You can help by gathering all the other potential witnesses. Is there somewhere they can wait until we're ready to question them?"

"I'll find a room." I thought about it. "Or two."

"Evidence technicians will be here soon," he added. "We'll need your help coordinating." He started to move away, then stopped and turned back. He heaved a sigh so deep his protruding gut lifted and dropped with a bounce. "What am I saying? You know the drill."

Unfortunately, I did.

"John's downstairs," I said, adding, "The tour guide," when Rodriguez looked confused. "I'll make sure he's okay. He saw the man who did this."

The rest of the tour group had been staged in a corridor down the hall; they were now being herded downstairs. I caught up with the guard who was bringing up the rear. "Where are you taking them?" I asked, sneaking a discreet look at his badge. I'd met him once before, but until I saw "Cornell," I couldn't come up with his name.

Tall, solid, and with military-cropped short hair, Cornell kept close watch on the trudging tourists as he answered, "Carr wants them held in the entrance hall until further notice. Not as much chance for them to get into trouble."

The group shuffled forward as directed, murmuring among themselves. A few shot backward glances toward where we'd left Mark Ellroy. They wore expressions of fear and disbelief. Couples held tight to one another. Others cast wary glances at their peers. I was happy there were no children in this bunch.

Cornell continued, "We've got everything under control. No one's getting out until we say so."

I knew his words were meant to reassure, but I also knew of secret passages that had helped another murderer escape.

"You're joining us?" he asked when I continued to accompany the exodus.

I shook my head. "I'm heading back . . . down." I caught Cornell's glum look of understanding, so thankfully didn't have to explain that I would be returning to where Lenore had met her death. "I need to relieve Frances. As soon as I can, however, I'll be up to help in the entrance hall."

I inched past the group when they turned down the next corridor. I reached the yellow staff stairway and trotted down as quickly as I could, my entire body pinging with awareness. My hands balled into fists as my pace picked up. I was angry—so angry—that another murder had been committed on Marshfield grounds that I felt almost eager to spring into action if I happened to cross paths with the killer.

In a twisted way, I almost wished I would. Whoever had killed Lenore and attempted to kill Mark Ellroy was not a member of the Marshfield staff. I was sure of it. Whoever it was must have posed as a docent, probably as he plotted his next major theft.

I was furious. Frustrated. My head buzzed with the need to *do* something. Adrenaline pumped under my skin, flushing me with a sense of invincibility. "Come on," I wanted to scream. "Let me at him."

I hurried through a narrow basement corridor toward the spot I'd left John and Frances, but all I could see were the backs of staff members from the laundry and maintenance departments. They clustered in the doorway, jostling one another for a better look as they all peered at the meticulous process of evidence collection.

Excusing myself as I made my way through the four-deep throng, I realized that despite their curiosity, they'd been effectively held back from trampling the scene by a slim band of crime scene tape. Bright yellow, flimsy plastic, it nonetheless worked like magic to keep everyone out of the stairwell. It kept me from entering the area as well.

I was grateful to see that our local law enforcement was on the scene much faster than they'd been in the past, but I hated the fact that we here at Marshfield had provided so much practice. I spotted Frances just out of the evidence technicians' way, a few steps up from the ground level. I called out to her. "Where's John?"

She'd glanced up at the sound of her name, her expression at once both annoyed and relieved. "There you are," she said. To the technician closest to her position, she pointed at me. "You can let her in. She's my boss."

The tech gave the briefest of nods then turned to me. He wore gloves and booties and carried a clear plastic bin full of items I couldn't begin to recognize. "You can walk in up to here." The tech drew an imaginary line on the ground about a foot from the doorway, where I ducked under the tape. "You can join your friend on the stairs," he said, "but don't come any closer than this."

"Got it."

He turned to the gaping group of staffers who had resumed staring. "Okay, enough. Everybody scatter. We've got work to do here and we don't need an audience."

"Where's John?" I asked Frances when I reached her.

"One of our security guards said he was needed for questioning and took him out." Pointing, Frances indicated upward. "He's waiting on the first floor."

"Who?"

"John," she said, with a look and a tone meant to deride me for asking.

"No. Who took him? Which of our guards?"

"Oh," she said, face flushing. "I missed looking at his name badge. One of the new guys."

"Was he dressed like a guard or a docent?" I asked.

Frances hesitated long enough to send me into a panic.

"But it was someone you've seen before?" I asked, desperate for answers.

"Sure, of course," she said. "I'd recognize him instantly."

I turned to the tech who had let me in. "I'm going up," I said.

He looked at me sharply. "Stay away from the second floor. That's a crime scene, too."

"First floor only." I was pointing even as I ran. What if the guard who had taken John was actually the killer, trying to keep from being identified?

Frances was right on my heels, apparently reading my mind. "You're not going to rush in there without help, are you?"

I didn't answer.

She tried again, a little more breathless now, as I reached the first-floor landing. "I'm sure he's one of ours. I'm sure of it."

I bolted through the door to find John alone in a soft chair, his face in his hands. He jumped to his feet as we burst in. "What else? What's wrong?"

There was no one with him. This room—another one that was off-limits to guests, in a section of the house they probably didn't even realize they were missing—had become one of our many storage rooms. With one door that we'd used to come in from the staircase and another across the room leading into the hallway, it offered excellent accessibility. Shelves lined two walls, wooden chairs stacked on them, neatly flip-flopped one atop another in sets of two.

"Where's the guard who brought you here?" I asked.

John twisted to face the door behind him, indicating as he did so. "He told me to wait right here. He needed to get someone."

"Did he say anything?" I asked. "Did you catch his name?"

The concern in my voice must have been apparent because John's already troubled expression grew even more alarmed. "I didn't know I needed to." He peered around me to look at Frances. "You know him, don't you?"

"I can't recall his name," she said stiffly. "But he works here. I'm sure of it."

I crossed the room and opened the oak door, peeking out into the quiet corridor. No one.

Angry anticipation danced in Frances's eyes when I turned back to them. "Say it," she said. "I know what you're thinking: that I should have accompanied John. But then who would have waited for the technicians, hmm? I can't be in two places at once, you know."

Frances was always able to turn any disagreeable situation into my fault. But there was no point in arguing right now. Clearly she'd realized her mistake. I pulled up my walkie-talkie and contacted Terrence.

"What's up, Grace?" he asked the moment he came through. There was no mistaking the impatience in his voice.

"I'm in the storage room just off the red staircase, first floor. John, the tour director, is here with me. According to him and to Frances, one of our guards brought John here claiming he needed to be questioned. Do you know anything about this?"

"Negative," he said. "But Rodriguez may have ordered that. I've assigned a few of our guys to him."

"But why would he bring John here and leave him?"

"Can't answer that. Gotta run." He started to sign off then asked, "Everyone there is okay, right? Nobody hurt?"

"We're fine."

"Check with Rodriguez, then. That's the best I can offer right now."

"See," Frances said the moment I signed off, "he's not worried. You're getting all worked up over nothing."

I was about to retort when the corridor door opened and one of our guards stepped in, looking sheepish. "Ms. Wheaton," he began.

"Aha!" Frances cut him off. "You see, there he is now. Where have you been, young man?"

He was about twenty-five years old, with a blond crew cut and high cheeks that flared red as it became apparent he'd been the topic of discussion. I'd seen this guy around, too. One of our newer employees. Worry that had been making my heart skip beats, now muted to a dull thump. "Is . . . is . . ." he stammered in a low drawl," . . . uh . . . everything all right here?"

"It is now," Frances said with a patronizing glare at me. "John says you brought him up here then left him alone. Why?"

"I . . . he . . ." The kid blinked several times, then closed his eyes briefly, as though to steady himself before answering, "One of the detectives instructed me to isolate this witness from everybody else. I did exactly that, but then wasn't sure about what to do next. I couldn't raise anybody on the radio"—he held up his walkie-talkie—"so I went looking for Carr."

"Did you find him?" I asked, moving forward to take the proffered radio out of his hands.

"No, ma'am," he said. "I ran up to the top floor where the other guest got himself shot and the Emberstowne fellow told me to come down here and wait for them. Not to leave the witness alone. Again." He swallowed, making his Adam's apple bob up and down like a yo-yo.

I examined the walkie-talkie, made an adjustment, then handed it back, while taking note of his name. "You had it on the wrong channel." I couldn't help the slim air of suspicion that had crept into my voice. "That's a heck of a mistake, Mr. Thrush."

"Won't happen again." He took up a position near the door. "I'm here until I'm relieved," he said. "Those Emberstowne detectives said it might be a spell before they got down here." He tried to smile. "At least they know where I have this man sequestered, so I guess something good came out of my leaving him here."

That remained to be seen. The kid's newness could easily account for his blunder, but I wasn't trusting anyone I didn't know. If what John had told me was correct, the killer had been wandering freely around the manor disguised as an employee.

John had gotten to his feet briefly when Thrush walked in, but he didn't seem to be able to remain standing. He made his way back to the soft chair and lowered himself into it with effort. "I need to get back to my group," he said to no one in particular.

"They're in good hands," I assured him. "Our security

staff has them in the entrance hall. They'll all be questioned before anyone can leave." Attempting to lighten his burden, I said, "I saw the other victim, Mark Ellroy. He seems like he's going to be okay. I couldn't tell for sure, of course, but it looked like he'd taken a bullet in the arm. The paramedics and the doctor from your group were all very calm as they worked on him."

"That's something, at least."

"What did he look like?" I asked. "The guy who was dressed like one of our docents? The one you saw Lenore talking to?"

The door to the room banged open. We all jumped as our visitor strode in. I'd been hoping for Rodriguez, but it was Flynn who entered, eyes blazing. He pointed to John, almost as though he'd been listening at the door, and demanded, "What did the guy look like?"

John turned a terrified face toward me.

"I'm asking the questions," Flynn said, "not her." He snapped his fingers in front of John's nose. "Come on, guy, we're running out of time here. What did he look like?"

To me, John had always epitomized restraint, eloquence, and strength. Reduced to near tears, his hands shook as he brought them up in supplication. "I don't remember."

"What's wrong with you?" Flynn shouted. The aggressive detective was clearly out of control. I'd rarely encountered him without his partner, Rodriguez, and I suddenly realized I hadn't ever appreciated what a loose cannon Flynn could be.

I moved forward. "Listen," I began.

"You." The word dripped with disdain and I was struck again by the change that had come over him. Freed from Rodriguez's tether, his true personality was unleashed. He pointed over my head, toward the opposite door. "Get out of my sight."

Frances gasped.

Tendrils of heat curled behind my eyes. "Excuse me?"

"Both of you," he snarled. "You get involved where no-body wants you. You screw things up and then everybody says how great you are. How much smarter you are than the *Podunk* police. Well, I've got news for you." He shook his still-pointing finger between us. "Neither of you are getting your noses in this one. This is police business and you're not going to make fools of us this time. You understand?"

Frances huffed. "Well, of all the—"

He advanced on her. "Get out of my sight or I'll have you arrested for obstruction. That goes for both of you."

This was stupid and I didn't have time for stupid. "You can't arrest us," I said.

"Watch me."

John cleared his throat. "He wasn't very tall. Average height."

We stopped arguing to listen.

Straightening in his seat, John leaned forward. "I'd put him in his mid- to late forties, graying hair, average build. No, wait." He closed his eyes a moment, concentrating. "Slim. Yes. I remember thinking his clothes looked baggy. He was wearing the regular staff uniform—the blue blazer and tan pants. Light blue shirt. Striped tie."

I knew what our standard uniform looked like, but I also knew John picturing the guy piece by piece might help him recall even more. Flynn looked ready to interrupt to ask for specifics other than clothing. I hoped he would keep his mouth shut and not disrupt John's train of thought.

Fortunately John started talking again before Flynn could blow it. "No facial hair. Light complexion but he had a summer tan." He pointed to his own eyes. "Pale here un-derneath, like he wears sunglasses. I never got very close to him, though. It could have been shadows playing tricks."

Again John closed his eyes. "Wait." We waited. A mo-ment later, eyes still clenched, John said, "He had some-thing sticking out of his collar. On his right side. Something pointed and dark."

Flynn rolled his eyes. "Lot of good that will do. He's probably changed clothes by now."

John opened his eyes and fixed a glare at Flynn. "It wasn't a piece of clothing. I couldn't get close enough to be sure, but I think it was either a birthmark or maybe a tattoo."

"You can't be sure, but now you got close enough to recognize a birthmark?"

Frances harrumphed. "With an attitude like that, it's no wonder you need Grace's help to solve these crimes."

Flynn turned purple, his face contorting in rage.

Frances had again chosen the most inappropriate moment to express a negative sentiment, but this time the unexpected support came as a welcome surprise.

The young guard stepped between them. "Can I be of any assistance here?" he asked. Flynn spun, looking ready to pounce, but apparently realized Thrush was part of the security team. I watched the short-tempered cop's shoulders relax.

"Yes," Flynn said. "This man needs to be interviewed. My partner and I will do it together, but I need to bring him upstairs while the task force questions the rest of his tour group."

I'd disliked Flynn before, but after this blow-up, I despised the twerp. He rocked back and forth, balancing on the balls of his feet. "You can come with me," he said to Thrush. "We'll get this guy upstairs while the GSW victim is being transported to the hospital."

"GSW?" Frances asked.

"They think they're so smart and they don't even know basic lingo," Flynn said to Thrush as he rolled his eyes. "Gunshot wound," he said to Frances in a condescending voice. To John, he said, "Your group will have to stay in town tonight."

"We're scheduled to leave in the morning." John was beginning to regain some of his vitality. I supposed dealing with idiots will do that for you.

"We'll see about that," Flynn said, "I can't promise. What I can tell you is that the victim upstairs isn't going anywhere. He's staying for a couple of days, at least. My partner and I hope to clear this in the next forty-eight hours and we'll need him here to identify the guy who killed the girl."

"You have someone in custody already?" I asked.

Flynn looked up with dead eyes but didn't answer. He grabbed John's elbow to hoist him to his feet, but John shook off the detective's grip. "I'm fully capable of getting up myself, thank you." Yes, John was beginning to regain spirit. "Mark Ellroy," he said to me. "He's going to need a place to stay once he's released from the hospital. We're only booked at our hotel here until tomorrow night."

I immediately understood. "If Mr. Ellroy is required to stay in town, he'll need a place to stay."

John nodded. "Can you take care of that?"

"Absolutely," I said. "I'll arrange to have his things brought over and we'll get him set up at the Marshfield Hotel."

Flynn seemed confused by our conversation. I felt no need to explain.

Apparently, however, John did. "Thank you," he said to me. To Flynn, he added, "This woman, who you so nastily dressed down, will be taking excellent care of your gunshot victim. It would behoove you to be nicer to her."

Flynn shrugged him off and led the small group out the door.

Chapter 9

I SENT FRANCES UPSTAIRS AND DECIDED TO stop by the entrance hall to see how things were progressing for the task force. The detectives on site weren't as pointedly rude as Flynn had been, but after providing me with minimal updates, they made it clear that they would prefer I wait in my office until summoned. Several of the incarcerated guests shot me looks of unrestrained desperation, but when I offered to have them moved to the Birdcage Room, where we could provide coffee and soft drinks, one of the task force detectives snarled, asking me if I thought this was a tea party.

"Leave this to the proper authorities," he said. "That would be us."

Truth be told, I was happy to be given a reprieve. As I started for my office again, I remembered my earlier state of mind—itching to take on the killer with my bare hands—and I gave a sad laugh at my own foolhardiness.

Who was I to take on such a monster? I'd gotten lucky twice. I wasn't about to push my good fortune by sticking my nose where it didn't belong. I had neither the skill set nor the resources to be any help whatsoever.

This morning I'd practically skipped up the stairs to our offices. Now, every trudging step I took made me feel as though I wore lead weights on my feet. My impression of Lenore was that she'd been misguided but ultimately harmless. She'd taken this vacation to get away from the fallout at the end of a difficult marriage. She'd been trying to do something positive, something for herself, and it had all been stolen away in a heartbeat.

Weariness borne of sadness kept me company all the way up.

I opened the door to Frances's office. She looked up when the door opened and spoke as though she'd expected me to walk through that very minute, as though we were continuing a conversation that was already under way. "The golden horn."

It took me a minute to remember we'd ordered an emergency inventory. "It's missing?"

Frances's eyes lit up the way they always did when she was about to impart bad news. "Right out of its display case."

The carved horn was a replica of an 11th-century oliphant, or hunting horn. Six originals were known to exist, but these had been carved from elephant tusks. The one stolen from us was a reproduction Bennett had acquired twenty years ago. Although he loved the graceful curves of the original horns, he didn't approve of owning real ivory. In fact, all the ivory items that his father and grandfather had accumulated in their lifetimes had been taken off exhibit and placed in storage. Bennett didn't want tangible proof of man's cruelty on display in his home, nor did he want to profit by releasing them to the marketplace. The hunting horn that had been stolen held all the beauty of an original, but had been carved out of solid gold.

"But . . ." I could tell from her artificially bored expression that she already had an answer for me and that I wasn't going to like it. "That display case is on camera."

"The viewfinder's angle was changed. Deliberately."

"For how long? Did no one notice?"

She held up a notepad. She made a show of perching her reading glasses on her nose, but I had no doubt she'd already memorized the facts and could recite them blindfolded. "I called down there the moment I found out about the theft," she said over the tops of the lenses. "This is what I found out: A note was sent to security, informing them that several cameras around the manor, including this one, would be adjusted during the DVD filming today. It was signed Corbin Shaw."

"What? Corbin knows better than to—"

"He didn't send the note." She waggled her brows. "At least, that's what he claims."

Dumbfounded, I tried to make sense of it all. "Is anything else missing?"

"Not so far. And before you ask, and I know you will, I have security trying to determine who adjusted the camera angles. I mean, if these were physically moved it ought to be pretty obvious who got close enough to the equipment to do it."

I suspected that whoever had gone to such lengths to reroute cameras would have taken precautions necessary to ensure anonymity. "Is security—"

"They're going over every minute of tape as we speak. They'll keep us informed."

"Thanks, Frances."

She gave me a look that said, "What did you expect?" and then asked for an update.

"The man who was shot, Mark Ellroy, has been taken to the hospital," I said. "I'll be heading over there soon to check on him. He may need help transitioning from his current hotel to ours. I'll see to his belongings, but there may be more I haven't anticipated." Frances's expression was one of pure skepticism and I couldn't imagine why. Continuing, I explained, "The police want to keep him in town until they have a chance to question him thoroughly."

"Can you do that?" she asked. "Up and move him without his okay?"

"I'll make sure I talk with Mr. Ellroy first before I touch anything of his."

She seemed to approve. "Poor man," she said. "His whole vacation will be ruined."

"Worse for Lenore."

"I wasn't forgetting about her," Frances said, miffed. "I'm thinking about what that poor man has to face next. Your detective friends have been made to look like fools twice now in the span of a few months, so they're desperate. You know how some doctors order fifteen more tests than a patient really needs to avoid being hit with a malpractice suit?" When I nodded, she continued, "I think the Emberstowne police are so worried about you showing them up again that they're encroaching on Mr. Ellroy's civil liberties. He should be allowed to resume his vacation if he likes."

That was a whole lot to assimilate at once. I blinked. "Would *you* be able to enjoy a vacation after the person standing next you was killed in cold blood?"

"I just think he should have been consulted before he was ordered to stay here."

"Point taken, Frances. And for the record, I agree. I'll talk with him." I glanced up at the office clock. "I don't want to leave here with the police still on-site, but they've made it clear I'm not needed." I took a moment to consider my options. "Flynn said they would be questioning John while the paramedics transport Mr. Ellroy. Maybe if I hurry down to the hospital right now, I can talk to him about relocating to the Marshfield Hotel before Rodriguez and Flynn arrive."

"Good luck avoiding those two."

* * *

AFTER ATTENDING TO A FEW MORE DETAILS, I
struck out for the hospital. Sunny, muggy heat engulfed me
the moment I stepped out of my car to hurry to the entrance. I wanted to rush, but found it difficult to move
quickly without working up a sweat. I skirted around an
ambulance idling outside the ER, and wondered if it was
the one that had transported Mr. Ellroy.

The moment the doors whooshed open and I stepped
through I lifted my arms, hoping to halt the outpouring of
perspiration. The hospital's brightly lit admissions area—
white tile walls, cobalt blue floors—was blessedly cool, but
my goose bumps weren't due to the chill. I knew I'd never
be able to escape the immediate reaction I always experienced when encountering that fake-fresh scent that every
hospital shares. I'd been in this one far too often with my
mother to ever permanently shake its effect. The appalling
aroma came in waves bearing hope, fear, and tension laced
with antiseptic, stale coffee, and bleach. I wondered if all
hospitals belonged to a co-op where they purchased the
same "Let's try to cover the odor of illness" fragrance to
pipe in by the gallon. Somebody ought to tell them it wasn't
working.

Today looked to be a slow day in the ER. Plastic steel-
frame chairs lined the walls. All empty. I walked through
the quiet passage to a high-top circular desk that sat between
two sets of automatic doors, both sets clearly labeled, NO
ADMITTANCE WITHOUT AUTHORIZATION in bold red letter-
ing. A young, uniformed Emberstowne cop lingered nearby,
watching a car commercial on a ceiling-mounted TV.

The woman at the circular desk didn't appear eager to
authorize my entrance. With tightly curled brown hair, a
trim build, and crisp movements, she gave off a vibe of efficiency and addressed me with one of those brisk up-and-
down assessments.

"You want to see a patient," she repeated after I introduced myself. Not a question. "A gunshot victim. And you don't have authorization."

"He was shot at Marshfield Manor."

"You already said that."

The Emberstowne cop perked up and turned toward us.

"I need to talk with him about where he'll be staying once he's discharged," I said. "I promise I'll be brief."

"We take our patients' right to privacy seriously here."

Arguing my case wasn't going to work. I switched tactics. "You're right," I said. "You have no reason whatsoever for letting me in to see him . . ."

Her eyes narrowed. She was waiting for the "but," so I gave it to her. "But I believe Mr. Ellroy will want to see me, given the choice. Do you think it would be possible"—I was treading lightly here—"for you to ask if I could have five minutes of his time?"

She started to answer, but I interrupted.

"If he says no, I'll leave. Easy as that."

She picked up a pen. "Spell your name for me, please."

I'd begun to do so when the doors to the right of the desk folded open like a double set of old-fashioned phone booths. The only difference was these mechanisms moved swiftly and silently rather than with an earsplitting screech. One of the paramedics who had helped stabilize Mr. Ellroy at Marshfield came through. He nodded to the attentive cop then lifted his hand in greeting when he saw me. "He's going to be okay," he said when he got to the desk. "Lucky that doctor lady was there. Not that we haven't handled worse stuff on our own, you understand," he added quickly, "but he was pretty worked up and she helped calm him down. They know each other?"

"They were all traveling as part of a group," I answered. "Is she still here?"

"Back there, talking with the doc on duty. Looks like the bullet—"

The woman at the desk cleared her throat. "Excuse me, this visitor is not family."

The paramedic rolled his eyes. "Yeah, well, this lady is involved. Cut her some slack." He shrugged as he addressed me. "I think it wouldn't hurt if you got in there. He's a little disoriented and wants to know what's going to happen to the group if he's stuck here in the hospital. He says he doesn't want to ruin anybody else's vacation."

"That's surprisingly thoughtful."

"It was," the paramedic said, "but he's got some powerful pain meds rushing around in there. Patients can get a little loopy."

The doors folded open again and the diminutive doctor from the group emerged. She headed toward us with purpose.

"Marlene?" I said.

"You're from the mansion, aren't you?" she asked, obviously recognizing me as well. "You're the woman who runs the place, right?"

"That's me." I extended my hand. "Grace Wheaton. We really appreciate all you've done for our guest."

She waved off my thanks. "He isn't rejoining the group, is he?"

"The police would rather he stay. Ultimately, I suppose it's up to Mr. Ellroy. That's why I'm here, to suggest he remain at Marshfield until the detectives have time to question him thoroughly."

Her mouth twisted off to the side in a reflective manner. I was sure she was about to argue about Mr. Ellroy's rights the way Frances had, but she surprised me by saying, "That's probably the best. After a trauma like this, he's going to need time to come to grips with all that's happened. This isn't going to be easy for him. And hanging with a bunch of tourists who are out for a good time isn't exactly optimal."

"Good point."

She winked. "You don't get to be my age, honey, without

picking up a little wisdom along the way. If you want my opinion—and you're going to get it whether you do or not—I think he should stay here for as long as he needs to. I can't remember where he's from. Maybe Colorado or something?" She shrugged. "Wherever it is, it's far enough that he can't drop what he's doing on a whim if he needs to come back. And he's going to need to work through all this. Closure has a mind of its own. Comes when it wants to and not a moment before. You tell him to take his time."

All this seemed to be enough for the efficient clerk because she jammed a laminated visitor card at me then pointed backward over her head. "Second bed on the left. The officer will escort you."

The uniformed cop straightened, looking eager to be of assistance. Any chance to do something more than just stand sentry, I supposed. "Thank you," I said to the woman, quickly excusing myself in case she changed her mind again. This time when the automatic doors folded open, I took a deep breath of the faux fresh air and walked through.

The second bed on the left had its curtains pulled back and I caught sight of my quarry immediately. He was shirtless, propped up in the bed, with bandages covering his upper left arm. I wouldn't describe him as chiseled, but he was definitely in good shape. He glanced up as I approached and I watched recognition dawn. Up close, he was as good-looking as I'd first thought: dark, tousled hair; expressive brows that arched at my approach; a strong jaw; and what looked to be the beginnings of five o'clock shadow. Like the bandaged Indiana Jones as Marion Ravenwood tended to his injuries.

"How are you feeling?" I asked.

"They gave me pain medication, but"—he winced—"it doesn't eliminate it. Just dulls it to an ache."

"What did the doctor say?"

"I got lucky. The bullet didn't hit bone and went right through. They stitched me up like Frankenstein."

"May I talk with you for a little bit, or are you too tired right now?"

"Please," he said, indicating the far side of the bed with a nod. I came around and saw a doctor's stool. "I could use a little company. Have a seat."

"If the doctor comes . . ."

"Let him get his own chair." He tried to smile, but the pain held him back.

I remained standing. "Mr. Ellroy—"

"For heaven's sake," he interrupted. "We're in an emergency room after a tragic afternoon at your mansion. If that doesn't put us on a first-name basis, I don't know what does."

That made me smile. "I'm Grace," I said.

"I remember, from John's introduction yesterday. I'm Mark, but you probably already knew that." He sent a quizzical glance directed toward the young cop, who hadn't left the immediate area. "Am I under surveillance?" he asked.

"No, sir," the uniform answered. "We're taking precautions to ensure your safety. In case this wasn't a random attack."

Mark's brows came together, forming three vertical lines between them. "That can't be . . . I'd never seen that man before." The lines between his brows deepened. "Wait. Do you mean that Lenore might have been targeted? On purpose? That someone was after her?"

The uniformed officer's cheeks flamed scarlet. "Forget I said that. I'm here to ensure your safety until the detectives arrive." He glanced at his watch. "They should be here soon." At that, he turned his back and moved far enough away to give us a semblance of privacy.

I had a lot of questions I wanted answered before freaky Flynn showed up, but as I was ready to start, Mark cleared his throat. His voice was shaky. "Lenore didn't . . . make it." He swallowed, then started again. "I . . . I have no words."

To buy myself a moment to search for an appropriate thing to say, I did as he'd originally suggested: I wheeled the doctor's stool closer and lowered myself onto it.

When I spoke I found it difficult to keep my own voice from trembling. "This was a terrible tragedy. I'm so sorry you were part of it."

Squinting, he squared his jaw. "What now? Marlene was good enough to stay with me through all this, but I can't ask John to keep the entire group in town until I'm released. Not to mention the fact that the police haven't even questioned me yet."

The young cop twisted his head toward us, then quickly fixed his attention on the emergency room's whiteboard as though he understood what all those scribbled notes meant.

Mark must have noticed it, too. "Could you give us a little privacy, Officer?" he asked without raising his voice.

"I'm here to protect you," the cop repeated, proof that he had indeed been listening. "But your visitor doesn't seem to be posing any danger. I'll step outside. Let me know if you need me."

Without his company, and with the nearest patient halfway across the capacious emergency room, we were left with only awkward silence. Around us, amid the occasional sounds of conversation, snapping plastic, and the clink of metal, hospital staff kept the area humming. A nurse hurrying by slowed her pace long enough to study the readouts on the monitor next to Mark's bed. Apparently satisfied by what she saw, she moved on again at a quick clip.

"I'm surprised Detectives Rodriguez and Flynn aren't here yet," I said in an effort to resume the conversation. "I'm sure Flynn will be plenty annoyed that I got to talk with you before they did."

"You tensed up when you said his name. Flynn, that is. Is there anything I should know about him before he shows up?"

"He's not particularly fond of me. Long story."

From the look on Mark's face, I realized that he thought Flynn and I had a sordid romantic history. As much as I would have preferred to set him straight, that wasn't why I was here.

"John wanted me to talk with you," I continued. "He thinks it may be best if the tour goes on as scheduled. I know he's working to get you a refund . . ."

"The last thing I'm worried about right now is a refund," he said, "although that's very nice of him."

"I know your group was staying at one of the hotels in town. I'd like to suggest you relocate to the Marshfield Hotel. On us. For as long as you need."

"That's incredibly generous," he said, looking concerned. "I know how beautiful your hotel is. In fact, I considered tacking on a few days before the tour on my own, but I couldn't get the extra time off."

"Where do you work?"

"I own a jewelry store in Colorado. It was my father's before me and his father's before that. My staff is covering for me while I'm gone. I felt guilty burdening them with full responsibility for this length of time, but they insisted I finally take a vacation." His eyes took on a wistful look. "It's been a while. And then . . . this."

"I'm so sorry. We'll do whatever we can to make you comfortable at our hotel. I can arrange to have your luggage brought over."

"Oh, that's above and beyond," he said.

"It's the least we can do. John said he'd release your belongings to us if you gave the okay."

He thought about that. "The vacation I'd planned is history," he said finally. "Part of me prefers to say thanks but no thanks and head home the minute they let me out of here."

I waited.

"But the truth is, I don't know that I *can* leave. So much has happened. I mean . . . in the blink of an eye, a woman was killed right in front of me. It happened so fast." I got the feeling he was talking to himself as much as to me. "To head home now, to pretend that this was all a bad dream seems wrong somehow. I need some sort of . . ."

"Closure?"

"Yes," he said, "precisely. I need to give this its due. Whatever that may be."

I understood what he meant. "Would you like me to arrange to have your things delivered to Marshfield, or do you prefer to wait until you're released?"

He thought about it. "I left my extra cash and some credit cards in the room's safe. It's probably better if we wait until I can clear that out."

"Makes sense," I said, pulling up my purse. "Let me give you my business card. Whenever you're ready, let me know."

"You've been very kind," he said.

"You've been through a lot."

"What do you think this was all about?" he asked. "Lenore struck me as a simple girl. I can't imagine anyone coming after her. Not like that."

"I can't either," I said. "The man who killed her . . . the one who shot you . . . did you get a good look at him?"

He pushed out a hard breath and I could tell the exertion hurt. "I've been trying my best to remember. I'm sure I'd recognize him if I saw him again, but it's like his face is a blur in my brain. I can't remember much, other than he was in uniform. Not a security uniform. More like one of your staff members. Blue blazer, tie, you know."

I nodded. People often had a hard time recalling details immediately following trauma. I held out hope that Mark would be able to come up with a better description after he'd had time to settle down. "John remembered a little bit."

Mark nodded. "I'm glad he got a look at him."

"Not much of one, I'm afraid, but it's a start." I thought about the missing golden horn. "Did you notice if the man was carrying anything?"

"I noticed the gun." Mark shook his head. "Otherwise, no. He called to Lenore."

"By name?"

"I don't think so." He struggled to remember. "Wait, no. He gestured for her to join him. He didn't say a word. I didn't know what was up, but I figured if a staff member was talking to her, she wouldn't get into trouble. But then I remembered I'd promised John, so I followed her. That's when I saw the guy in the blazer pulling her toward the stairs."

His eyes clouded with the memory. I was about to tell him he didn't need to continue, but he went on. "Whatever was happening between them wasn't right—I could see that much—so I went into the stairwell after them. By the time I got there, he'd . . . he'd . . ." Mark widened his eyes and bit his lips tight. He held up a finger as he looked away. Composing himself, he said, "This is so wrong. I didn't even really know Lenore, but I can't help feeling responsible."

"It's not your fault."

"Then why do I feel like it is?" His voice cracked again but he calmed himself by breathing deeply through his nose. "I went after them, catching the door as it was about to close. That's when I saw her go over. And then the guy turned on me."

He swallowed. I knew there was more.

"I froze. I was stupid and froze. That's all the guy needed—that second or two. He pulled out a gun and shot me. Right there. Ran off down the stairs."

I didn't know what to say.

Mark broke the silence. "Wait," he said, staring at some middle distance. "He dropped something and then picked it up." Looking at me, he added, "I don't have any idea what it was."

"Thanks," I said, "that's very helpful. You'll want to mention that to the detectives when they talk to you."

"You know, if the killer had picked anybody else to call

over," Mark said, "he might have gotten away without being noticed at all. We were all so high-strung about Lenore after that problem yesterday." He ran a hand along his bandaged arm. "Maybe my getting shot is a good thing after all. Maybe I'll be able to help identify the guy and put him away."

"Let's hope so. In the meantime, you're starting to look a little tired and I don't want to—"

"What are you doing here?"

I spun to see Flynn advancing on me. Rodriguez trailed behind, the tip of his tongue caught between his teeth as he walked and scrawled notes at the same time. He glanced up and acknowledged my presence, but I caught a sense of weariness in the older detective's eyes. "Let's not jump to conclusions," he said in a loud enough voice for me to hear. "I knew she'd be here, partner. Cut her a little slack."

Flynn's eyes blazed. He ignored Rodriguez's suggestion and took a position across Mark's bed. "You're interfering with a police investigation."

"No, I'm not," I said. "I know you'll want to keep him close for the next few days. You wouldn't want me to leave the poor man without a place to stay while you interrogate . . . er, I mean . . . question him."

Okay, so I threw out that word *interrogate* on purpose. Flynn grated on every nerve I possessed. Ever since we'd first met after Abe's murder, I'd taken pains to avoid him. Harsh, abrasive, and quick to judgment, Flynn was— apologies to Sherlock Holmes—as tenacious as a lobster.

Fire practically shot out of his eyes. "You think this is funny, don't you?"

Rodriguez took an easy step forward, smacking his lips as though he'd just finished a giant plate of barbecue. "Ms. Wheaton has business with Mr. Ellroy, same as we do. Let's not get ahead of ourselves here."

Rodriguez, at least, took time to listen. What would happen to the Emberstowne homicide division when their cool-headed lead detective took his retirement and ambled home? I didn't want to know.

"Ms. Wheaton," Rodriguez continued calmly, now addressing only me, "my partner does have a point. I hope you won't mind if we take over now?"

"I was about to leave."

"Thank you for stopping by," Mark said to me. "I'll call you the minute I'm released."

Flynn fixed me with a strange look. "Gave up on the gardener, did you?"

"What?" I asked.

To Mark, he said, "Watch out for that one."

I didn't realize what he meant until I was outside in the sweltering heat again and the infamous lightbulb went on in my head. Or maybe it was the sun. Either way, I spun in a rush of belated anger, facing the doors that *whooshed* shut behind me. "You jerk," I said it aloud, meaning it for Flynn. He'd believed I'd been there to flirt with Mark. And Mark, who probably assumed I had a history with Flynn, was likely convinced he was facing a jealous ex-boyfriend.

I gave a grumble of sheer frustration. It was time to go home.

Chapter 10

"I SWEAR, GRACE, NO ONE COMES HOME AS OF-
ten as you do saying, 'There's been a murder at work.'"
Bruce finished seasoning the pasta, tasted it one last time,
and pronounced it done, even as he shook his head. "I'm
starting to get a little paranoid."

He placed the turquoise earthenware bowl in the center
of the yellow checkered tablecloth and directed me to start
serving the salad. Scott poured wine, a white this time, and
we all took our places around the cheery kitchen table.

I'd grabbed a quick sandwich when I'd first gotten home,
but there was no way I was passing up Bruce's homemade
frutti di mare. My roommates usually waited to have dinner until after they closed Amethyst Cellars for the night.
Because I enjoyed their company—not to mention Bruce's
cooking—I often joined them, even though that meant I
had to keep from overindulging earlier.

Scott passed me a plate loaded with bruschetta slices.
"I'd say it's better than Grace going *in* to work saying that
there's been a murder at *home*."

I shuddered. "Don't even say that. Marshfield has just had a run of bad luck."

Bruce dug in. "I'll say." A moment later he closed his eyes. "Mmm," he said, "I think I may have outdone myself this time."

Scott and I enthusiastically concurred. Bootsie wound her way between the kitchen chair legs to stare up at me and yowl with polite indignation. "I fed you," I said. She yowled again and the boys laughed. Bootsie's pupils were huge and soulful, which I'd come to learn meant a leap into my lap was imminent. "Can you wait until I'm finished eating?" I asked.

She seemed to understand. Winding her way between the table and chair legs again, she took up a position near the door to the dining room and sprawled, watching us.

"You seem to have gotten over your allergies," Scott said.

I was about to answer but instead I put down my fork. They both looked up.

"What's wrong?" Bruce asked.

"Do you realize that we went from talking about the murder of a young woman to my allergies—which yes, you're right, have abated—in the space of one minute? Doesn't the fact that we were able to shift subjects so quickly seem wrong?"

"You're right." Scott put his fork down, too. "But that doesn't make us callous, or uncaring, does it?"

Bruce looked a little alarmed, as though we were all about to stop eating after the first two bites. "I think it's a coping mechanism."

Scott agreed. "Think about it. We don't have any idea how to handle the fallout from a murder, yet we've scrambled to do our best ever since the first time you brought one home."

"Wow, doesn't that make me feel good?" I said.

Bruce chimed in again. "That's not quite accurate.

Makes it sound as though it's your fault, and it isn't. I think what Scott means is that there are no rule books to follow, no guidelines. Unless we strive for normal, we risk getting sucked into depression. I can't believe that would serve anyone. Not even the memory of the recently deceased."

"You're probably right," I said. "The crime is too horrible to deal with. We aren't cops, we aren't psychologists. We don't have the skills or tools to deal with this kind of trauma."

"Scott and I have the luxury of distance. We can separate ourselves from all that's happening at the manor. You, on the other hand," Bruce pointed to me with his filled fork, "have been able to use your emotion as fuel to help solve the crimes."

"Not intentionally."

"Maybe not. But don't beat yourself up about how you handle all this. I think you're more than living up to your name. You've shown grace in situations that would cause anyone else to wring their hands and run away."

"I had to bring Bennett up to date on all that's happened. Do you have any idea how difficult it is to explain that we've suffered yet another murder?"

"Does he feel responsible?" Scott asked.

"Of course he does. As do I."

I took a bite of pasta. No longer hungry, I was nonetheless eager to get back to normal, like Bruce had suggested. How hypocritical of me. I'd complained that we were in too much of a hurry to resume our ordinary lives and now it was I who was scurrying back to a place where comfort reigned.

It wasn't until we cleared the plates and began our kitchen cleanup that the subject of the murder came up again. "The man who was shot," Bruce began as he dried a dish with a blue cotton towel, "you said he's going to be staying at the Marshfield Hotel?"

"The hospital is keeping him overnight for observation.

I'm to pick him up around nine tomorrow. We'll set him up in a nice room at the hotel." I stopped in the middle of sweeping the floor. "Why did you ask about him?"

Scott and Bruce exchanged a look.

"What?" I asked.

They hadn't conversed without me in the room since they'd gotten home, yet it was clear they were communicating. "Nothing," Scott said.

"Not nothing. Fess up."

Again the shared look. Bruce threw his dish towel over his shoulder and waited as though he expected me to say something.

I looked over at Scott. Up to his elbows in soapy water, he paid more attention to me than he did to his dirty dishes.

"What?" I asked again.

One of Scott's eyebrows rose. "Is there anything else you'd like to tell us about this Mark Ellroy?"

Completely lost, I looked from one to the other. "Not really," I said slowly. "I told you he lives in Colorado, didn't I?"

Bruce cut to the chase. "You didn't mention if he was single."

"I don't know if he is or not."

"He was *traveling* as a single, right?" Scott asked.

"That doesn't mean anything."

Bruce wagged his head. "You should have seen yourself talking about him. Everything was doom and gloom until you got to the part about visiting him in the hospital. Then your face lit up."

"It did not."

"Did, too," Scott said, picking up another dish to scour. "Like night and day. Is he good-looking?"

I turned my back to them, resuming my sweeping job. Bootsie decided it was time to play and, with her rump up, watched with rapt attention as I navigated nonexistent dirt out of the far corner. As soon as I went back for more, she pounced, then scampered away the moment her little paws hit the bristles.

I glanced back over my shoulder to find my roommates waiting for an answer. "He's not bad."

"Aha!" Bruce said with undisguised glee. "I knew it."

"I thought you two were rooting for Jack."

"When was the last time you and Jack spoke?" Scott asked.

"A week ago."

"What did you talk about?"

"Things."

"Things like relationships or things like pruning roses and when to put down more fertilizer?"

I bit my lip. "He's had a rough go of it. You know that. He needs time."

"You had a rough go of it, too, and you've rallied," Bruce said.

"Listen," Scott added, rinsing suds off his hands before wiping them dry, "nothing against Jack. He's a good guy. We like him. But you've got to do what's best for Grace. Right now that may mean exploring other opportunities. Nothing wrong with that."

"You don't think flirting with a victim—an attempted murder victim, no less—is a little tacky?"

"You're not flirting with a victim. You're establishing a bond based on a shared experience."

"The shared experience in question being a murder," I reminded him.

Scott said, "I'm telling you, your face lit up when you talked about him tonight. We're just saying not to close the door on any possibilities."

"Sorry to disappoint you guys, but you obviously missed that part about him living out West. I'm not ready for a long-distance relationship." I gestured with the broom, causing Bootsie to jump.

The two of them shared another glance before returning

to the dishes. Bruce grinned at me over his shoulder. "Whatever you say, Grace."

I was about to start sweeping again when Scott asked, "When do we get to meet him?"

THE NEXT MORNING I LEFT FRANCES A VOICE-mail on the office phone, letting her know I'd be late because I was overseeing Mark Ellroy's transition from the hospital to the Marshfield Hotel. I also made a few other key calls, letting our bell captain know I'd be contacting him later once I found out where Mark was staying. I'd forgotten to get that information from John.

When I finally left my bedroom, dressed and ready to go, Bootsie bounded down the stairs ahead of me. She took the steps double-pawed, her rear white legs bouncing like a jackrabbit's. I usually fed her before leaving in the morning. The poor thing probably thought I'd forgotten.

She crawled around my ankles, mewing pitifully while I opened a fresh can and scooped out two tablespoons. "Yum," I said as she started in on her breakfast, "you like that, sweetie?"

I left her making little smacking noises, and thought about how much fun it was to have her as part of the family. I remembered Ronny Tooney's involvement when she'd first arrived, and how much he'd helped me with the last murder on Marshfield grounds. As much as I'd appreciated his assistance, I sincerely hoped he hadn't heard about this new problem. If so, he'd be on my doorstep in no time.

The thought gave me pause as I let myself out the back door and made sure the lock held. We'd been having troubles with it popping open lately, and I always worried about Bootsie getting out. After I ensured the lock was secure, I checked our yard and driveway for some sign of Tooney. Coast was clear. Good.

Today would be another warm one. Barely eight-thirty

in the morning and already my skin had gone clammy in the damp heat. I pushed my bangs back, knowing I'd fight that battle all day. One of the worst things about having blond hair—or at least the kind that I had—was the fact that when the temperature and humidity rose, my tresses went stringy and flat. I'd spent time with the blow dryer this morning, but I knew that after five minutes in this heat it would look as though I'd just stepped out of a shower.

Not that it mattered. Despite Bruce's and Scott's contentions, I wasn't eager to see Mark Ellroy for anything other than professional reasons. Yes, I thought as I opened the driver's side door, he was handsome. He seemed nice. But that was the extent of it. I'd noticed his dimples. I was a sucker for dimples, and when he'd smiled—which had been only once, given the circumstances—I'd been treated to a truly handsome view indeed.

I lowered myself into the driver's seat and reached to pull the door shut. As I did, a hand grabbed the top of the window and yanked. I screamed, nearly toppling sideways, as my grip instinctively tightened on the door handle.

"Tooney!" I didn't care that I shouted. "What is wrong with you? Why did you sneak up on me like that?"

"Oh, Grace, I'm sorry." He instantly let go and stepped away from my car as though to demonstrate he was no threat. "I called out to you. I thought you heard me."

Still furious, my heart beat like a mad thing. "I didn't," I said, and slammed the door.

My rage was so hot it took me three tries to get the key into the ignition. The moment I did I started up the car, jammed it into reverse, and turned to make sure I was clear to back up.

It wasn't until I'd gotten onto the street that I chanced a look back.

Tooney stood there, hat literally in his hands, looking sheepish and hurt. He mouthed, "I'm sorry," and started for the sidewalk. I heaved a resigned sigh. Mere moments ago,

I'd thought fondly of this man. When would he learn not to startle me like that?

I pulled back into the driveway and lowered my window without shutting off the car.

"Just once, Tooney, can you give me a little forewarning before you pop up in front of me and scare me half to death?"

He returned to the car, face suffused with relief. "I did, Grace, I swear. But you seemed really preoccupied. I shouldn't have stuck my hand in the door like that. I was wrong. It's just that I heard you had another problem at Marshfield yesterday, but nobody will tell me exactly what happened."

With a start, I remembered Terrence's story about Tooney having rescued Lenore. I could afford to be generous with the man. He deserved that much.

"I have to go to the hospital to pick up one of the victims from yesterday."

Tooney's eyes lit up. "Can I come along?"

"You really haven't gotten any updates, have you?"

He must have noticed the hesitation in my voice. "What happened out there, Grace? They're not releasing any names yet. It must have been pretty bad."

"Where's your car?"

He shrugged. "In the shop again. I walked."

I gestured toward the passenger side. "Get in, I'll drive you wherever you want to go." When he brightened, my heart lurched. I was about to kill his happy spirit.

"Home would be best, I guess. If you won't let me go with you to the hospital."

I waited for him to get in. "Where do you live?"

He provided an address that wasn't far out of my way. "Before we get moving, I think I'd better bring you up to date on what's going on at Marshfield."

Surprise registered on his face. "Sure, I'd like that. Do you need help?"

I was about to shut down that idea, but thought better of

it. "I don't know yet. What I do know is that you may be called in for questioning."

"Me? Why?"

"It's unlikely, but possible." Oh smooth, I chastised myself. I'm trying to break bad news and I start by telling him he may be brought in for questioning. "What I mean to say is, there was a murder at Marshfield yesterday. Again. This time it was someone you met."

"Who?"

I told him about Lenore.

"Aw, that poor kid," he said. Staring out the windshield, he blinked rapidly. "Stupid shame. What's the world coming to when a little thing like that can't even go on vacation and be safe?"

I didn't have an answer for that. Worse, I hated that it had happened on Marshfield grounds. "I thought you ought to know."

"I appreciate it," he said.

I still hadn't put the car in gear. "You okay?"

He scrunched up his face and stared out the front windshield. "I think I'd prefer to walk home, if you don't mind."

"I understand. I'm so sorry."

He didn't look at me as he nodded acknowledgment and alighted from the car. "You'll let me know if there's anything I can help with, won't you?"

This time I didn't feel as though it was Ronny Tooney wannabe detective asking. This time the request felt personal. "Sure, Tooney."

Again, the nod. He gently closed the car door and walked away.

I MADE IT TO THE HOSPITAL A BIT AFTER NINE. Because they'd admitted Mark the night before, they'd moved him into a regular room and I was able to snag a visitor's card without any drama this time.

I knocked and he called for me to enter. When I did, I found him fully dressed in a blue polo shirt and gray Dockers. "What do you think?" he asked, using his uninjured arm to point toward his chest. "My slacks were fine, but my shirt was completely ruined. They have a liaison person here who helped me pick this out from the hospital's shop."

"You look great," I said, and when he smiled at the compliment—full dimple alert—I wished I hadn't sounded so enthusiastic. "That is, except for that." I pointed to the sling. "Otherwise, you look completely recovered. Yesterday I thought you were a little pale."

"Losing a lot of blood will do that to you." Mark's voice dropped a notch. "I hope you know how much I truly appreciate you taking care of everything. The police suggested I stay in Emberstowne for a while longer. You're making the transition that much easier."

"How did the questioning go yesterday?" I asked.

"Your friend Flynn came at me with guns blazing," he said, watching my reaction. "I felt more like a suspect than a victim."

"That's Flynn."

"What's his first name?" Mark asked.

I didn't know. For that matter, I'd never learned Rodriguez's first name either. A new mystery. This time, fortunately, an innocuous one.

I was about to answer when a chipper middle-aged nurse came in carrying a clipboard. "We still do our discharges on paper," she said to Mark. "These are instructions for your follow-up care. I'll need to go over them with you and your wife before you're released."

My first thought was, *Oh, he is married*, but my second thought—inspired by Mark's openmouthed surprise—was the more correct one. The nurse assumed *we* were married.

"Oh, I'm not—" I began.

"She isn't my wife," Mark stammered, then added, "That is, I don't have a wife. I mean, I'm not married."

The nurse made an "Oops" face.

"I'll wait outside," I said.

Mark waved down the suggestion. "No big deal. You can stay."

The nurse continued smoothly as though she hadn't just embarrassed us both. "Most important is that you call us immediately if you run a fever, or if the site of the wound gets hot or red. If you see any signs of infection, you'll need to come in right away . . ."

As she went through every warning and talked Mark through the steps for keeping his injury clean and germ-free, I moved toward the window and stared out. The parking lot view was uninspiring, the asphalt so hot it shimmered.

How did I get in these situations? I wondered. I didn't mean being mistaken for Mark's wife, although that had been weird enough. I meant getting involved in murder investigations. The number of recent incidents at Marshfield had to be throwing off the law of averages like crazy. The chances of so much happening in such a short span of time could be no greater than infinitesimal.

Yet, here I was again. I sneaked a sideways glance as Mark listened attentively to the instructions the nurse recited while indicating important points on his discharge papers.

He was a good-looking man. Very good-looking, if I were to be honest with myself. Mid- to late thirties, he was a few years older than me. Age-wise, we could easily be mistaken for husband and wife. Still, I'd been trying to avoid thinking about him in any way other than professionally because . . .

I turned my attention back out the window. Because . . . why?

Jack came to mind, of course. I knew he'd been through

a lot in his youth and again in recent months, but the fact that he backed away from me every time life got complicated made me wonder if he had what it took to maintain a long-term relationship. I had my doubts. Bruce and Scott had their doubts, too. We'd only touched on the topic yesterday, but over recent weeks my roommates and I had discussed the situation ad nauseam over countless bottles of wine, never coming up with a clear answer.

"Deep wounds take time to heal. They can't be rushed," the nurse said, breaking into my reverie. I turned, but she was still explaining to Mark.

For a moment I thought she'd been talking to me.

After final signatures and instructions we were out the door. Mark refused a wheelchair, and when we stepped out the hospital's front doors, he recoiled in the heat. "Whoa," he said, blinking in the brightness, "I've been outside for all of ten seconds and I'm already missing the hospital's air-conditioning."

"My car is right over here." I unlocked the passenger side and opened the door for him.

"Shouldn't I be holding doors open for you?" he asked with a smile.

"Not with a bad wing." I walked around to the other side, got in, and started the engine, making sure to set the air-conditioning to high. "Where are you staying?" I asked before putting the car into gear. "I should have asked John, but I forgot."

"Oak Tree Hotel," he said.

I set off without comment.

We traveled in silence for about half a mile. Although I was eager to resume our conversation about how questioning had gone the night before, I didn't want to appear nosy or intrusive.

Mark must have read my mind. "Aren't you going to ask me more about Flynn?"

"Actually . . ." I gave him a quick glance, both to make

eye contact and to do a surreptitious assessment of his general health. I was sure he'd be fine, but I remembered how weak I'd been after I'd suffered a gunshot wound, "I'm extremely curious about how the rest of the questioning went. I'm sorry to hear that Flynn made you feel uncomfortable."

"You never told me what his first name is."

I laughed. "That's because I don't know it."

From my peripheral vision I could see him react. "But I thought . . ."

I waited for it.

"My mistake," he said quietly. "I thought you and Flynn had a history."

"We do have a history. Though not a romantic one, thank goodness."

Now Mark laughed. "I have to admit I wondered how a lovely person like you could ever get involved with such a hothead."

He'd said, "lovely person," not "nice girl" or "gorgeous woman." Neither condescending nor obsequious. I liked that.

"Do they have any leads?" I asked, forcing my mind back to the investigation.

"If they do, they didn't mention them," he said. "I got the impression they don't have a lot to go on. Aside from what I was able to remember about the guy and whatever description they were able to get from John, they're flying blind. They did ask me if I noticed any tattoos or possible birthmarks on the man. Did you hear anything about that?"

"John mentioned it yesterday. He wasn't a hundred percent sure about it, but it's a start, I suppose. It bothers me that he was wearing one of our blazers." The road ahead was nearly empty, but frustration made me grip the steering wheel hard. "*Of course* Lenore had trusted him. Why shouldn't she?"

Mark didn't have an answer for that. He stared out the side window. "I wish I could have saved her."

We were silent again for several blocks, until I banged the steering wheel. "Darn! I forgot to notify the bell captain before we left. Do you mind if I pull over a moment and make a quick phone call?"

He assured me that would be fine. "It's nice to meet someone who abhors distracted driving as much as I do."

I pulled to the shoulder and dug out my phone. The bell captain said he'd arrange to have one of his staff meet us at the Oak Tree Hotel at once.

Though considered decent lodging in Emberstowne, the Oak Tree was midrange at best. That meant no bellboys, no concierge. Bare bones. Clean, convenient, but no frills.

When I hung up and started to put my phone away, Mark pointed to it. "I left mine in the room to charge yesterday. Haven't been able to make any calls since."

"Oh no," I said. "Were you able to get in touch with your family?"

He gave a sad smile. "No real family to speak of. But I *was* able to get in touch with my employees to let them know where I was in case there was an emergency."

"I'll bet they're worried about you."

"I held back the gory details. That can wait until I get home. No need to get people worked up."

We were back on the road a moment later and were soon pulling into the Oak Tree's parking lot. The six-story hotel was architecturally insignificant—in other words, blah. A multi-story hotel built in the 1970s before Emberstowne implemented architectural ordinances, it sat in a sea of asphalt two blocks off the town's main thoroughfare. A few small green plants dotted its perimeter, doing little to soften the structure's drab lines.

I was surprised John's tour company would have chosen a nondescript hotel like this one when there were so many more upscale venues available in town.

Again, as though Mark could read my mind, he said, "You heard how we got stuck in this hotel, didn't you?"

I shook my head.

"We were originally booked at the Waltham Arms," he began.

"Ah, the union strike." I remembered what Corbin had told me. This was high season and rooms were in demand. "You were lucky to get a hotel this nice on such short notice."

"So we were told." He didn't sound convinced.

I spotted Arthur, one of our bellboys, waiting outside the Oak Tree's front door. Sweat poured from his thick, dark hair into the collar of his white long-sleeve shirt. "Have you been here long?" I asked as we started in. The cool air felt like heaven after the short walk from the car.

"No, ma'am. Just got here." He glanced expectantly at Mark. "Lead the way, sir."

I let them walk ahead of me. "I'll wait for you down here," I said. The last thing Mark needed was for me to encroach on his personal space by accompanying him to his room. Besides, I had work to do.

I caught the eye of a twenty-something kid behind the reception desk. No doubt a recent graduate with a major in hotel management, he was fresh-faced and eager to help. "I'm here to settle the bill for Mr. Mark Ellroy. He's checking out right now." I handed over one of Marshfield Manor's credit cards.

"Yes, ma'am," he said. "Would you like a receipt?"

"Please," I said, then amended, "Make that two."

Moments later, I'd pocketed one receipt to give to accounting and folded the other to give to Mark. I had no idea how long they would take upstairs, so I made my way across the linoleum floor, past the reception desk to the lobby beyond. With wicker furniture, fake palm trees in all four of the room's corners, and sliding glass doors that faced the back of the property, the lobby overlooked a tiny courtyard and a small outdoor pool. I settled myself in one of the chairs with a view of reception to wait. Across the room, attached to the ceiling in much the same way as one had been at the hospital, a television blared the morning news.

There was one other person in the cool room with me. I wouldn't have given him a second glance if the network anchor on the booming TV hadn't announced breaking news in the Marshfield Manor murder investigation. My lobby companion had been hidden behind a newspaper, but the moment the Marshfield segment was announced, he crumpled it to his lap and spun in his seat, turning to stare over his shoulder at the broadcast above him.

Breaking news? And I hadn't heard anything about this? Before I could think twice about it, Flynn's face filled the overhead screen. The unflattering close-up distorted the young detective's nose, making it look extra wide. The old TV gave his face a sickly, yellow sheen. Three microphones had been thrust into Flynn's personal space, but the shot was so tight I couldn't see who held any of them. "We are pursuing a very strong lead in yesterday's murder at Marshfield Manor. We can now confirm that Lenore Honore was killed at the scene," Flynn said, mangling the dead woman's last name.

"It's pronounced On-or-ay," I corrected under my breath.

The man with the newspaper twisted back in a flash. His glare hit me with a force so hard I nearly felt the impact. He didn't speak, but I could see calculation behind his dark eyes. His expression shifted a heartbeat later. I couldn't place it except to say that it seemed like he recognized me. I didn't recognize him.

Then I remembered that Corbin's group was staying here at the Oak Tree for the duration. We'd halted production until our homicide detectives gave us the all clear. That might account for crew members sitting around at the hotel, waiting to be called back to work. This man could be part of Corbin's team, but that didn't explain the malevolent stare. He turned back to watch the TV in time to hear Flynn saying to expect an arrest soon.

"Within the next twenty-four hours?" A reporter persisted.

Flynn's mouth twisted into a smirk. "Within the next twelve, if it's up to me."

"We understand there was a second victim."

Flynn shook his head. "No further commentary."

Thank goodness for that.

When the scene shifted back to the anchor for summary, the man across from me faced forward again, snapping his paper up as he did so, effectively rendering himself invisible. I thought hard, trying to place him. I'd interacted with many of Corbin's team, but I couldn't pinpoint where I might have seen him before. For the half minute or so that I'd gotten a look at him, I'd noted that he was shiny-head bald, about forty years old. His clothing suggested an early morning workout: navy blue swishy pants, black flip-flops, and a white long sleeve T-shirt with a terrycloth towel draped around his neck.

That irksome feeling of not knowing who he was made me want to initiate conversation, if only for the chance to see his face again. My plan was foiled, however, when the man jumped to his feet. He jammed the newspaper under his arm and stormed out the back doors toward the pool.

I waited a couple of beats, then gave in to my curiosity and followed to the doors in time to watch him disappear around a tall group of shrubs. That was odd. No, it was more than odd. I stood staring long after he was gone, attempting to sort out my disquiet. What was it exactly that bothered me? I'd encountered rudeness before in my life, but a peculiar sense of dread stole over me when I thought about the man's glare. Could he have had anything to do with Lenore's killing? Or the missing items from Marshfield?

Chapter II

IT WAS PREPOSTEROUS FOR ME TO MAKE SUCH a leap, but events over recent months had served to make me ever suspicious, ever aware of oddities. I ran my hand through my hair, trying to sort out facts from feelings. It would do little good for me to call Rodriguez to report a non-encounter with a curious stranger in a second-rate hotel.

Instead, I turned and made my way to the front desk. "Hello," I said to the twenty-something young man again. "I thought I spotted a friend of mine in the room over there. But he disappeared before I could say hello." I gestured backwards. "Did you happen to see him?"

I had to give the boy credit. He valiantly tried to tamp down his "Are you kidding me?" expression. "I'm sorry ma'am. I've been very busy here. What is it you need?"

I tried a different approach. "I thought I saw someone I knew. He's . . . ah . . . forty-four," I guessed, "not terribly tall. Bald. That is, his head is completely shaved. I saw him for a moment, but I don't know where he went."

The kid worked hard at being polite. He picked up paper

and pen. "If you give me his name, I can give him your message."

"Oh, no," I said flipping my hands forward in a dramatic gesture. "It's not that important. I wasn't even sure it was who I thought it was. It might not be. I mean, I didn't even know that he was in town. Maybe it isn't even him. That's why I was asking. Just to see if it was who I thought it was."

Stop talking, I told myself. I backed away as I babbled, thoroughly embarrassed, wishing I could duck out the front door.

One of the reception desk phones rang right then, sparing us both further discomfort. "Thanks, anyway," I said with forced cheer, and returned to the lobby, taking a seat out of the young man's line of sight.

I thought about what Flynn had proclaimed on the news broadcast. I should have been excited to learn that the police were close to an arrest, but the truth was that I didn't buy it.

I considered sneaking out the front door to wait, in the hopes that the bald guy might come around the far side, but at that moment Mark and Arthur returned. Arthur gripped the handle of a black suitcase, which he rolled while carrying a laptop case slung over the opposite shoulder. "Ready to go, Ms. Wheaton?" he called. I nodded and he headed out at a quick clip.

As I passed the front desk, the young kid said, "I hope you find your friend."

"What was that all about?" Mark asked.

"A man in the hotel," I said, waving my hand in dismissal, wishing I'd minded my own business. "I . . ." How to explain my sense of unease without sounding like a total idiot? "I thought I recognized him, but I was mistaken. By the way, here's a copy of your bill."

He took the receipt, folded it one-handed and tucked it into his pants pocket. "Thank you again. That was unnecessary, but I truly appreciate it."

Arthur had taken off ahead of us, probably intending to

crank up the Marshfield car's air-conditioning as soon as he could.

Mark and I followed, returning to the blast-furnace outdoors. I squinted in the blinding sunlight, stopping in my tracks because I couldn't see. "Yikes," I said, my eyes instinctively clenching shut. The sun was so intense that it actually hurt. I put a hand up to shield my face, blinking to try to accustom myself to the brightness.

"You have light eyes," Mark said. "That means you're more susceptible to the sun. And today's a scorcher." He reached into the pocket of his shirt. "Here," he said, proffering a pair of sunglasses. "You can use mine."

"Thanks, but I've got a pair in the car. I'll be fine in a minute."

The words died on my lips because just as my vision acclimated, I spotted Jack walking toward us. Beneath his khaki shorts, his knees were crusted with dirt, his tan T-shirt dark with sweat, his shoes filthy. As he crossed the street, he tugged off muddy gloves and stuffed them into a back pocket. He'd apparently been landscaping at the church across the street.

"Grace," he said, smiling, "I've been meaning to call you."

He had? Warmed by the thought, I was cautious all the same. "Anything wrong?"

"No," he said drawing the word out. "I wanted to see what you were up to." His attention was not on me, but on Mark.

I could read Jack's mind from the expression on his face. With Arthur out in the parking lot, Jack couldn't know I was here on official business. What he saw was me exiting a second-rate hotel in the morning accompanied by a strange man.

"How's your dad?" I asked changing the subject before Mark picked up on the vibe.

Jack shrugged. "It's been rough. But we're getting through it. My sister's there at least once a week."

Mark extended his hand and introduced himself. "Sorry to hear your father is ill."

Jack and I exchanged a glance as the two men shook hands. Gordon Embers wasn't ill, but that was too much information to share.

"Jack Embers. I'm . . ." He looked about to say that he was a friend of mine. "I'm the landscape architect at Marshfield Manor. Grace and I . . . ah . . . work together sometimes." There was a look in his eyes that I read as disappointment. To me: "How have you been?"

I was still off-kilter from my clumsy attempt to identify the bald guy with the clerk at the front desk. "Good," I said, for lack of anything better. I was unsettled. Truth be told, I was a little angry, too. If Jack had bothered to keep in touch, if he'd taken time to talk with me instead of buzzing in only when Marshfield garden business required he do so, he would have known exactly why I was here this morning escorting Mark Ellroy out of the Oak Tree Hotel.

If he couldn't be bothered to keep in touch, why should he care that I might have spent the night with another man? I hadn't, of course, but my face flamed nonetheless.

Jack gave a lopsided smile. "You look happy," he said. To Mark, he nodded. "Nice meeting you." And then he was gone.

Mark and I resumed our trek to the parking lot. "I know it's none of my business, and you've already set me straight about Flynn. If I'm overstepping, please feel free to say so, but do you and the landscaper have a history?"

I opened my mouth to reply, but he interrupted.

"Forget I asked. It's really none of my business, sorry."

I knew I should resist the urge to explain, but Mark's polite inquiry and that tiny undercurrent of attraction I was feeling for him made me spill. "Jack and I went out. Once."

"I assume it was a disaster."

We turned the corner at the hotel's edge. "Actually, it went very well." I expected surprise to register on Mark's

face. When it did, I continued, "Up until the very last minute. A problem arose that had nothing to do with our being
out together, but had everything to do with another murder
on Marshfield property."

"You're joking."

I shook my head. "Jack was a suspect. So was his brother."

Mark's brows came together in concern. He gestured
behind us. "That guy? I know I just met him, but he seems
like a decent sort."

"He was innocent. His brother, too," I said, wondering
how deep to take this. "But what they had to endure to prove
their innocence was pretty rough. They're still recovering."

"How long ago was this?"

"Not very."

Mark didn't comment, but I could feel the questions he
wanted to ask. Thankfully he let the subject die and we
made it to the parking lot to find Arthur sweating next to
the idling Marshfield car. "All set," he said as he rounded
the car to open the passenger door. "Mr. Ellroy?"

Mark shot me a rueful smile as he started for the car's
far side.

"Unless you'd prefer to ride with me?" I asked. The
question popped out of the blue. Why hadn't I thought of
that earlier?

He smiled, showing those deep dimples again. "I'd like
that very much."

I turned to Arthur. "I guess we'll meet you there."

Within seconds, Arthur had hopped into the vehicle and
pulled away. Mark and I opened our opposite car doors and
waited a minute for the stuffy air to clear. "Sorry," I said.
"It's a little hot box."

"You need a convertible."

"Yeah, right," I said, thinking about the gorgeous 1936
Packard Phaeton convertible Bennett had once offered me.
"On a day like today, there isn't enough sunblock in the
world to get me into a convertible."

"Ah, that explains it," he said.

"Explains what?"

His eyes twinkled. "With those light eyes, that lovely blonde hair, and fair skin, you seem like a person who'd burn quickly. And yet"—he gestured toward me across the top of my car's roof—"you have the most flawless complexion. Whatever you're doing, keep it up."

He climbed into the passenger seat.

Had he just flirted with me? I took a moment to process the possibility, then joined him in the car. "Thanks," I said as I started the engine. "That was a very nice thing to say."

"One thing you'll learn about me, Grace," he shot me a sidelong smile, "that is, if I'm fortunate enough to spend more time with you . . ."

Okay, so he was definitely flirting. Even better, I was enjoying it. I delayed putting the car in drive and turned to him. "What's that?"

"I don't lie. I won't even fib to protect a person's feelings. Gets me into trouble sometimes, but it's who I am. So when I look at you and tell you you're a beautiful woman," he smiled into my eyes, "believe it."

"Oh," I said in a small voice. "Thank you."

He didn't break eye contact. "Have I made you uncomfortable?"

Time for me to share the truth. "A little."

"I apologize. It's just that the moment John introduced you to our group, I had the strangest feeling that I was destined to get to know you."

"You did?"

"Isn't that odd? I've never had a sense like that before and I confess I don't believe in fate or woo-woo supernatural stuff. What I do believe is that everyone makes his or her own luck. But I couldn't help feeling that I ought to get to know you." He looked away. "Of course, I never imagined circumstances like these. I would give anything to change recent events . . ."

He broke off and I decided it was a good time to get moving. I pulled out of the lot, realizing that Mark's words had taken a good bit of sting out of the pain I'd felt from Jack's sudden appearance.

What had become obvious to me—too late to avoid the hurt, of course—was that I really didn't know Jack at all. I'd fallen for him—the part of him that was strong, upstanding, and reliable. What I could never have anticipated was how he would pull away from me at every unexpected turn.

Unusual situations had shaped Jack's behavior years earlier, and I'd tried my best to be patient. Nevertheless, it was hard to maintain so much as a cordial relationship with someone who didn't believe in communicating. When things got rough, he preferred isolation, avoiding anyone with the capacity to hurt him. I blamed myself for some of my own heartache. I'd missed the fact that he was still too broken inside from prior tragedies to be able to sustain a romantic relationship. He needed help, but was too proud to ask for it.

Mark proved to be an easy person to talk with. I learned that he was an only child and had inherited the jewelry store a relatively short time ago. His father had died five years prior, and his mother two years before that. He was thirty-seven years old, held a master's degree in business administration, and had three dogs.

"Three!" I exclaimed with delight. "What kind?" I turned into the entrance gate at the manor, and waved to the guard as I drove in. We still had another two miles to the hotel.

"Two golden retrievers and one mutt. The goldens were my parents' dogs. They're brothers and were still pups when my mom died. I took them in when Dad got sick and they've been with me ever since. The mutt is mine. A cross between a Lab and a Border collie, his name's Bubba and he's almost twelve. Getting up there. The other two watch out for him, though."

"You must have a big house."

He shrugged. "Too big sometimes," he said quietly.

"Having a jewelry store must be fun. People buy jewelry for happy occasions."

He didn't smile.

"Did I say something wrong?"

He was quick to try to make me feel better. "Not at all. I've come to realize that as lucky as I am to have this thriving business, it isn't the best fit for me. I . . ." He looked out the window. "This is probably too heavy for a first real conversation."

"I don't mean to pry."

"I know you don't," he said, looking at me again. "But I might as well be up-front with you. I still have a hard time. I was married. For ten years. Very, very good years."

I took a little breath of surprise.

"She died," he continued softly, "exactly sixteen months after my father did. I lost everyone I cared about in the span of three years." He looked out the window again. "That was a rough time for me."

"I'm sorry." I gripped the steering wheel, not knowing what else to say.

Now that he'd opened the wound, Mark was quick to share more, and I got the feeling it was cathartic for him to do so. "While Madison was alive I enjoyed the jewelry store, but only because she loved it so much. Now, however . . ." His voice trailed off. "There's nothing there for me. My favorite part of owning the business is the financial dealing that goes on behind the scenes. In fact, I've started to think about a new career."

"Doing what?"

He snapped out of his reverie. "That's what this trip was supposed to be about, you know: starting fresh, a new beginning. Getting a handle on where I want to be, what I want to do." His voice grew with excitement. "I could easily sell the store and all its contents, and let me tell you, the temptation is strong. The only thing holding me back is the thought that I'd be selling off all my father and grandfather worked for, for so many years."

"But if you aren't happy . . ."

He smiled at me. "We make our own happiness. I think there's more out there for me. There is so much I've missed while I've been sitting home brooding and feeling sorry for myself. I've been alone now for almost four years and life is short—a fact that I've recently been reminded of all too clearly. I think it's time to reassess. Don't you?"

I didn't answer, but he didn't seem to mind.

"But what about you? I've monopolized the conversation, talking about myself. Tell me about you. I know you're the woman in charge at Marshfield, but that's the extent of it. What are your goals, your aspirations? Have you ever been married?" He asked this lightly. "What do you do for fun?"

I gave him a brief synopsis of how and why I'd returned to Emberstowne after more than twenty years away. I told him about the huge Victorian home I'd inherited—and all the maintenance and repair work that came with it. I talked a little about my roommates, Bruce and Scott, and their wine shop.

"You miss your mom, don't you?"

"Every day."

He nodded. "I understand." Changing the subject, he said, "I stopped in at Amethyst Cellars my first afternoon in town. It's great."

"I'm lucky. Bruce and Scott are like brothers to me. I don't know what I'd do without them." I made a sharp turn onto the hotel property and started up the driveway to the front gate.

"No other roommates, or significant others?" he asked.

I'd specifically avoided any mention of my former fiancé, Eric, and declined to share any more about my current situation with Jack. "There is someone special in my life . . ." I said with a grin. "I have a little tuxedo cat. She's actually still a kitten. Bootsie."

"I love cats," Mark said. "Except I'm allergic."

"That's funny, so am I."

"You're allergic, but you have a cat?"

I thought about Bennett's reaction when I'd told him about my allergies. I shared with Mark the same advice Bennett had given me. "I seem to have developed a resistance. Keeping hydrated, changing my bedsheets really often, and washing my hands a lot helps. It's really not so bad."

We reached the canopied front door, where uniformed bellboys unloaded vacationers' vehicles. I spotted Arthur waiting just inside the vestibule, standing next to Mark's luggage. I pulled to the curb and stopped the car.

Mark laughed. "Bootsie is a lucky kitten."

I remembered all I'd been through from the time Bootsie had shown up on my driveway until the day I knew she was mine to keep. "I'm crazy about her."

"I'd love to . . ." He seemed about to say, "meet her," but apparently thought better of it, "see a picture. Do you have any?"

I didn't. "Do you have pictures of your dogs?"

"You know," he said, "I don't. We'd both better get that rectified before our beloved pets disown us."

We alighted from the car and I accompanied Mark through the sweeping front doors, across the bright marble floor. "This way," I said, walking past the collection of tourists waiting to check in.

"Wow," he said, looking around. "This is a far cry from the Oak Tree."

"It's a wonderful hotel. I hope you'll enjoy yourself here."

"I know I will."

I led him to the concierge desk. "Hi, Twyla," I said to the woman behind the tall counter. "Is everything ready for Mr. Ellroy?"

It was. We'd taken pains to ensure that Mark's transition

from the Oak Tree to our hotel would progress without mis-hap. She had the key ready to his suite on the top floor, and handed him a linen packet of information, which she took time to explain. "You may dine in any of our restaurants on property. Just charge it to your room."

When she was finished, Mark thanked her then turned to me. "This is too much," he said. "You're being far too generous."

"Mark," I said, using his name for the first time, "let us do what little we can to help." In an impulsive flirtatious move of my own, I placed a hand on his arm. Despite the hotel's air-conditioned bliss, he was warm. I liked that. "Okay?"

"Okay," he said, treating me to another dose of dimples.

"We'll get your bags up to your room. No need to tip Arthur. He's been taken care of." The bellman had been waiting at a discreet distance. I gestured him forward. "Everything will be taken care of." I thought it would be awkward for me to accompany Mark to his room, so I pulled out one of my cards. I started to hand it to him, but drew it back when I remembered I'd given him one already.

"Hang on." It was time to stop worrying about Jack and start considering what might be good for Grace. I grabbed a pen from the top of Twyla's desk and scribbled my cell phone number on the back of the card. "Arthur will help get you settled, but if there's anything else you need that the staff can't assist you with, let me know."

Mark took the card and smiled. "What if everything is great and the staff caters to my every whim?"

"I don't understand."

"Can I still call you?"

I tingled from fingertips to toes. How long had it been since I'd interacted so playfully with a handsome man? I felt like a teenager, wordless and tongue-tied. "Sure," I said so quickly it sounded like a bird chirp. I backed away from Mark, Arthur, and Twyla, grinning like a lunatic, and waved. "See you all later."

Chapter 12

BACK AT THE MANSION, I MADE MY WAY UP TO the office, reliving my conversations with Mark. I'd felt all gangly and obvious when I'd left him there, but for some reason, I wasn't embarrassed. I got the sense that Mark liked me enough to see through such awkward moments. I felt comfortable around him. The story he'd told me about his parents and his wife had touched my heart. The poor man had suffered. And yet he remained kind, likeable, and quick to put me at ease. I especially appreciated what he'd said about always telling the truth.

I stopped before opening the door to Frances's office. The only reason Mark and I had met—the only reason we'd been afforded this chance to get to know one another was because someone had died. Lenore hadn't deserved such a violent end to her short life. I didn't know the woman well, but from what I'd heard about her recent divorce and the little she'd told me about the voice in her head forcing her to touch and do things, I sensed that her life hadn't been particularly easy.

I pushed aside the sadness and opened the door, but before I could say hello, Frances was on her feet, her expression panicked, her eyes wide. She held up both hands, then placed a finger to her lips, rolling her eyes with animated drama, clearly communicating there was someone in my office.

"Oh, hello . . . Lois," she said to me, delivering the line like a sixth-grader trying to win elocution points in her school play. More eyeball gesticulations. Still using her stage voice, she continued the spontaneous performance. "I'm sorry. Ms. Wheaton isn't in the office . . . right now." Using both hands she scooted me toward the door. "Why don't you try again in about an hour?"

If Rodriguez and Flynn were here I'd want to talk with them. I needed to know more about this great lead they were pursuing. I started to ask, "Who . . ." but Frances slammed me with a look.

"I said you should come back later. Got that? Later." I watched an idea spring to her mind. "Why don't you call me, Lois?" Again she pointed to the door, ushering me out. "Go back to your office and give me a call." Frantic nods. "Okay?"

Hillary appeared in the doorway between Frances's office and mine. "For goodness' sake, Frances, anybody with half a brain could tell you were faking it." She bestowed a smile that was as phony as my assistant's performance. "Why don't you want Grace talking with me? Have something to hide, do you?"

Frances glared, first at Hillary then at me. There was a difference, however. I detected deep-seated loathing with Hillary. With me it was mere impatience. A silent chide: "Why didn't you leave when you had the chance?"

"Hillary," I began. "How can I help you?"

Frances sent me a baleful look and went back to work, muttering to herself.

Hillary bit the insides of her cheeks as she faced me. "I

don't know why you keep that woman on staff," she said, talking as though Frances wasn't there. "She's a menace."

"I'm not about to discuss Marshfield personnel with you," I said. Then, because Frances was listening, and because I rarely got the chance to give her kudos, I added, "Not that it's any of your business, but Frances is a major asset to Bennett's organization. We're lucky to have her."

It wasn't a lie. Frances was a gossip, a stickler for the old rules, and unpleasant more often than not. But she tackled every one of her responsibilities with unrivaled tenacity. I knew that when I left her in charge—which I'd done on occasion—the manor ran smoothly as long as no major decisions needed to be made. She annoyed most of her colleagues, but not one could claim she didn't do her job well. Despite the fact that her negativity drove me up a wall, I'd reluctantly learned that I could depend on her.

I'd flabbergasted Frances with my declaration, but Hillary continued as if I hadn't said a word. "You'd better watch yourself," she said in a low voice. "I could take your job over in a heartbeat. All I'd have to do is mention the idea to Papa Bennett and," she snapped her fingers, "you'd be gone like that."

I pinched the bridge of my nose. Talking with Hillary was like walking through a minefield. While there were a number of ways to push her buttons on purpose, there were also a million hidden explosions just waiting to happen. I never knew exactly what might set her off.

"Let's start again. What brings you in today?"

"You." She pointed toward my office. "Can we talk in there? I prefer not to share my grievances in front of the rank and file."

I glanced over at Frances, who rolled her eyes. Hillary had come to the manor as a teenager back when Frances had already been working here for a decade or so. There was history between them, none of it pleasant.

"Go ahead," Frances said. "There's nothing I care to hear anyway."

Hillary's voice was strained. "I don't need your permission."

"To make a nuisance of yourself? No, you seem to accomplish that feat well enough on your own."

Hillary didn't shriek, but her gargled exclamation bespoke pure fury. "I deserve . . . no, I *demand* your respect. Don't forget, I am Bennett's daughter."

Frances had been writing while Hillary bellowed. Now she looked up, put her pen down, and smiled. "Stepdaughter."

Hillary sucked in a breath, then continued with forced calm, "We're family. That's all that matters."

Frances perked up, looking like the cat that ate the canary. She sent me a meaningful glance and for the briefest moment I knew what she was thinking: Frances was one of the few who knew my secret. She was aware of the fact that my grandmother and Bennett's father had been in love. She knew that chances were strong that my mother was an illegitimate child born of that affair. *Don't say it*, I pleaded silently. *Please.*

The light in Frances's eyes dimmed ever so slightly. I breathed again.

Frances turned her back to us. "I have work to do."

HILLARY SETTLED HERSELF INTO ONE OF THE wing chairs opposite my desk and folded her arms across her chest. "Who gave you the right to halt the DVD filming?"

"Is that what this is about?"

"I came here to star in the DVD. Papa Bennett all but promised me that I would be part of the filming. Who better to be the face of Marshfield?"

She didn't wait for me to answer. Give her credit for that.

"When I showed up ready to work this morning, I found out that you'd cancelled everything."

"Postponed," I corrected. "Didn't you hear about the woman who was killed here yesterday?"

"Of course I heard," Hillary said in a snit. "Who hasn't?"

"Don't you think we can show a little respect . . ."

"The manor isn't open to visitors today. Nobody's going to know what goes on behind closed doors. And the woman was killed in one of the staff stairways, right? Corbin isn't filming there, so what's the big deal?"

"What's the big deal?" I repeated in disbelief.

"This was a perfect opportunity for you to let the film crew have the run of the place all day."

"Even you aren't that callous."

"You blew this one. You had a chance to make things easy for Corbin, for his team . . ."

"For you?"

"Yes, for me. What's wrong with that?"

I wasn't about to debate the subject. "The DVD team stays out as long as the police are here. I think they'll be packing up soon. It usually . . ." I caught myself. Usually? Did I really know that much about police procedure now that I could spout such proclamations with authority? I began again. "I think they should be wrapped up today. Maybe tomorrow. The evidence technicians need to be certain they've gotten all they need and the detectives want to make sure they've questioned everyone who was here that day. By the way, is there anything you care to share regarding your whereabouts when Lenore was killed?"

She blinked. "Absolutely not."

"Where were you?"

"Does it matter?"

Rather than push one of Hillary's buttons to send her flying into a rage, I picked a careful path around the prickly topic instead. Hillary wasn't a murderer, but that didn't mean she wasn't above lying to protect her own interests.

I trod carefully. "I know you couldn't have been a witness to the crime because you're a good person and if you had seen anything suspicious you would have reported it to the police immediately." She relaxed, visibly. I thought about Mark's "white lie" proclamation, but didn't feel a trace of guilt. I wasn't lying. Hillary wouldn't knowingly withhold evidence in a crime of this magnitude. Would she?

"Of course I would have reported it," she said. "I don't like the idea of a murderer in my father's house."

I wanted to be like Frances and correct her by saying "stepfather," but I held my tongue, my eyes on a bigger prize. "The thing is, if you were anywhere near the stairwell, or even nearby, you may have seen something you don't even recognize as relevant. That's why it's imperative you think back." I decided to give her an out—an opportunity to amend her claim that she wasn't anywhere in the vicinity of the murder. "In all the excitement, you may have forgotten where you were at the time."

She squirmed in her seat, looking so much like an uncomfortable teenager that I had to remind myself she was more than a dozen years older than me. "I may have," she said. "Forgotten, that is."

"You've been staying here for about a week," I began in an attempt to guide her memory back to yesterday's events, "and you'd probably already had lunch . . ."

"Why do you care?"

Because, I wanted to say, if we find out who killed Lenore and injured Mark, we may have our thief on our hands. And if we do, then you, Hillary, will no longer be under suspicion for stealing from your stepfather. What I said was, "The sooner we get this thing solved, the quicker we can bring the killer to justice. We can't bring Lenore back, but we can make Marshfield Manor safer. For our visitors and for the people who live here." This last part I delivered with a meaningful look.

"I don't plan to live with Papa Bennett permanently," she said with undisguised pique.

"I didn't think you were. He told me you were only staying with him for a week or two." He'd actually told me he wasn't sure how long Hillary planned to remain on property, but this was my chance to dig.

"Do you know that Papa Bennett actually suggested I get a room at the Marshfield Hotel?" She pointed to the floor. "This is my home. This is where I grew up. Why would I want to give all this up to stay in some shabby hotel?"

"I'd hardly call it shabby."

She waved my comment away as though it meant nothing. "What I mean is, until I find my own place, I prefer to live with *family*." Again, she stressed the word.

"I thought you had a place near the coast."

To say her demeanor morphed from annoyed to flustered was understatement. "Well, of course there was that," she said, using the past tense. "But you know how things are these days."

Uh-oh. "What are you saying? You still have your home, right? You haven't sold it?"

She laughed, but it was forced. "Sold it? No, of course not."

We both turned at the sound of conversation from Frances's office. A moment later, my assistant appeared in the doorway. "The detectives are here," she announced.

Hillary jumped to her feet. "I'd better go." Was it my imagination or was she in a hurry to get out of my office?

At least I'd get a chance to ask Rodriguez about the news conference this morning. I stood up. "Send them in." To Hillary, I said, "You'll excuse us?"

She was already crossing paths with them at the door, mumbling a quick greeting and ducking out under Frances's watchful gaze. My assistant locked eyes with me. "What's up now?"

I shrugged, then ushered the two detectives in. "You can keep the door open, Frances," I said as my assistant made a move to grab the knob. She glanced up at me in surprise, nodded, and took her leave.

Flynn had already flopped into one of my wing chairs. He leaned his head back, his right ankle perched on the opposite knee, fingers laced across his chest, the picture of relaxation. Or at least the picture of a person trying to look relaxed.

In contrast, the more polite Rodriguez waited for me to offer him a seat. "Thank you," he said as he lowered himself into the open chair. "How are things going?"

"I was about to ask you the same thing," I said.

Flynn's right foot shook hummingbird fast, and he sucked his lower lip as though trying his darnedest to keep from spouting off. I wanted to ask him directly about his announcement this morning on TV, but the man looked ready to blow.

Focusing on Rodriguez, I asked him about the killer wearing a Marshfield blazer. He assured me they were following up on that lead, but encouraged me to continue checking on my end as well. I said I would, then brought him up to date about Mark Ellroy's move to the Marshfield Hotel and how we were keeping the mansion closed to visitors today. He nodded slowly as I spoke, in quiet agreement.

"Well done," he said when I finished. "We spoke with Mr. Ellroy yesterday, as you know. We plan to visit him again today in the hope that he'll be able to remember more about the circumstances. Humans have a great capacity to shut out unpleasantness, and until a person relaxes, his mind protects him. There may be more he's able to tell us now that he's settled."

Flynn cut into our conversation. "Quit psychoanalyzing. That's how we've let too many killers get away. Instead of thinking, we should be doing."

"I can't believe you actually said that," I said.

He sat up, both feet on the floor. "We need you to answer some questions, so you can quit getting all snippy on me."

"Snippy? You want to see snippy?" Just being in the same room with Flynn got my blood boiling. "What was up with that news conference this morning?"

Rodriguez heaved a sigh. "You saw that, eh?"

Flynn shot his partner a look of contempt. The concept of teamwork was lost on this man.

"I did." I directed my glare at the younger man. "You're on the verge of making an arrest?"

Flynn worked his jaw but remained silent.

"Who is it?" I prodded. "Who are you about to charge? Or do you already have a suspect in custody?"

That was too much. Flynn leaned forward and banged on my desk. "We were given bad information. From you."

"Me?"

Behind Flynn, Frances appeared in the doorway. "Do you need help?" she asked.

Flynn must not have heard her. "Not you precisely," he said with enough wiggle in his voice to undermine his righteous indignation. "Your people."

I looked to Rodriguez for confirmation.

The older detective seemed worn out, ready to abdicate all responsibility. Ready to let Flynn have his way with me—interrogatingly speaking. "Let's not get ahead of ourselves here," he said.

From behind them, Frances piped up. "I heard that you were going after the dead woman's ex-husband. Is that right?"

Flynn's head whipped around. "How did you hear that?"

I allowed myself a smile. "Frances knows everything."

She marched forward, wagging a finger. "Word gets out if you're not careful. And I daresay you're loose with the lips, young man."

I expected Flynn to spring out of his chair like Wile E. Coyote popping from a high-powered ejection seat. The guy clearly had anger management issues. Didn't they administer psychological tests to potential cops anymore?

Frances kept going, unfazed. "Now, I don't know this ex-husband fellow from a bum on the street, but it seems to me that if you're here hollering about getting bad information, then maybe you jumped the gun on your little news conference this morning?" She looked up at me over the top of Flynn's head. "I think that makes a good case for thinking first, acting later, don't you?"

After delivering her final line with an emphatic head shake, she turned and stormed out of the room.

I usually heard my clock tick when the office dropped silent. This time the sound was drowned out by Flynn's breathing, fast and furious from between clenched teeth.

Rodriguez cleared his throat. "An understandable mistake."

I waited.

Flynn resumed his purposeful pose, trying again to look relaxed. He spoke in a deceptively soft voice. "One of your staff members noticed a man leaving the grounds yesterday with an oversized briefcase."

Large bags, backpacks, and briefcases were not allowed inside Marshfield Manor. "Could he have been escaping with the stolen item?"

Rodriguez looked at Flynn, signaling his intent to resume control of the conversation. "At first that's what we thought. One of your staff stopped the man, who claimed he was here on business. Your staffer called security to examine the briefcase, but they found nothing suspicious inside and allowed the man to leave. A moment later he disappeared into a crowd and was gone. You have to understand, all this transpired shortly before anyone was alerted to the shooting upstairs. There was no reason for your staff member to sound an alarm."

"But you think he's the killer?"

Flynn's jaw tightened. Rodriguez glanced over at him, then answered, "We only have a description at this point.

No name. But the man's description matches that of Lenore Honore's ex-husband."

"That's good news."

"No," Rodriguez said. "We *thought* it was good news." He ran his bottom teeth over his top lip. "This morning we expected to be able to issue a warrant for Lenore Honore's ex-husband's arrest." Another huge sigh. "But the man has an airtight alibi. He's in the hospital with appendicitis. In New Mexico."

"Oh."

From the look on Flynn's face, he wanted to be anywhere but here. "So who is this mystery businessman?" I asked. "Seems to me if you find him, you'll be a lot closer to finding answers."

Flynn shifted position, delivering the unmistakable message that he didn't care to be discussing the issue with me.

"That's one of the reasons we're here," Rodriguez said, ignoring Flynn's behavior. "We wanted to ask you if you'd had any visitors yesterday who fit the description. This situation could be cleared up very quickly if we find that the individual in question did indeed have business with you."

"Not me," I said. "Except for the film crew and tour groups, I didn't deal with anyone other than Marshfield staff members yesterday."

Rodriguez perked up. "Then maybe this is a valuable lead to follow. We've asked the staffer who stopped the man to go over security recordings. There's a chance he'll show up on the tapes."

Even Flynn lost his bored expression for a few seconds. "Did Bennett Marshfield have any appointments yesterday?"

"I don't know of any. He's out at an auction today, but I'll find out for sure and get back to you."

"Quickly," Flynn said.

"That reminds me." I'd debated bringing the subject up,

but it wouldn't do any harm. "I had an odd interaction with a man today."

"What does this have to do with the murder?" Flynn asked.

I faced Rodriguez. "You know the film crew is staying at the Oak Tree Hotel, right?"

He nodded.

"I was there this morning to help Mark Ellroy transition to the Marshfield Hotel; while I waited for him downstairs, I saw a guy who didn't seem right."

I explained about the man's interest in the morning's news conference, and how he'd glared at me when I'd absentmindedly corrected Flynn's pronunciation of Lenore's last name. The younger detective glowered. I plunged on, explaining how the man in the lobby hadn't looked at all familiar, but that he'd seemed to recognize me. And I told them about the anger. "He wanted to put distance between himself and me," I said. "That much was abundantly clear."

"And you got all that from a glare."

I wasn't about to let Flynn badger me. "It wasn't simply a glare. It was malevolence staring straight at me."

Rodriguez had pulled out his notebook and was scribbling as I spoke. "What can you tell me about him?"

I described the guy as best I could, mentioning that he looked ready to work out or head toward the pool. "He was shaved-head bald," I said, then stopped.

"What?" Rodriguez asked.

"It didn't dawn on me until this minute, but his head was a different color than his face."

Flynn made an unpleasant noise.

"Explain," Rodriguez said.

"His head was pale, but his face was tan. As though he'd been out in the sun with his head covered." I was putting two and two together as I spoke. "For years. Like . . . he may have shaved his head only recently."

Rodriguez's heavily lidded eyes widened slightly. "Hmm," he said as he continued to write notes.

"Nothing against the law about that," Flynn said.

"The man Mark Ellroy and John Kitts saw," I said, my train of thought gaining steam, "what did they say about him?"

Rodriguez licked his thumb and paged back in his notebook. "Middle-aged. Slim. Head full of graying hair. Light complexion, though tan. Possible tattoo or birthmark on neck." He looked up. "You see any kind of birthmark?"

"No, but . . ." Now I was really convinced I'd seen the murderer. "He was wearing a towel around his neck. I'll bet he shaved his head so that no one would recognize him."

Rodriguez didn't share my enthusiasm, but he didn't dismiss my concerns either. "Would you recognize this man if you saw him again?"

"Absolutely."

"And you say he's staying at the Oak Tree Hotel?"

"I assume so. He was there, at least."

"Worth a look." He hoisted himself to his feet and gestured toward the door with his chin. Flynn followed his partner's lead. "You'll get back to us about Mr. Bennett's appointments?" Rodriguez asked.

"Right away."

Chapter 13

I HAD A LOT OF WORK AHEAD OF ME, NONE OF which had anything to do with the latest murder, yet I nonetheless found myself staring out my office windows trying to piece the puzzle together. My mind wandered, as it often did, and I recalled this morning's interaction with Jack. I didn't know what it was about him that kept me hoping for more.

I wondered what Jack was thinking right now about the alleged tryst I knew he imagined I'd had with Mark Ellroy. In the Oak Tree Hotel, no less. Jack's erroneous assumption disturbed me more than I cared to admit. Unfortunately, there was nothing I could do about it unless I called him to explain and, oh, wouldn't that be awkward?

Like two rival spirits on my shoulders, my logical side urged me to have patience with him. "It's too soon," she whispered. The other spirit didn't attempt to keep her voice down. "You have one life," she reminded me. "Why waste it waiting when he may never come around? If you meant enough to him, he would share more of his life with you. Let him go. Move on."

I blew out a breath, still staring. I didn't even notice Frances at the door until she cleared her throat. "The Mister sent word that he'll be down soon," she said. "He's back early from his errand."

"Thanks, Frances."

She sidled up to the desk. "What you said earlier, about me knowing everything."

I arched one brow. "You have more to share?"

"I don't know if you'll want to hear it."

She sat, letting me know I was going to hear this whether I wanted to or not.

The look on her face, her position at the edge of the seat, and the way she'd come in as I'd been thinking about Jack, shot flashes of apprehension from my stomach up to my heart. Frances had an uncanny way of knowing exactly what I was thinking.

"What is it?" I asked.

She hesitated. It was about Jack. I was sure of it now.

"Spill it, Frances," I said with more than a little sharpness to my voice.

Rather than get her back up, she worked her mouth. "You've been fair to me, more or less," she began. "I'm not saying I want to start a fan club or anything, but you've done a better job taking over for Abe than anybody expected, especially me. And because you've been fair to me, I think you ought to know sooner rather than later."

This was definitely not going to be good.

When she looked up, her tadpole eyebrows were as far apart as I'd ever seen them. "He should have told you himself." She pursed her lined lips. "I suppose it falls to me, though. It always falls to me."

Just get on with it, I wanted to scream.

"Our landscape architect."

"Jack?" Who else could it be?

The briefest of nods. "He used to have a girlfriend. Years ago. Before the trouble."

I remembered. He'd told me about her. About how she'd left when he'd been accused of murder.

Becke, I thought, as Frances said, "Becke."

"What about her?"

"Last name was Anderson way back when, but she got married. Moved to Westville."

Did I know where this was going? Yes, I thought I did.

"She's back," Frances said, confirming it. "Divorced now. With kids in tow, not two weeks ago. She's staying with her folks until she finds a place of her own. Word is the minute she learned that Jack had been cleared, she raced back to rekindle the old flame."

"And?" I couldn't stop the question from tumbling out. "Are they? Rekindling?"

Frances wore a decided scowl. "They've been seen together."

"Have *you* seen them together?"

She nodded, watching me. "I can't say that they were exactly acting like lovebirds, but I can tell you they were friendly. You know, warm."

Rather than wilt under her scrutiny, I resumed staring out the window. "He doesn't owe me anything," I said. "We have no commitment to each other. He has every right to live his life the way he wants."

Frances didn't say a word. Silence lay like a dead thing between us. Finally, I couldn't stand it and turned to face her again.

Her eyes narrowed. I could tell she'd been waiting for my attention.

"Is that what you think?" she asked softly. "That he doesn't owe you anything?" She made a noise that sounded like *pheh*. "That fool owes you his life. His brother's, too. One of these days he's going to wake up and realize that. And when he does, you're going to be long gone. Mark my words."

She stood up and trundled out of the room.

"Thanks, Frances," I whispered.

* * *

BENNETT AND I MET AN HOUR LATER IN ONE of the few third-floor rooms that hadn't been converted into office space. I was certain a great deal of history had been lost when the second and third floors of the west wing were redesigned for administrative use. I was glad, however, that the architect had minimized our commercial footprint by keeping most of the home's original details intact.

This room, about fifty feet down from my office, sat ten steps inside the administrative area; just beyond it, double doors led into the third-floor Gathering Hall, where a guard was posted whenever the mansion was open to visitors. At one time this gorgeous space had been Warren Sr.'s bedroom, but the noise from guests reveling so close to his quarters late into the night had inspired him to find a quieter location for sleep. The thing was, he loved the view from this spot, as well as the room's layout. Expansive, as most rooms in the mansion were, this L-shaped sanctuary boasted a unique feature of having a separate, sunken reading area. Along the wall of windows, three steps down from the main area, a pair of rose-hued velvet chairs faced one another overlooking the western expanse of the estate. Even after Warren had given up the room for sleeping, he was said to return here often to enjoy his nightly brandy while watching the sun set.

"Welcome to the 'man cave,' Gracie," Bennett said when I arrived.

The description was apt. "I didn't realize you knew that term."

Bennett smirked. "I hear more than people suspect."

"I believe it. Why the Sword Room today?" I asked.

"The Sword Room," he repeated, chuckling. "I've always referred to it as 'the old bedroom.' But I like yours better."

Warren had decorated the room with every weapon he'd ever had the pleasure to meet. Although several of the more historically interesting pieces were now displayed in glass cases in other areas, this room housed the bulk of his collection. To the right and left of the fireplace were dozens of swords. Crisscrossed, and rising from the top of the wainscot to the bottom of the room's crown molding, they formed a herringbone pattern of deadly metal with an oak beam running vertically down their center, locking them in place. Over the marble fireplace mantel a broadsword with a winged hilt claimed the place of honor.

I knew from Marshfield history that this handcrafted sword had been presented as a gift to Bennett's father by a dear friend who had emigrated from Japan before the start of World War II. When it became clear he would be moved to an internment camp, he asked Warren Jr. to keep the sword for him. Upon his release, when Warren attempted to return it, his friend refused. He said that Warren's letters had kept him confident of the future throughout his ordeal, and because of the strength he derived from his friend's support, he wanted Warren to keep the sword as a gift.

A powerful, frightening weapon with wide, wavy edges, its grip sported a cruel-looking jagged wing. Even though it wasn't extremely valuable in the financial sense, its sentimental worth rendered it priceless.

"Have you ever taken that down?" I asked.

"Of course. What young man wouldn't?" His eyes got a faraway look. "I haven't touched in years, though. I should."

"The maids keep it dusted and we have a service come by once a year to make certain all the swords are maintained." I said. "It's kept in pristine condition. Nothing stopping you."

"Why don't you give it a go? You told me you fenced in college."

"College foils are nothing compared to that." I laughed. "I probably couldn't even lift it." On the floor next to the fireplace was a brass plate I hadn't noticed before. Levered doors were set into a horizontal frame. "What's that?"

Bennett chuckled. "My grandfather enjoyed smoking cigars and had this chute installed to dispose of stogies when he was finished with them. Over time, the servants came up with an alternate use and decided to make life easier for themselves by using it as a place to discard fireplace ashes." He pointed vaguely north. "It empties out near the trash in the basement. When my grandfather discovered this new efficiency, he regretted not installing a chute next to all the fireplaces in the house." Bennett shrugged. "You can't think of everything, I guess."

Another tidbit of history I hadn't known. "You keep a lot of precious items in here." I pointed across the room to a new addition. "What's that?"

His eyes twinkled. "We'll talk about that later." He guided me to the two seats in front of the windows and gestured for me to sit. I did. "Hillary hates this room," he said as he took the chair facing mine. "She thinks all the weaponry makes it barbaric. Hence, it's ideal for safekeeping." He spared me responding by changing the subject. "Speaking of unpleasantness, how is Frances?"

"Better," I said. "Surprisingly."

His smile was wide. "Working your magic on the poor soul, are you? You bamboozled me after only a few weeks. Took a little longer for her, but then again, she's a lot tougher than I am. I'm just a cream puff inside."

"Uh-huh, right. Tell that to the sellers you negotiate with on a regular basis." I returned his contagious grin then sobered. "I need to bring you up to date on the police investigation."

I told Bennett everything I'd learned. He asked about Mark's move to our hotel, Rodriguez and Flynn's updates, and had pointed questions about our security. "I hired Terrence because of his track record," he said with more than a trace of frustration. "Marshfield Manor has always been a refuge, a bucolic location where visitors come to enjoy beauty and peace. Yet we've had three murders since he's been here."

"The same could be said about me."

"You're not in charge of security."

"True, but I am in charge of the manor, which means I share responsibility."

He sat back, steepling his fingers under his chin. "Why so protective?"

"Is that what it sounds like?" I wrinkled my nose, thinking about it. "I suppose it's because Terrence and I started at the same time. We're both the new kids on the block and we've both had to work under difficult circumstances because of the murders."

"Don't forget the recent thefts, too."

I hadn't forgotten. "Chances are, these murders and the thefts would have happened whether Terrence and I were here or not. So far I can't blame either of us for actually *causing* any of them."

"Go on."

"It seems to me that if you aren't going to blame me, you can't blame Terrence either. But if you are blaming him, then I have to share in that as well."

A skeptical frown. "I doubt that sort of logic would hold up in a court of law."

"Does it need to?"

"Tell me what to do, Gracie. If hiring a top-of-the-line security expert isn't keeping our guests safe, then what's left? All the money in the world isn't going to stop bad things from happening, but I don't want them happening here. Do I close the mansion to tourists for good?"

"No," I said immediately. Although I understood where he was coming from, the idea of closing the mansion was too severe to consider. Doing so would effectively kill Emberstowne, which relied on tourism to survive. "Marshfield just has had a rash of bad luck."

"Bad luck," he repeated. "Making a success of yourself in life means creating your own luck. I'm not about to sit back and let the fates wreak havoc on my home and my life.

That said, let's table the idea for now with the understanding that if we can't get a better handle on the situation soon we will have to consider more drastic measures."

"Understood," I said.

"Speaking of luck, let me satisfy your curiosity."

I followed as he got up and crossed the room, coming to stop at the small cherry wood chest I'd noticed earlier. It sat waist-high atop a gilt-metal stand in the room's far corner. "You got this at the auction yesterday?"

"No. Yesterday's event was a bust. I won this treasure at an auction two months ago. It only arrived at my solicitor's office last week. I couldn't wait to bring it home."

"What is it?" I asked.

He didn't say a word but merely placed both hands atop the shiny cherry wood. The chest was about the size of a small carry-on suitcase, with three roses carved into its lid.

"It's lovely," I said.

"You haven't seen anything yet." He opened the lid, revealing a diamond tiara, which sparkled in the light.

"Oh my," I said, stepping closer. "You didn't tell me you'd been to London and stolen the crown jewels. This is stunning."

"It is, isn't it," he said with undisguised glee. "That diamond," he pointed to the tiara's central stone, "is eight carats by itself. The sapphires making the V-shape around it total another twenty-five. The smaller diamonds in the curlicues are a half-carat each."

I had no words. "Breathtaking," I said. "I've never seen its equal. What is its provenance?"

He smiled. "Don't worry. It's perfectly legal."

"I had no doubt."

"This little beauty was created for a gentleman in Greece for his new wife, not all that long ago. An artist was hired for the job back in the early 1900s. He was given an unlimited budget and the command to please the Grecian's wife. She directed every step of the design process and was said to have been overjoyed when the tiara was finished."

"There's more, I'll bet."

He smiled and continued. "She wore it exactly once, at a ball the couple threw to show it off." He lowered his voice in an aside. "Back then, famous people threw lavish parties. These days, famous people do outrageous things on reality TV. But I digress . . ." He took a deep breath. "That night, the wife went to bed, taking the tiara with her."

"Something bad's coming, isn't it?"

"The artist had become so enamored of the tiara that he broke into her room and professed his undying love, begging her to run away with him—with the tiara, of course. She ordered him away, and when she attempted to call for help, he killed her."

"Wait a minute," I said. "If she's dead, how do we know about him professing his undying love?"

Bennett grinned. "Too smart for me, are you? They caught the artist as he was about to climb over the estate's outer wall with the tiara tied into his shirt. He broke down and confessed. Speculation was that he didn't care a whit about the woman. She was rather vile, controlling, and—if the rumors are true—homely as sin. Because of that, and the artist's professions of love, rumors started. Word got out that the tiara had the power to cast spells, making the woman who wore it obsessively desirable—no matter her looks or personality. The artist jumped on this as a defense. He claimed he had acted in madness. Astonishingly, his passion was considered temporary mental illness and he was acquitted."

"That's terrible. The poor woman."

Bennett made a wry face. "I agree. It was further speculated that the jury, made up of townspeople who despised the woman, was inclined toward leniency. In any case, the tiara was returned to the husband, who believed in its powers so fully that he secreted it away where no one would ever find it. And no one did until after his death. He died a pauper and his estate was sold for back taxes. Another collector snapped the tiara up."

"Recently?"

"Mid nineteen forties. Right after the war. The man who bought it planned to bestow it upon his wife for their anniversary."

"Another tragic ending?"

"Not right away. She was killed by an intruder a few years later. But the tiara wasn't lost. The husband held on to it for decades. He never remarried and it was said he went mad at the end of his life."

"So this is cursed. Death and madness to all who own it."

"Considering the husband was over a hundred years old when he died last year, I don't think his dementia could be attributed to the tiara. I decided to take my chances." His expression dreamy, his voice lowered. "Indeed, I *had* to have it. It's as though I needed to possess it because it already possessed me. I was oddly compelled . . ." He turned to me, his eyes crinkling with mirth. "Just kidding. Did I get you?"

I tapped his arm, playfully. "Not for a second. But I am concerned that something this valuable isn't more secure."

"It's safe." He must have read skepticism on my face because he changed the subject. We crossed the room to resume our seats by the window. "Any news on the missing items?" he asked.

"We think the killer was in the process of stealing the oliphant when he encountered Lenore. He was spotted carrying an item that might have been the golden horn. Detectives Rodriguez and Flynn are tracking down a lead. They're looking for the identity of a man seen carrying a briefcase when he left the property yesterday."

Bennett's eyebrows rose.

"I take it he wasn't here for an appointment with you, then?" I asked. "Rodriguez asked me to check."

"I would have told you. Did no one stop him?"

I gave him the rundown of how the man's briefcase appeared to contain only papers. "And you have no idea what he was doing here?" I asked.

Bennett worked his mouth. "No," he said finally. "That doesn't mean he wasn't here to see someone else."

"Hillary?" I asked.

"Have you talked with her?"

I shook my head. "She came in here to take me to task for halting the DVD filming. At the time I hadn't yet heard about the man with the briefcase so I didn't know to ask."

"That girl will be the death of me."

"Don't say that," I snapped. "Bite your tongue."

He chuckled. "Did your mother used to say that?"

She had. "Why?"

"Because my father adopted that expression a long time ago." He got a faraway look in his eyes. "So many similarities, Gracie. Are you sure you don't want to find out for sure?"

He hadn't broached the subject of DNA testing since we'd first discovered our possible blood relation. "I've told you about my sister," I began. "If you and I are related, that means you're related to Liza as well. You don't want that on record. She'd be here faster than a shot to see how much she could weasel out of you."

"Worse than Hillary?"

I thought about my estranged sister. How she'd taken off with my fiancé a year before. They were married now, heaven help them both, and although she hadn't come running back for a handout lately, that didn't mean she wouldn't be darkening my doorstep soon. "She's worse," I finally said. "Hillary wants your money, yes . . ."

He laughed. "I love a girl who speaks her mind."

"But Hillary also wants family. She has no one besides you."

"Besides *us*."

"I shudder to think what would happen if she knew there was that possibility . . ." I let the thought hang, then returned to the original subject, leaning forward in my chair. "Besides, the test can't prove beyond a doubt that we are related. It can only prove the likelihood. What if the results show that we can't possibly be related?" I asked.

He reached forward to grab my arm. "That's the thing," he said, "they won't."

"If you're so certain of the results, then why bother to do it at all?"

"So that no one—not even Hillary—can ever contest my will."

I froze. "What? No, Bennett. No. You can't include me. Not even a little bit. That wouldn't be right."

He pointed at me. "Your reaction tells me I'm making the right decision."

I resorted to my "serious" voice. "Bennett, you can't."

"Of course, I can. But I understand your concerns. How about this . . ."

I watched him warily. His eyes twinkled, which meant he was up to something.

"You don't tell me what to do with my will, and I'll stick around so you won't have to worry about what's in it. Deal?"

"Bennett . . ."

"That is as good as you are going to get for the moment."

I took a deep breath. "You can be exasperating."

"One of my charms," he said. "Deal?"

"Deal."

As I relaxed again, he added, "Think about the blood test. Make an old man happy." When I opened my mouth to reply, he cut me off. "That's the last I'll say of the matter."

"Okay."

He grinned. "For now."

I shot him a warning look that didn't have the impact I'd hoped for. "Changing the subject," he began again, "I'd like to meet the young man who was shot. Do you think you could coordinate that? I'd like to convey my sincere apologies."

"I'm sure that can be arranged."

"Good." He stood up. "Let me know when and I'll make myself available. You know I have so many social conflicts to work around." He rolled his eyes.

"You keep busier than half the people I know. I'll bet you're on your way to some fabulous event right now."

He gave a short laugh. "Not so fabulous. A boring meeting with my lawyer." He waved his hand as though shooing a fly. "Routine stuff."

We parted ways at the Sword Room door. I didn't want to think about death and inheritance. I also knew that Hillary had been trying in vain to get him to leave the entire estate to her instead of to Emberstowne. She promised on her solemn honor to keep her stepfather's vision alive. The only person I think she'd actually fooled into believing that she'd follow through was herself.

I wasn't afraid that Bennett would change the trust, but I knew he had personal effects numbering in the thousands. Maybe he intended to leave me something personal. I shook my head. The idea of a world without Bennett was not one I wanted to contemplate.

While I would be honored to be included, the truth was that we'd only gotten to know one another over the past year. Any overt generosity on his part toward me—without any explanation as to why he thought me worthy of inclusion—could render his entire will suspect. Hillary could weasel in by the tips of her fingers and create doubt, perhaps significant enough to land her a larger share of whatever Bennett intended to leave. That would be the exact opposite of Bennett's wishes and I couldn't allow that to happen.

If he insisted on including me, Hillary's reaction posed a real risk. If I consented to a blood test and it proved Bennett and I were probable blood relatives, what then?

Chapter 14

RONNY TOONEY MET ME OUTSIDE MY BACK door the next morning. I'd called him and requested we meet, so encountering him this time wasn't a shock. "How's Bootsie?" he asked when I closed the door and made sure it locked securely.

"She's doing very well," I said. "If we had more time, I'd invite you in to see her."

Tooney's face registered pleasure. "Things sure have changed from when we first met," he said. "Are you getting tired of constantly ordering me away?"

"What can I say? You've worn me down."

His pudgy, homely face creased into an expression of great delight. So much so that I couldn't help myself from saying, "You know, Tooney, you're a pretty handsome fella when you smile like that. I'll bet you're quite the heart-breaker."

His glee disappeared in a flash and I realized I'd inadvertently struck a nerve. I wanted to apologize, but sensed that would only make things worse.

"What did you want to see me about?" he asked.

Taking his cue to change the subject, I launched into my request. "Remember a few months ago you told me that former employees often donated their old uniforms to the resale shop or sold them on consignment at secondhand stores?"

He nodded, his doughy face somber. "You said you stopped that practice. You told me you now require employees to turn in their uniforms whenever they retire or quit."

"Exactly right. But that was like closing the stable after the horse ran out. There are still quite a few old uniforms circulating, and from what I understand they've become collectible. We inadvertently created a secondary market for Marshfield blazers when we started demanding their return."

"What do you need from me?"

"You heard that the killer was dressed as a Marshfield employee, right?"

He nodded.

"The police are following down all the leads they can," I went on, "but I keep remembering how you brought this to my attention months ago. You saw a vulnerability that others missed."

He brightened. "I did, didn't I?"

"I'd like you to investigate. Track down this lead."

"Won't the detectives run me in for interfering?"

"I'll talk with Rodriguez," I said. "He wants me to continue looking at how one of our blazers got into the wrong hands, and you're the one I trust to get this done."

You'd have thought I'd given Tooney a million dollars. "I won't let you down."

"I know you won't."

A flicker of fear crossed his eyes. "Can I . . . that is . . . when I need to report back, would it be all right if I came in person? To Marshfield?"

My heart gave a little tug at his simple request. I'd banished him from the manor after he'd been caught impersonating a cop during Abe's murder investigation.

"Sure," I said. "I'll leave word with Terrence."

I gave him a rough description of the killer as provided by Mark and the tour director. "It's not much to go on," I said, "but it may help if someone remembers someone buying one of those blazers. And when you talk to people, keep in mind that the killer might have a birthmark or tattoo here." I fingered my own neck in emphasis.

"I'm on it," he said.

RATHER THAN PUT MY CELL PHONE ON speaker on my drive to Marshfield, I sat in my driveway and put in a quick call to Rodriguez to remind him about Tooney looking into the matter of the rogue blazer. The detective had encouraged me to follow up on my end, but I wasn't entirely certain he'd be thrilled to know Tooney was on the case. He surprised me, however, by telling me it was a good plan.

"We can use all the help we can get," he said. "I'll be in touch with him today. We're following up with anyone who had contact with Ms. Honore before her death, and Mr. Tooney certainly qualifies."

"That doesn't sound too promising." If they had solid leads, they'd be tracking those down, not following up with a private-eye wannabe who'd accidentally crossed paths with Lenore. "Is the task force stalled?"

He heaved another of his deep sighs. "My partner won't admit it, but we got nothing. Zero. What about Mr. Marshfield? Did you ask him if he had any business appointments that day?"

"I did, and he didn't."

"That's something then. The man with the briefcase may wind up being a suspect after all. But he didn't resemble the description that the tour guide and the victim gave us. Right now that's all we've got: an average, possibly slim, middle-aged guy. You have thousands of people in and out of the mansion every single day. That description fits probably twenty percent of them."

"Except for the birthmark or tattoo," I said.

"The one that no one is really sure exists?" he asked. "The tour guide wasn't positive, and the victim didn't even remember seeing it until we asked about it. If it's there, it's small and easily hidden. To be frank, our best lead may be the one you gave us."

"Me?"

"The guy you saw in the lobby of the Oak Tree Hotel. He acted suspicious, right? He's our best hope for a lead right now."

My wild suspicion was their best hope? If so, that was terrible news. "I'm sorry," I said.

"Not your fault." His voice was resigned.

"Where is Lenore right now?" I asked. "That is, where has she been taken?"

"Autopsy is complete. Her neck was broken, most likely before she was pushed."

"This killer was ruthless."

"All that's left is for us to release the body and she can go home for burial."

"Who's taking care of that?" I asked. "Does she have family?"

"Her ex-husband put us in contact with a sister. I talked with her. She's understandably distraught." He made a sad noise. "At least we can feel good about that. Lenore will be taken care of by someone who loves her."

I thought about my sister and how much I would not want her taking care of me. But all I said was, "Yeah."

"Any updates on your inventory?" he asked. "Has anything else gone missing?"

"We've checked and double-checked inventories and believe nothing else has disappeared except the golden horn. I've got a call in to our insurance company, and I did have a chance to talk with my friend at the Kane Estate again. She doesn't have anything further to offer in terms of suspects, but she said she would be willing to talk with you if you ever have questions."

"Appreciate that, but we don't see any connection at this point. We will eventually get in touch if there's reason to. In the meantime, thank her for us, will you?"

I promised I would. "One more thing," I said. "I plan to allow the DVD filming company to resume as soon as you give me the all clear."

"Consider it given," he said. "We've catalogued all the samples and photos we require. If we need to come back and revisit the crime scene, I'll contact you."

"Fair enough."

"One more thing, Ms. Wheaton. Do you believe there's any chance the thefts are tied to the DVD film crew?"

I thought about the people I'd met. Even though I'd harbored suspicions about Donald Lee Runge and Harry Hinton, I didn't have any reason to suspect they'd actually stolen anything. Neither one closely resembled the killer's description. "It would be hard for any of the film crew to steal while our security is watching."

"Don't they have access to the back areas, and don't they have knowledge about your security protocols? Either could make things easier for a determined thief."

"True," I agreed, "and it's possible. I just don't have any proof."

Rodriguez heaved another deep sigh. "Join the club."

FRANCES LOOKED UP WHEN I WALKED IN. SHE held up her left wrist. "You're late."

"Are you keeping tabs on me now?"

With a huff, she slammed a palm onto her desk. "Do you have any idea how much trouble you could have gotten into?"

"What happened?"

She glared. "Nothing. That's exactly my point."

I raised my hands. "I give up. What are you talking about?"

"You arrive every morning at the same time. Give or take ten minutes. You're very predictable, as you should be. If you're going to be late, you call and tell me. Today you're late and you haven't called in. We're all well aware of your tendency to get into trouble, and I don't like it one bit."

I glanced at the clock. My talk with Tooney and subsequent phone call with Rodriguez had set me back about a half hour. I suddenly understood. Frances had been worried—about me. After our little adventure together a few weeks ago, we'd been getting along a great deal better, but this was unprecedented. "I apologize, Frances," I said. "I didn't realize the time."

"You need to do better," she said again with a huff. "What happens if you get into trouble again? It will fall to *me* to contact the police. How am I supposed to know whether you're running late or a killer is holding you hostage?"

"Let me bring you up to date." I told her about my plan involving Ronny Tooney, and I let her know that, unfortunately, the police weren't coming up with any solid leads.

"They should bring that woman back," she said. "Tank. The detective from Michigan. She was good."

"I've thought the same thing, myself."

"Hmph," she said, returning to work on whatever project she'd begun.

I took that as a cue that our conversation had ended, but as I reached the doorway to my office she spoke again. "If they were smart, they'd put the three of us in charge of this mess. We'd have it cleared up in a hurry."

With one hand on the jamb, I turned. "The three of us?"

"You, me, and that Tank," she said with a shrug. "Who else?"

* * *

I CALLED CORBIN TO MAKE ARRANGEMENTS for resuming filming the next morning. "Thank heavens," Corbin said. "My crew was going stir crazy at that hotel."

A little light sparked in my brain. "While I have you on the phone," I began, "do you have anyone on staff who looks like this?" I went on to describe the man I encountered in the Oak Tree lobby.

"Doesn't sound like any of the crew," he said, "but if I find that any of my guys has shaved his head recently, I'll let you know."

"I'd appreciate it," I said.

"Will you be around for the filming again?"

"As much as I'd love to, with everything that's happened recently, I need to be in my office as much as possible. But don't worry. Our head of security, Terrence Carr, will be with you and his team will help make sure everything goes smoothly."

"I understand," he said. "But you ought to know that Mr. Marshfield is quite insistent about you being part of the project."

As soon as I'd hung up the phone, Frances appeared in the doorway. "He's on his way out, you know," she said.

"Who is?"

"Carr. Ever since he got here, we've been having nothing but murders."

I thought about how Bennett and I had had the same conversation. "The same could be said about me."

"You, at least, have had a hand in solving the crimes. What has Terrence done? Nothing, to my mind." She seemed to be waiting for me to say something further. When I didn't respond, she said, "Thought you'd want to know. The Mister is none too pleased."

A few hours later, my cell phone rang. I glanced at the

display before answering, not recognizing the phone number. "Grace Wheaton," I said.

"Yes, hello," the male voice said, "I'm calling to register a complaint."

Even as I wondered how on earth a guest could have gotten my personal number, I asked, "How may I help you?"

"The accommodations here at the Marshfield Hotel are much too luxurious. Everything is far too pleasant. If I stay here another day I won't ever be able to return to my ordinary life in Colorado."

I'd recognized Mark's voice by the time he'd gotten halfway through his spiel and decided to play along. "I'm sorry to hear that. What on earth were we thinking when we put you there? I'll make arrangements to have you returned to the Oak Tree at once."

He began to laugh, as did I. "No thanks," he said, "I think I can tough it out a little longer."

"How are things going?" I asked, hoping for an update on the investigation.

"Your friend Detective Flynn had me visit the police station to look at some mug shots."

"And?"

"Nothing. I can't say that I'm able to describe the killer perfectly, but I have no doubt that I'd recognize the guy if I ever saw him again."

"I hope you don't."

"That makes two of us."

"Is everything else going well?" I asked. "Anything you need?"

"Now that you ask, there is something . . ."

My heart fluttered a little faster. "Sure, what is it?"

"I'd love to have dinner with you," he said, quickly adding, "and just so you don't think of me as some kind of loser who takes advantage of others' generosity, I'd like to find a great little spot in town where the magical Marshfield credit card won't work and where I get the chance to take a lady out. I was hoping you'd be free tonight."

I felt myself blush and thanked heaven he couldn't see it. What was with me, anyway? "That sounds wonderful. What time?"

"There is one small glitch," he said.

I was about to ask what that was, but then remembered. "You don't have a car."

"Bingo."

"I'll pick you up then. What time?"

We settled on seven o'clock. "I'll make reservations," he said. "Any suggestions as to where?"

"Surprise me."

I heard the smile in his voice when he said, "A challenge. I like that. See you at seven."

As I shut my phone and started to put it away, movement near the door caught my eye. Frances stood there, her eyes bright with interest. "And?" she asked.

I tamped down my grin. "Mark Ellroy and I are meeting for dinner."

Her two little tadpole eyebrows attempted to leap off her forehead. "Oh?" she said.

Why did I get so much enjoyment out of surprising Frances?

"Business or pleasure?" she asked.

"A little of both, I think."

She nodded, which for Frances was as good as approval. She rearranged her face into a glower. "Behave yourself."

Chapter 15

EVEN THOUGH I COULD HAVE STAYED AT work until it was time for our date, I decided to head home at five to give myself a chance to change clothes and gussy up. "Hey Bootsie," I called when I got in. She came running. I often thought the little kitten was more dog than cat. I picked her up and rubbed her face, which was one of her very favorite things.

"I've got a date tonight," I said.

She closed her eyes and nuzzled for more.

"You're going to be alone here all evening. That okay by you?"

A noise must have caught her attention because she perked her head, wriggled out of my grasp and jumped to the floor in a bound. A second later, she'd disappeared around the corner and I heard her tiny paws pad on the wooden stairs.

"I'll be there in a minute."

I made sure she had food and water, then followed her upstairs to get changed.

Forty-five minutes later, I was ready to go. It took only about twenty minutes to drive back to Marshfield. I didn't want to be ridiculously early, so I snuck one last look in the mirror to ensure that my summer dress was still a good choice—it was—before I grabbed my clutch purse to head down. As I picked it up, however, Bootsie bounded in. "You've been busy," I said, noting the dust on the top of her head. "Exploring the basement again?"

She jumped into my desk chair and circled the seat three times before staring up at me with her sad, large-pupiled eyes. She opened her mouth in a loud meow. "What do you want?" I asked.

She circled the seat again. Meowed again.

I glanced at my computer on the desk behind her. "Hmm . . ." I said, leaning forward to power it up. Plenty of time.

As soon as my Mac sprang to life, I ran a quick Google search on Mark Ellroy. I found four LinkedIn accounts, including one for a jeweler in Denver. Bingo. There were about a dozen other hits with the same name. One was a doctor in private practice in Vermont, another a male model whose racy photos popped up during my image search. I clicked out of that fast. There wasn't much more than that, except a Facebook account for a Mark Ellroy who looked to be about twelve years old.

As a lark, I searched my own name and was shocked by the number of hits. I didn't need to click to know why. Every single mention of my name was associated with either Abe Vargas's murder, or Zachary Kincade's, the two men who'd met their demise here at Marshfield Manor in recent months. I was especially sad to see my predecessor's name there.

I tapped the screen. "Hey, Abe," I said softly. "I hope you think I'm doing a good job."

One of the links had my name listed along with Lenore's. Posted by the local newspaper, I was sure it carried an account of the investigation. I knew how far the police were from finding the killer and I didn't want to rehash all that negativity tonight. I opted not to click.

A quick glance at the time posted in the top right-hand corner of my screen made me realize I needed to get moving.

I shut down the computer. "Good night, Bootsie," I said. "Don't wait up."

MARK STEPPED OUT FROM THE HOTEL AS I pulled up. The evening had not yet shrugged off the warm blanket of the day and I watched him wince as he hit the heavy wall of heat. He wore a red polo shirt that set off his dark hair, black pants, and a black sling for his injured arm. He opened the door. "May I?" he asked.

"Of course."

As he settled into the passenger seat, he turned to me. "You look lovely," he said. "Absolutely lovely."

"Thank you."

"Allow me to apologize for my appearance."

"Why?"

He smiled ruefully and pointed to his arm with his free hand. "I don't know why I didn't think about this before, but it's impossible to wear a sport coat over a sling without looking ridiculous. I hope you don't mind I'm a bit more casual?"

"I think you look great," I said sincerely.

He shot me a beaming smile. "Thank you."

"Where to?" I asked, putting the car into gear.

"You wanted a surprise, right?"

A little excited, a little nervous, my skin zinged. "I did."

He shot me a sidelong glance. "Any dietary restrictions?"

"None."

"All right then, drive out to the front gate and I'll give

you directions from there." He pulled papers from his pants pocket and, using one hand, unfolded them on his lap. "No peeking."

For the first time in a long while, I let myself relax. Tonight, I decided, I'd have fun. It was about time.

Mark's directions took us through Emberstowne, during which I convinced him to allow a detour past my house. "That's it," I said as I pulled up onto the driveway.

"Beautiful."

"You're very polite," I said. "It needs work. Lots of it. Time and lack of funds are holding me back. But there's a glimmer of hope ahead."

"I can't wait to see what it looks like when you're finished."

"I can't wait to show it to you." Backing onto the street, I asked, "Where to?"

He directed me until we wound up at the very outskirts of town where a small copper-roofed restaurant snugged up tight next to a bed-and-breakfast in an odd juxtaposition of old and new. I'd been past here a hundred times, but because the site was a bit off the main road, I hadn't paid much attention to its quaintness until now.

Though larger and in better shape, the yellow Victorian mansion reminded me of my home, with its wraparound porch and pointed gables. White-trimmed peaks were detailed with deep pink, and bright impatiens and petunias burst out from window boxes and decorative planters that perched in every available space. Next to it, Bailey's restaurant was a modern add-on, but its lines and design complemented its neighbor well.

I pulled into the gravel lot adjacent to the restaurant, my tires crunching as we rolled past a half dozen cars parked there. "The website said it was out of the way," Mark said as I turned off the engine. "It's not as prestigious as the dining room at Marshfield, but then again, I'm not dressed for elegance."

"I've never been here before."

His eyes lit up. "I'm glad to hear it."

Mark was able to manage his way out of my car with one arm and we crossed the lot together, walking next to one another but not too close. I took in the evening and the setting. We were surrounded by tall trees, the heady fragrance of green, and accompanied by a chorus of frogs chirping nearby. A tiny wooden bridge spanning a two-foot-wide creek connected the lot to the restaurant's cobbled sidewalk.

"This is beautiful," I said as we stepped inside. Soft lighting, buttery woodwork, and linen tablecloths gave the room an inviting, gentle air. Couples sat at tables spaced far enough apart to provide quiet privacy. They chatted and smiled at each other over fat cream-colored candles whose flames flickered and danced.

A motherly hostess with crinkly eyes and beaming smile led us to a table at the rear of the restaurant, next to a wide window. "Oh my," I said as we took our seats, "what a gorgeous view."

We overlooked a small pond centered in a wide garden of luscious greenery and bright blooms. What made the space special was the way it was encircled by tall pines—creating this hidden gem in the center of a giant forest. Pink, red, and salmon impatiens edged lush flower gardens of purple, gold, and white. Ornate benches were tucked behind wide tree trunks, giving their occupants a little privacy from restaurant-goers' eyes. Paths led out from the pond area, one toward the bed-and-breakfast, and the others deeper into the woods. I could envision myself getting lost out there, hiding among the fresh foliage, reading a book with my back up against a tree trunk and hoping no one would find me until I turned the last page.

"This is even better than it looked online," Mark said. "Smaller, too. I was afraid it would be big and impersonal. This is cozier and much more intimate. I hope the food is as great as the ambiance."

Our waiter overheard. "The food is excellent here," he said as he handed Mark a wine list. "The restaurant has only been open a few months and we haven't built up a following yet. It's growing every day. Your first time here, I take it?"

We admitted it was.

"You'll be back," he said with a smile. "But let's make *this* evening memorable first. Would you like a few minutes to decide on a beverage?"

Mark's eyes reflected our table's candlelight. "I have to confess I'm not much of a wine connoisseur," he said as he perused the leather-bound list. To me: "Would you like to decide?"

Although Bruce and Scott had been tutoring me with regard to wines, I was still far from an expert myself. Our waiter seemed to sense my hesitation and after a few pointed questions, wherein I discovered that Mark preferred reds, like I did, he suggested we opt for a bottle of claret he'd sampled. "Smooth, with a velvet finish," he said. "You won't be disappointed."

"A new restaurant, a new wine, a first date," Mark said. "Sounds like a perfect combination."

The waiter's eyebrows rose ever so slightly at the "first date" comment, but he didn't remark. A moment later he returned with our choice, going through all the ceremony that comes with ordering a bottle of wine at a fancy restaurant, and finally Mark and I were left alone to talk.

"I don't want our entire evening to be taken up with discussion about the investigation," he began, "but it is the rhinoceros in the room."

"It is," I agreed, "and I truly don't mind starting there. I do have a few questions for you."

He sat forward, as though eager to hear anything I'd say. "I thought you might."

"Have you talked with Rodriguez or Flynn since we last spoke?"

His gaze flicked out toward the pond for a second before he turned to me with a sardonic smile. "How do those two keep their jobs?" he asked. "Rodriguez isn't the worst, but that Flynn . . ." Turning to face me again, he said, "You remember I told you that I was down at the station to look at mug shots."

I nodded.

"They called me again this afternoon to tell me that I'm free to go."

"What?"

"They said they're finished with me. They'll get in touch whenever they need me again—*if* they need me again. What's wrong with these people?" He leaned forward, at once angry and eager. "I'm a material witness. I got closer to the killer than anyone did." With a sudden thoughtful frown, he added, "At least, anyone who's alive to tell. John saw the man, but not up close and personal"—he indicated his injured arm as his voice rose—"like I did. They should keep me nearby until the case is closed."

"I'm so sorry." I was, but not only because Rodriguez and Flynn appeared to be making a tactical error. If Mark was free to go, then this first date was likely our last. I was surprised by how much that prospect disappointed me.

He sat back and took a sip of his wine. "No, I'm the one who's sorry. I didn't want to talk about all this and here I go, first thing out of my mouth. I didn't want you to know until later that I'd be checking out in the morning. I wanted to enjoy our evening together."

I kept my voice neutral. "You're heading home then? In the morning?"

He tilted his head slightly. "Unless, of course, you wouldn't be opposed to my finding a hotel in town for a few more days." The candlelight danced again. "I'd originally planned to be on vacation through next week and it would be a shame to return home when there's so much here I'd rather see and do."

His flirtation was dragonfly light, but it was there all the same. As was the little twist in my stomach, which thrilled at the prospect of him staying in town longer. I wasn't fooling myself. I knew he had a home and business back in Colorado and this relationship probably wouldn't go anywhere beyond the next few days, but I wanted—no, I needed—this. I needed to feel attractive. I needed to feel desired again. It had been far too long.

"Why not stay where you are? You know you're welcome at the Marshfield Hotel for as long as you care to stay."

He sat back with a short laugh. "You've been generous and gracious to a fault. I couldn't imagine staying in a better location. But it isn't right to impose."

"It's more right than you think." I scooched forward in my seat, wine forgotten, intent on convincing Mark to remain our guest awhile longer. "Bennett Marshfield, the owner of the estate, asked to meet you." I answered Mark's reaction. "Seriously. I told him I'd check with you to see if you're willing. How would it look for Bennett to find out you're staying at a local hotel instead of at Marshfield?"

"I feel guilty taking advantage," he said, then asked, "Why does he want to meet with me?"

"Bennett feels personally responsible for everything that happens in his home. He's beside himself over Lenore's death and your injury."

"That's very kind of him, but it wasn't his fault."

"Either way, are you willing?" I held my breath. I was surprised to discover how much I wanted Bennett to meet Mark.

"Are you kidding? Of course. I'd be honored."

"There's the added bonus of keeping you close to the investigation. Even if Rodriguez and Flynn don't think they need you, I know I wouldn't mind."

Mark shook his head, but he was smiling. My heart was thumping a happy beat and I hoped the restaurant's dim lighting provided enough cover for my warm cheeks. "You're quite convincing. Thank you. I would be very pleased and very grateful to stay."

"Excellent, it's settled."

The waiter appeared to take our order. As soon as he left us alone again, Mark picked up his wineglass, tipping it toward me. "Let's hope the lead you gave the friendly detectives pans out before I have to return home next week. Maybe then I'll be able to be of some real help."

I'd been about to take a sip of wine, but I stopped myself. "What are you talking about?"

"Rodriguez told me you saw some man acting suspiciously at the Oak Tree Hotel when you were waiting for me there."

"Oh yes, that. I can't believe that's their best lead."

Mark shrugged. "It's more than they had before. They asked me if I'd seen a bald guy walking around the hotel at all, and what he might have been doing. I told them I didn't make a habit of noticing bald men, but that the description vaguely rang a bell."

"There was nothing especially remarkable about the man, other than the fact that it looked like he'd only recently shaved his head," I said. "I wouldn't be surprised if you didn't notice anything about him."

"So why did you report him to Rodriguez?"

I told him about waiting downstairs and how Flynn had appeared on the television. I mentioned the man—describing his looks and his clothes—and his reaction to the news broadcast and subsequent abrupt departure. "He'd been sitting there quietly until the news came on. After I spoke aloud, he became irate and stormed off." As the words tumbled out, I could hear how ridiculous this sounded. "All I can tell you is there was something not right about his reaction. I didn't like him. And even though we'd never met before, I could tell he didn't like me."

"How could anyone not like you?" he asked with a smile. "But to get back to the case . . . Rodriguez didn't mention that the man was wearing workout clothes. Or, at least I don't remember him mentioning it."

"What difference does that make?"

"I might have seen the guy you're talking about. The workout room at the Oak Tree isn't much. I think the entire area isn't bigger than fifteen by fifteen. There are two treadmills, a bench, and some free weights. I try to exercise every day, even when I'm out of town. I was limited by the arm, but decided to go on the treadmill for a while that morning. There was a guy in there with me. Bald. Just the two of us for about, oh, twenty minutes. I wouldn't have even thought of him if you hadn't mentioned the workout clothes."

My heart started its trip-hammer beat again, but this time for an entirely different reason. "Did he have a tattoo on his neck? Some kind of birthmark?"

Mark made an uneasy face. "I'm sorry to say I didn't pay much attention to him." He stared up at the ceiling for a moment, concentrating. "He could have, but honestly, I can't say for certain. I do believe his scalp was paler than his face, though. That feels familiar. Your hypothesis about the killer shaving his head in order to disguise himself is a good one. I have to tell you, though, I really believe I would have recognized the guy. Even without hair."

Disappointed, I agreed. "It looks like Rodriguez and Flynn may be back to square one."

"Let's hope not."

Over dinner, Mark asked me more about Bruce, Scott, and Bootsie. I told him about how the roof had finally gotten repaired, though I left out mention of Bennett's assistance. I talked about our plans: clean out the garage, fix the back door, redesign the landscaping. At that last one, he winced. "Has your friend Jack offered to help you with that project?"

I didn't know how to answer that. "He has offered," I

began slowly, trying to decipher Mark's expression. I was discovering that the man knew how to read people, but I wasn't certain if I was detecting wariness or challenge in his dark eyes when he waited for me to talk about Jack. "That was a while ago. I don't think he's interested anymore."

Mark spoke in a low voice, "I wouldn't be so sure about that. But . . ."

I waited.

"You and I are here together tonight. Not Jack. I'm sorry for bringing up something painful for you. Don't deny it. I can see it in your eyes."

"We've never actually . . ."

"No need to explain," he said, still keeping his voice so low I had to lean forward to hear him. "I only asked because I want to know where you are right now. If you're open to a new relationship." He closed his eyes briefly. "I'm sorry. I don't mean to move so quickly. It's just . . ."

"That you'll be leaving soon," I finished.

He made a face. "Makes me sound opportunistic, doesn't it? Again, my apologies. Let's enjoy dinner and not worry about what comes next."

Too late. I was already thinking about what might come next.

Chapter 16

WE DROVE BACK TO MARSHFIELD SHARING
stories about our childhoods, laughing a lot, and completely
avoiding the topic of the murder. I felt a buoyancy in my
heart I hadn't experienced in a long time, and every so often I stole a glance at Mark, appreciating his easy warmth
and those delightful dimples.

Because it was after ten at night, we were required to stop
at the visitor's gate for entry onto Marshfield property. "Hi,
Joe," I said to the guard, who bent down to peer into the passenger seat. "I'm driving up to the hotel to bring our guest
back." There was no real need for me to explain, but I did.
Joe gave us a thumbs-up and opened the gate for our passage.

"Did that make you uncomfortable?" Mark asked once
we'd cleared the entrance area.

"A little, I suppose."

My headlights cut a lonely glow along the dark access
road. Mark adopted a thoughtful expression for about a half
mile. "Would you mind pulling off for a moment?" he
asked, pointing just ahead.

My pulse quickened but I complied, making a right off the smooth asphalt onto an unpaved strip that I knew led to one of our maintenance outbuildings. I pulled far enough in so that no cars passing by would even notice we were there.

I shut off the engine, feeling excitement take hold of me. Enjoying every delightful moment.

I cracked the window, allowing cool air to drift in. Mark followed my lead. Although it was still warm outside, the humidity had all but dissipated and a breeze had even kicked up, brushing us with sweet softness. Frogs chirped in the distance, leaves shushed overhead.

As though prearranged, we both unbuckled our seat belts and turned to face one another. I wondered if he could hear my heart beating.

Mark's mouth curled into a smile. "Right about now I wish I were staying at a different hotel."

He must have read my mind.

"But all those people . . . people you work with . . ."

"Scandalous."

He moved a little closer, his gaze never leaving mine. "I can't bear the thought of watching you drive away tonight without us having the chance to say good night properly."

He was very close now. I could feel the man's warmth, smell his aftershave—a scent that touched something deep and needy within me. Behind him, all was dark. We were surrounded by nothingness, alone, whispering as though afraid to shatter the mood.

"You have a reputation to uphold with your subordinates," he said softly. "I understand that."

Shivers ran up and down my spine. Heady with anticipation, I could do little more than nod.

"The thing is," he said, gesturing toward his left arm, "I have this to contend with. And we're like two teenagers in our parents' car. Not exactly ideal. Not what I would want for a woman as special as you are." Staring at me with an exhilarating intensity, he reached to brush a few strands of hair away from my eyes. "You are breathtaking, Grace."

I could barely speak. "Thank you."

"More than that, you have a kind spirit. Such compassion."

I didn't know what to say.

He ran a finger along my cheek, smiling. "I wish I had a month here," he said. "Longer."

His hand had moved along the side of my face in a slow caress. I reached up to lace my fingers with his. "Me too."

"Do you think . . ."

"What?"

"No, I'm being silly. We've only begun to get to know one another." He looked away and then back to me again, smiling, but much more hesitantly this time.

"What's silly?"

"I don't know that I'll be content to return to life as it was when I get home. Not after meeting you." The intensity was back as he stared at me and tightened his jaw. "Not after all that's happened here. I've learned the hard way that life is too short. I don't want any more of it to slip through my fingers."

"What are you saying?"

"I know long-distance relationships aren't ideal. I know there are pitfalls. But would you be willing to give it a try? At least until I return home and decide what to do about the store. I told you that my heart isn't in it anymore. I need to decide what comes next for me. What to do about my future."

I hadn't expected this. "I don't know . . ."

"Don't promise anything. Just consider it. In a week you may question why you ever bothered going out with me this once."

I doubted that.

He must have read my mind again because he placed a warm finger across my lips. "Don't give me an answer.

Let's wait. I need you to want this as much as I do. And I have a sense you're not there yet. It's okay," he added hastily when I tried to speak. He took his hand back. "Fair enough?"

I nodded.

He smiled then, and sat back. "Do you know how much I want to take you in my arms right now?"

I couldn't help myself. I whispered, "What's stopping you?"

He took a deep, shuddering breath and let it out slowly. The sparkle in his eyes had changed into something fierce, a longing look that sent tingles all over my body. "I'm a healthy, mostly able-bodied man attracted to a gorgeous, amazing woman, who—incredibly—seems to be interested in me." His voice rumbled. "I want you more than you can imagine."

His gentle fingers skimmed my face again. "But by acting on my base instincts I risk too much, Grace." Hearing him say my name sent another flush of pleasure racing through my chest, "I want more than a few enjoyable evenings with you. There can be much more between us. If we do this right."

He leaned forward and whispered, his breath tickling my ear. "Before we take that next step, I need you to know you can trust me."

Every nerve ending in my body zinged with tension, begging for release. But when he eased back and I saw the disquiet in his eyes, I knew he was right.

I ran a trembling thumb along his right eyebrow. He closed his eyes, grasped my hand, and brought my palm to his lips. He opened his eyes again and smiled. "So," he said breaking the wonderful spell, allowing me to breathe freely again, "are you busy tomorrow night?"

Unfortunately, I was. "I promised my roommates I'd help out—"

Mark placed a finger across my lips. "It's okay. You have

a life and commitments," he said. "You don't need to explain anything."

"Hey . . ." A thought occurred to me as we released our connection. "Would you be willing to meet with Bennett tomorrow evening? It would have to be fairly early because he turns in by ten. What do you think?"

"A perfect solution for my lonely night," he said. "I look forward to it. Where should I go?"

"I'll check with him and get back to you." We held each other's gaze for a long moment, but there seemed little more to say. I twisted forward and prepared to start the car.

"Grace," he said, stopping me mid-motion.

I turned.

"Tonight has been the best evening I've had in a very long time."

I'D LEFT A NOTE FOR BRUCE AND SCOTT AND so I wasn't terribly surprised to find them waiting eagerly to hear all about my date with Mark.

Bruce was reading the newspaper in one of the wing chairs. Scott reclined on the sofa, glasses perched on his nose, mystery novel in hand. Bootsie had curled up on his chest. All three perked up the moment I walked in.

Bootsie stood up and stretched, then leapt off the sofa to rub up against my legs, meowing as though to chastise me for being away. "Hey sweetie," I said, picking her up. She gave a little grunt as I did so but didn't squirm away as I took a seat across from Bruce.

"So?" Scott said, sitting up. "How did it go with the mystery man?"

"You two should go to Bailey's," I began, purposely coy. "It's a lovely little restaurant adjacent to a bed-and-breakfast. It's a perfect location for out-of-town guests."

"Perfect for other out-of-the-way needs, too, I imagine." Bruce folded the newspaper and glanced up at the clock.

"But I'm betting you didn't check out its comforts, did you?"

"No, of course not," I said, pretending I hadn't been tempted in the least. "For goodness' sake, this was our first date."

Scott picked up on that "First? Does this mean there will be a second?"

I grinned. "Saturday."

"Not tomorrow night?" Bruce asked.

"I'm working with you two at the wine shop, remember?" Before they could absolve me of my duties, I added, "Besides, Mark is meeting with Bennett tomorrow night. Turns out we're both busy."

"You should Google him before you get serious," Scott said.

"Already done. Bootsie suggested it before I left. There wasn't much, but I found his LinkedIn account up there."

Hearing her name, Bootsie nuzzled my hand with gusto, reminding me that I was supposed to be rubbing her face. I complied, saying, "There's a good baby," in my talk-to-the-kitty voice.

"What about Jack?" Scott asked. "Understand I'm not rooting for the guy, I'm asking because I'm curious. You were really into him for a while there."

Still playing with Bootsie, I said, "He's made it clear he's not ready for a relationship." I looked up. "I'm beginning to doubt he'll ever be."

"He had his chance," Bruce said.

"Exactly."

Scott leaned back, ready to dive into his book again, but before he opened it, said, "You're glowing, you know."

I raised one hand to my cheek as I stood. "Am I?"

Bruce agreed. "I haven't seen you this happy in a very long time. I'd wish you sweet dreams, but there's no doubt you'll have them."

* * *

FRIDAY MORNING I CALLED BENNETT AND asked him about his availability. He was delighted to hear that Mark was willing to talk with him and suggested they meet at the mansion that evening after dinner. "My chauffeur, Grant, will pick him up and return him to the hotel when our business is complete."

"Business?" I asked.

"Gracie," Bennett said, "there's a real danger of him suing us, claiming our security was so lax that it nearly got him killed. Frankly, I'm expecting it. Before that happens, however, I want to meet him face to face. I like to know something about my adversaries before we get into court."

"I don't believe Mark has any intention of suing. He's not that kind of person."

"Oh?" Bennett's tone changed. "What makes you say that?"

I debated for just one instant. "He and I went out last night," I said haltingly. "On a date."

"Oh," Bennett said again, this time with a knowing cadence. "I see. That changes things. I have even more reason to meet with this young man tonight. What are his intentions?"

I laughed. "At the moment we've simply agreed to go out again Saturday night." Bennett was quiet for a moment. Long enough for me to ask, "Are you still there?"

"You told me he lives in Colorado, correct?"

"That's right."

"He has a business out there. His own business."

"You have a good memory."

"Will he want you to move out there?"

"Bennett," I exclaimed, "we've only gone out one time. There's no talk about moving or getting serious."

"You're in your thirties. Many young women are married, or at least engaged by now. I think once you find the right fellow you'll fast-track it to the altar."

"I have a life here."

He made a noise and I took it to mean that my answer had pleased him. "You're sure he's single?"

"He's a widower."

Bennett didn't respond to that except to say, "I look forward to meeting him."

"Be nice," I said.

"Not to worry. I'll be on my best behavior."

Chapter 17

FRANCES AND I WORKED QUIETLY IN OUR RE-
spective offices for the next several hours. I'd left a message
on Mark's cell phone about plans for tonight with Bennett.
I asked him to call me if there was any problem but I hoped
he'd call me either way.

So deep was I in the week's departmental reports I
barely paid attention to sounds coming from Frances's
area until two female voices, rising in intensity, brought
my attention back to the present in a hurry. Even as I stood,
I recognized both combatants: Frances arguing with Hillary.

Hillary had her back to me when I came around the
corner. White linen pants and matching jacket. One fist
jammed into an angrily thrust hip. "Why do I need an appointment to see one of *my* employees?"

Frances snorted. "Grace doesn't work for you, she works
for the Mister. And you'd better watch your step, or you
may find yourself working for *her* someday."

Uh-oh. I couldn't let Frances go down that road. "What

did you need, Hillary?" I asked, changing the trajectory of the conversation.

She whirled on me. "An appointment, apparently. Since when do I need one? And why is she"—Hillary pointed without looking at Frances—"acting as gatekeeper?"

Without waiting for me to reply she stormed right at me, expecting me to move out of the way to allow her passage through the door. I leaned against the jamb and folded my arms, effectively thwarting her progress. "I asked Frances to screen visitors." I hadn't, but it sounded good. Behind her, Frances smirked. "What do you need?"

Hillary gave an indignant head-waggle. Under the white sweater, she wore a boatneck silk shell of bright blue. It set off her blonde highlights so perfectly it was like she'd planned it. I was sure she had.

"I need to talk with you," she said, then added with dripping sarcasm, "obviously."

"In regards to what?"

Frustration worked over her features, but I had to give her credit for holding her tongue in check. "Can we talk in your office?" Over her shoulder, she added, "Privately?"

I relented. "Come on in." I watched her shoot an "I told you so" look at Frances, so I added, "But leave the door between our offices open."

"Are you kidding? All she'll do is eavesdrop."

My assistant's grin grew bigger when I said, "That will save me having to bring her up to date when you leave."

To my surprise Hillary didn't protest further. "Fine," she said walking past when I stepped out of her way. "This shouldn't take long."

Once we were settled, Hillary wasted no time. "Corbin says I have to get an okay from you if I want to be in the final cut." She waited.

"What about Bennett? What does he say?"

"He says it's up to you. I have no idea why."

"I have no idea why either."

"Speaking of my stepfather . . ." She leaned forward and spoke in a conspiratorial tone, "I have another reason for talking with you today."

I waited.

"If you and I were to work together, it could benefit us both."

"Work together how?"

"Maybe you and I can figure out a way to convince him into giving me a bigger stake here. You know I respect what you do here and I'd keep you in charge of the manor, no matter what."

She must have misinterpreted my look of shock because she continued as though I'd encouraged her. "It's lucky I've been here lately to keep an eye on him. I mean, I'm sure you've noticed," she gave a slow, weighty wink, "that Papa Bennett requires more supervision lately. He seems to be losing touch with reality."

Anger rushed up fast and hot, requiring every ounce of my resolve to keep me from leaping to my feet and throwing her out on her fancy little rear. I almost couldn't speak. "How dare you?" I slammed both palms onto my desk. "Don't you ever say such a thing."

Her eyes widened and her jaw dropped.

I wasn't finished. "Your stepfather is sharper and more on top of things than people half his age. Including you. Don't even go there. Do *not* attempt to undermine his authority. It's beneath you."

She worked hard to rearrange her face back into a semblance of calm. "Ooh," she said lightly with a forced smile. "That must have come out wrong. I didn't mean any disrespect to Papa Bennett."

Yeah, right, I thought.

"What I was trying to say was . . ." She bit her lower lip and inched forward in her chair, buying time. "I think Papa Bennett may be losing out on some excellent promotion."

My expression didn't change, so she talked faster. "He's

all for this DVD, right?" Without giving me a chance to interject, she went on, "I'm thinking that if he and I were to appear on camera together—family values and all—people may be more interested in watching it. That's better for business, isn't it?"

She was working hard to save face. When it came to his relationship with Hillary, I worried about Bennett—always. He longed for family, for people to care as deeply for him as he did for them. Hillary's relentless entreaties, her never-ending quest to get Bennett to change his will was maddening. Worse, it was hurtful to Bennett.

He deserved better. I thought about his desire to have our DNA tested. Maybe relenting would ultimately prove to be the best option. If we were blood relatives, Hillary would be obliged to back off, wouldn't she? I swallowed my anger and decided to push that decision aside for now.

"You're here because you want to be in the DVD? That's it?"

She clearly had more on her mind, but whatever had transpired between us kept her silent. I read that on her face in two heartbeats. "That's it."

"Fine. You're in." She started to get up but I remembered the last time we'd talked and stopped her. "You seemed to be in quite a hurry to leave when the detectives were here," I said. "What's up with that?"

"Those two make me nervous." She gave a high-pitched giggle even though nothing was funny.

I leaned forward and lowered my voice. "You don't have anything to hide, do you?" I asked. "You know you can tell me."

For a split second she looked tempted but then laughed again. "Don't be silly." Jumping to her feet, she said, "It's getting late. I have to run. Thanks for letting me be a part of the DVD appearance. You know I'm always willing to go the extra mile to help out Papa Bennett." By the time she got to the end of this little speech, she was at the doorway, beaming brightly, and wiggling her fingers at me. "See you later."

Moments later, I heard the outer door slam shut.

Frances came around immediately, holding aloft a pink "While You Were Out" slip. "Your friend Ronny Tooney called while her highness was whispering betrayals into your ear." The look of distaste on her face made me wonder which one of the two she despised more: Hillary or our would-be detective. "She's got a lot of nerve trying to make the Mister look bad. That girl is a bigger fool than I gave her credit for." Frances waved the pink slip again, signaling a change in topic. "Tooney says he might have a lead on the item you asked about."

"That's great."

"He's on his way," she said. "I told him to meet you in the rose garden. That way he stays outside and in plain sight." She held up a fleshy arm to check her watch. "He should be here soon."

"You think of everything, Frances."

"Uh-huh." She turned and strutted toward the door. "And don't you forget it."

I HADN'T HAD A CHANCE TO WANDER through the rose garden much this season, so I took the opportunity to stroll while I waited for Tooney to show. The enormous walled garden, nearly the size of a football field, featured hundreds of roses of all sizes, colors, and varieties. I had a preference for pink- and salmon-colored flowers and I made my way to the center where petite clump roses were trained to grow along trellises that formed a fragrant walkway.

I meandered at will. With four entrances to the garden, one at each corner, and low foliage throughout, it would be easy to spot Tooney the moment he arrived. A brick path struck off on a diagonal from the central sidewalk and I took it, breathing in the sweet, summery scent of new blooms.

A small conservatory anchored the garden's southern end. Our master gardener, Old Earl, often sat on a stool inside the humid, glass-roofed structure, potting new cuttings and waxing nostalgic for the days when he'd been in charge of the entire estate. I started for the conservatory to say hello, but when I cupped my hands over my eyes to peer through the dusty glass, I realized the place was empty.

I turned around and nearly jumped.

"Jack," I said, shocked to see him less than ten feet away from me. "Where did you come from?"

He pointed toward the conservatory's far side. "Around the corner." His khaki shorts were dirty at the hems, his blue T-shirt was stained with sweat, and it looked as though he had forgotten to shave this morning. "Were you looking for me?" he asked.

"No." I snapped at his assumption, then amended, "Sorry. You startled me. I was looking for Old Earl."

"What do you need him for?"

I waved away the question. "I didn't. I'm out here to meet someone and I thought I'd duck in and say hello while I waited."

"Meeting someone? The guy you were with the other day?"

"No," I said, but not so sharply this time.

Jack shifted his weight. "How are you doing?"

"I'm okay. You?"

He watched me. "Been better."

Awkwardness rushed up to engulf us once again.

"The guy from the other day," Jack said, "he's the one who got shot, isn't he?"

"That's right."

Jack's face creased into a smile bigger than I'd ever seen on him before. "I'm sorry to hear that. It dawned on me later who he was. At first I thought . . ." He didn't finish the sentence. "I guess that doesn't matter right now. You were probably helping him move to the Marshfield Hotel when I ran into you. Is that it?"

"You got me."

He heaved a deep sigh. "Davey mentioned the other day that you and Bennett were taking care of the victim. Makes sense." I'd never seen Jack like this: rambling, nervous, shifting from foot to foot. "How is he? The victim, I mean. I forgot his name."

"Mark."

"Yeah, that's right. Mark. I take it he's doing well? Has he been able to help the cops find the killer?"

"Not yet," I said. All the while Jack had been talking I'd been waging a war in my head. Should I tell him that Mark and I had gone out together and were planning to do so again? I tried to come up with a decent segue, but Jack was still talking.

"Things are getting better," he said. "In case you were wondering."

I remembered what Frances had told me about Becke being back in town. "Yes, I've heard."

He brightened. "You have?"

"Word gets around."

It was either my tone or my expression, but Jack started to get the message. Yet he persisted with the cheerful commentary. "What you did for me and my family has made a difference. Now that people realize I'm not a killer, business has really picked up. I've got a handful of clients already and more waiting in the wings."

"That's great."

"I have you to thank for it."

Irritation strangled me. He'd had weeks to start this conversation, but he'd waited until *after* he'd seen me in the company of another man to start talking again?

He took my silence as encouragement to continue. "All

these new clients make me believe the folks in Embers-towne are trying to make up for lost time."

"What about you? Are you making up for lost time?"

I could tell I'd confused him. He took a step closer. "If you're talking about us," he began, "I'd like to apologize—"

"I'm talking about Becke." Even as the words rushed out I couldn't believe I was actually saying them. It wasn't that I enjoyed making him uncomfortable. Rather, I wanted to get this topic out in the open so we could deal with it and move on. Maybe then I'd stop second-guessing my feelings for Mark.

His expression swung from disbelief, to indignation, and finally to repentance. "What have you heard?"

More in control of my emotions than I'd ever been around Jack in the past, I didn't see reason to provide answers. "Enough."

Staring at the ground, he rubbed a hand across his forehead as he sought to explain. "I don't know what you think—"

"It doesn't matter."

His head snapped up. "Of course it does. You're hurt."

"I'm not," I assured him. That was a lie, but it felt good to say. "I'm simply moving on. We tried. It didn't work."

"*You* tried." His tone was melancholy. "It's my fault. I kept pushing you away. I've isolated myself for so long that I don't know how to share. Especially with you, after all that happened. But I really am trying to relearn how to be there for another person."

"You seem to be doing very well with Becke." As the snippy comment fell out, I thought: *So much for pretending not to be hurt.*

"Becke." He said her name with more helplessness than affection. He ran his hands up the sides of his face. "Would you at least give me a chance to explain?"

"You don't owe me any explanation."

"Are you seeing someone?" he asked.

I was spared answering because at that moment my phone rang. I pulled up the handset to check caller ID. Mark. Pleasure flooded my entire body and I smiled. "I should take this," I said.

"You *are* seeing someone." He nodded toward the little phone. "And you're happy, aren't you?"

"I have to go."

I spied Tooney entering the walled garden from the far entrance. He was on his cell phone as well. As I started toward him and hit the button that connected me to Mark, Jack grabbed my arm. "You're not seeing Tooney, are you? Romantically, I mean."

I burst out laughing. "No," I said, feeling ridiculously good all of a sudden. Jack stepped back, looking embarrassed he'd asked. "Thanks," I said. "I needed that." Into the phone, I said, "Hey, how are you doing?"

I was so glad Mark had called. Even though he was fully apprised of the plans for the evening, it was great to hear his voice. "I'm kind of feeling as though I'm meeting your parents," he said with a chuckle. "I've got butterflies in my stomach."

"Bennett can be imposing at first, but he's a wonderful man. You're going to love him." Truth was, I hoped that would be the case. Bennett's recent grilling about the possibility of Mark taking me away from Marshfield made me ever so slightly apprehensive. "Just do me one favor."

"Anything."

I loved the sound of that. "Don't . . ." I began, then hesitated.

"Come on. You can tell me."

"Bennett will probably not even mention it, but he may try to quiz you about the relationship you and I . . . have. Er . . . might have," I was suddenly flustered, ". . . are thinking of having. You know what I mean."

"I do. And I should try to keep him in the dark?"

"I think that would be best."

"Got it. Have fun tonight with whatever you have planned."

"I will. Let me know how it goes with Bennett."

"You know I will."

Tooney had seated himself on one of the stone benches that were interspersed along the paths. He patted the spot next to him when I approached. I sat.

"What have you got for me?" I asked when he hung up.

He scratched his nose then lifted his chin toward Jack, who was still in the garden, checking on rosebushes. "After all you and Embers have been through, how come you're not dating him?"

I was about to chastise Tooney for being nosy, but stopped myself. Even though it was none of his business, I found myself admitting, "I'm seeing someone else."

Tooney sat back. "No way."

"What? Don't tell me I've surprised you? I thought you kept up to date on everyone's comings and goings."

He seemed more taken aback than I would have expected. "Who's the lucky guy?"

"Mark Ellroy."

"The shooting victim?"

I nodded.

"Well, I'll be. Gotta confess, I didn't see that one coming."

He looked so nonplussed I had to laugh. "It's about time I managed to keep at least some of my personal life personal, don't you think?"

"I'm falling down on the job."

"Not if you have an update on the jacket for me."

"It's not much."

My heart sank. I didn't know what I'd been hoping Tooney might turn up, but the hangdog look on the private eye's face spoke volumes. "Give me what you've got."

"I found the jacket."

"That's huge," I said. "How on earth did you find it? Where is it? Better yet, where *was* it?"

He waited for me to settle down. "I turned it in to Rodriguez. The detective isn't sure they'll be able to get much from it forensically speaking, but they'll give it their best shot."

"Tooney, that's fabulous. What do you mean this isn't much? It's incredible. You've done what Rodriguez and Flynn weren't able to do. How did you find it?"

He held up a finger. "What would you do if you were the killer?"

I shrugged.

"You'd get away from here as fast as you could, right?"

"Right."

"But I got to thinking about the guy you saw at the Oak Tree Hotel. The one who acted kind of suspicious."

"Go on."

"For argument's sake, let's say he is the killer."

I nodded, wishing he'd talk faster. "Spill it."

He shook the finger, silencing me. "Why is the guy still here?"

"I don't know. Why?"

"That," he said, "is the million-dollar question. He's staying for a reason—a good enough reason that he risks being caught."

I thought about it for a moment then told him about my contact at the Kane Estate. "According to her, the mansion suffered a few smaller thefts before the major heist—a heist that appeared to have been planned from the start. Do you think the killer is remaining here because his job isn't finished yet?"

"Was anything stolen the day Lenore was killed?"

I told him about the missing golden horn. "It's very valuable, but I wouldn't consider its theft a major heist by any stretch."

"That's what I suspected. He wants more."

"Are you going to tell me where you found the blazer or not?"

"Indulge me another minute. You're still the killer."

Biting back my impatience, I nodded.

"Word gets out fast about Lenore's murder and pretty soon everybody in Emberstowne knows that you were wearing a bootleg Marshfield blazer. You've got to get rid of it in a hurry."

I waited.

"If you're staying at the Oak Tree, you can't very well toss it into the trash can for the maids to clear, can you? You can't risk being seen stuffing it into a Dumpster, and you sure as heck can't wear it anywhere. It's got to go away where no one will find it for a long time. You've got to stash it where no one will think to look. And maybe even more important, where there are no security cameras to record your actions."

"You're making me crazy," I said.

"Working under the assumption that the guy you saw was the killer, I cased the joint."

My eyebrows arched.

Tooney's cheeks went pink. "I've always wanted to say that."

"Get on with it."

"I walked around the Oak Tree lobby, the outside, and the pool area trying to think of what I would do if I had to dump a sizeable piece of clothing fast. And just as I was standing outside the front doors it hit me."

I tried picturing it. When I'd exited the hotel with Mark, Jack had come across the street from his landscape project.

"The church?" I asked.

Tooney nodded encouragingly. "What's there? What's outside the church?"

"A parking lot," I said, picturing it again. At the far end of the parking lot was one of those giant metal boxes where kindhearted people donated their used clothing. "Tooney," I exclaimed. "You're a genius!"

He blushed. "Nah. It took me four times of standing out

front to figure it out. Only took you a couple seconds. I had to ask the church permission to dig through, of course. With the way I dress and my reputation around town, if they saw me they'd probably think I was scrounging for free stuff."

"So, it was in there?" I asked, eager for him to continue.

"The guy was clever. He'd stuffed it into a plastic garbage bag and tied it shut so it looked like every other bag in there. He even added other clothes to plump the bag up. I wound up having to dig through two dozen bags before I found it."

"Good work. And Rodriguez has it now?"

"Yeah, but they don't think there's anything they're going to get from the blazer."

"What about hair samples, or DNA, or maybe even fingerprints?"

"Lifting fingerprints from fabric is tough. I heard about a new technology in Scotland that's making news—I keep on top of all that, you know—but I don't see them getting any good prints from this stuff. As far as hair and DNA, sure, that's great—but only if you have samples to compare them to. If the Kane Estate people share their samples we might get a match, but that's a long shot. There's no centralized database of DNA or hair for everybody on the planet."

I knew that, but I also knew that some offenders' samples were kept on file. Of course, if the Kane Estate people couldn't find the culprit with the help of federal authorities, what chance did we have with our inadequate police department?

Picking up the thread, Tooney continued, "For instance, *you* could probably get away with murder if you wanted. I bet you haven't ever done anything bad enough to get even your fingerprints on file."

I said, "I'll keep that in mind if I ever intend to plot anything." But I was thinking about that donation box. "Can't the police get a list of guests from the Oak Tree?"

"Oak Tree's being very cooperative. But no names on the list match any known suspects. He's probably using an alias anyway. That'll slow us down."

"Then we'll have to think of a different way." I stood up. Tooney followed. "What's next on your agenda?"

"Find out who sold the blazer. We have to also consider that the killer may have stolen it. Buying risks having a nosy old lady remember your face. Could have been that much easier to steal when her back was turned. Most of these little secondhand shops don't have security cameras, so we're out of luck there. I've asked a few of them to check their stock and report back any discrepancy. But you know how a lot of these mom-and-pop stores are. They're not great at the bookkeeping."

"Keep on top of it," I said, thanking him again. "Great work."

He tipped an imaginary hat. "My pleasure. I'll be in touch."

Chapter 18

FRANCES DIDN'T HAVE MUCH TO SAY WHEN I brought her up to date on Tooney's progress other than, "About time that nuisance of a man did something right."

I let it roll off. "The best part is that it proves that the man I saw in the Oak Tree lobby is the killer."

She froze. "Haven't you learned anything yet?"

"Don't you see?" I tried again. "The jacket being found so close to the hotel makes it extremely likely—"

She folded her arms. "He *saw* you. Or have you forgotten that?"

"Of course he saw me," I said, pooh-poohing the point she was about to make. "I'm sure he saw a hundred people that morning. I highly doubt I've registered as even a blip in his brain. Even if I did, he can't possibly know that I reported him to the police."

"That kind of logic is what got you into trouble before. Or don't you remember?"

"I'm not trying to apprehend him. All I'm doing is reporting what I see. There's nothing wrong with that."

She made a noise that sounded like *"Hmph,"* and turned her back. "Time for me to leave. You better watch your back over the weekend. No telling what kind of trouble you'll get into when I'm not around to keep tabs."

"Your concern is touching."

She threw a sarcastic glance over her shoulder and began rummaging in her cavernous purse.

"That reminds me," I said, remembering trouble we'd run into in the past, "if I need to reach you over the weekend . . ."

She stiffened.

Unsure now, I plunged on. "Do you have a number you prefer I use?"

She straightened then turned. "I check cell phone messages occasionally," she said crisply, "but I can't promise I'll call back. I may be out of town."

This wasn't the first time Frances had been cryptic about her weekend plans. The few times I'd tried to reach her on days off were exercises in futility. I wondered where she went almost every weekend. And why it was such a big secret. With too much on my mind, this would have to be a mystery for another day. The woman had a right to privacy—even though she didn't respect the privacy of anyone else.

I acknowledged her answer. "There really shouldn't be any need to call you. I wouldn't worry about it," I said.

Her shoulders relaxed almost imperceptibly. "I'll see you Monday," she said.

I headed into my office. "Have a good weekend, Frances."

"Pheh." As the outer door closed behind her I could have sworn she said, "Be careful."

I MADE IT TO AMETHYST CELLARS SHORTLY before six. Bruce and Scott had hired a few part-timers for busy nights such as these, but even with the extra help we would be swamped tonight. I was glad I hadn't backed out on my friends. Though the tasting room was spacious and inviting with recessed lighting and warm cherry wood décor, I could barely see any of their strategically placed trinkets because the place was packed cheek to jowl with groups of happy people celebrating their Friday night.

I ducked behind the main tasting bar and said hello. Bruce, who was pouring a tempranillo into four glasses while extolling the virtues of this particular red, didn't acknowledge he heard me. There was a small utility area behind the bar, where we all stashed our personal items. I tucked my purse into a corner, tied on a burgundy apron, and caught the attention of a middle-aged man and his wife who hadn't been helped yet.

"Welcome to Amethyst Cellars," I said, pulling out two tasting glasses. "Is this your first visit with us?"

TWO HOURS LATER THE CROWD HAD THINNED considerably. The pre-dinner wave was over and we would experience a less busy, though still steady, business until the after-dinner crowd flocked in an hour from now.

"You need a break?" Bruce whispered when the foursome I'd been serving had sipped their last and were preparing to leave.

"Let one of the other women go on break. They've been here longer than I have," I said, "but I will sneak five minutes to hit the ladies' room, if you don't mind."

"You worked all day at Marshfield and then came here. You probably haven't even eaten dinner."

He was right about that, but I didn't want him to worry. "I snuck a couple of chocolate-covered strawberries when no one was looking."

"That's not much. Get yourself something to eat. That's an order."

"I will."

I ducked into the utility area to grab my purse, deciding
to hit the ladies' room before I ventured out for a quick bite.
I passed two other foursomes and one couple on the way, but
my attention was drawn by a man standing alone, facing the
far wall of wine bottles. Handwritten index cards described
the wines on the wall. Not every wine was covered, but
there were at least forty 5 x 7 cards explaining the nose, the
flavor, and the finish of individual wines. It was a fun, eye-
catching wall, a real conversation starter, not to mention a
marvelous way to generate interest in wines that might otherwise go unnoticed.

People stood and studied that wall all the time, so that
wasn't what piqued my interest. What caught my eye was
the fact that this man wasn't studying the cards; he was
glancing sideways, as though to keep tabs on the tasting
bar. And he appeared to be alone, which was highly unusual for Amethyst Cellars on a Friday night.

He wore a blue baseball cap and a nylon jacket with its
collar pulled high up on his neck. Of average height and
slight build, I didn't know precisely what had made me halt
my trek out the door, but whatever it was also compelled me
to duck behind a tall display of bar accessories to continue
my surveillance. I couldn't get past the idea that I'd seen him
before and that the vibes I'd gotten from him were negative.

He craned his neck to better observe the bar area just as
a group meandered by, blocking his view and making him
stretch to see. I sucked in a breath when recognition hit.

It was the man from the Oak Tree Hotel.

Or was it? I couldn't be sure. If it was the guy, why was
he here?

Momentarily paralyzed with indecision, I fought
through the shock of seeing him and grabbed for my cell
phone, deciding to place a quick call to Rodriguez's cell. I
knew that by the time the detective got here, the man was
likely to be gone, but I had to try.

The man fidgeted constantly, always looking over his shoulder toward the bar where I had just been working.

Where I should have been working.

He must have followed me here. I should have been more alert. Frances was right again.

I had started to dial Rodriguez when common sense smacked me in the head. I couldn't very well stand in the middle of Amethyst Cellars and report seeing the man. The fact that I was peering around from behind a tchotchke display had already garnered me odd looks. And I'd be required to raise my voice to be heard over dozens of conversations. No, I had to find a quiet place to make this call.

Noise levels being what they were in tiled washrooms, I opted for sneaking outside. Scott, at the auxiliary tasting station to my left, had noticed my weird movements and mouthed a query I didn't quite understand. He was too far away to call out to, so I waved him down and decided to make for the door.

I stopped short as Frances's words of warning clanged in my brain again. If this man was the killer, I could be getting into serious trouble here. But only if he spotted me, right?

I slunk along the far wall doing my best to blend in. Belatedly, I realized my apron was a dead giveaway. I yanked it off and slid it up onto a nearby table.

Halfway to the door, I had a brilliant idea. So brilliant that it caused my already speeding heart to race faster, and my breath to come in quick gasps. Take his picture! My cell phone had a camera. All I needed was a good, clear shot.

Keeping behind a happy group of wine drinkers, I caught Bruce's attention. "Go help that man by the wine wall," I said, gesturing. "Make him turn around. I need to get his picture."

Understanding registered in my roommate's eyes as he excused himself from the couple he'd been helping and came out from behind the bar.

Bruce strode past two groups, crossed in front of the guy then grabbed a bottle from the wall with expert nonchalance, as though he'd trekked there for that sole purpose. I gave him credit. Much better than singling the guy out right away. The guy sidestepped away, momentarily distracted from his surveillance of the bar. Wine in hand, Bruce started back, then turned as though the thought had just occurred to him. "Is there anything I can help you with?"

The guy shook his hat-covered head.

Bruce donned his best wine connoisseur demeanor, hefted the red wine he held, and said, "If you want to sample anything at all, let me know." He pointed. "I'll be right over there."

The guy turned, following Bruce's direction. Whether it was an instinctive move or because it gave him an excuse to look at the bar full on didn't matter. Bruce had gotten him exactly where I needed him to be. I was out of the guy's line of sight—barely—but able to snap a quick shot of his profile as Bruce held his attention for those precious few seconds. "We've got a wonderful special on this malbec today. If you like reds, it's worth a look."

The guy shook his head and returned to staring at the wall.

Bruce didn't make eye contact with me until after he'd gotten back to the couple he'd been helping. "Here's the malbec I was talking about . . ."

My heart was still beating madly despite the fact that all I'd done was take a man's picture in the middle of a busy room. My hands shook as I tucked the phone into my pocket, and now I did head outside, happy to breathe the fresh air and find a quiet place halfway down an adjacent side street to make the call to Rodriguez.

With it being high season, tourists were milling everywhere on this gorgeous, warm evening. All thought of grabbing dinner was forgotten as I feverishly sent the photo to Detective Rodriguez's cell phone. Then I dialed.

"I got him," I said when the detective answered. Without waiting for a reply, I spoke quickly, bringing Rodriguez up to date on what had happened in the last ten minutes.

For the first time since I'd known him, Rodriguez was not slow to respond. "He may be on to you," he said. "Where are you now?"

"Outside the wine shop."

"Get back inside. Right now. Don't leave the premises for anything. Don't go near him, don't engage him. Don't try to stop him from leaving. I'll be there in five minutes."

He hung up.

I hurried back into the shop, easing the door open with caution just in case Mr. Killer happened to be on his way out. I had nothing to worry about, however. Five twenty-something women were chatting and laughing as they spilled out onto the street, and I was able to slide in unnoticed.

I stole a glance toward the wall where I'd left Mr. Killer, but another group of tourists was blocking my view. I skirted the mass of humanity around the bar and snagged my apron from its hiding place. As I tied it back on, I stole another surreptitious glance at the wall. Still no luck. Bruce caught my eye and held up both hands in an "I don't know," gesture.

Had the man left?

Concerned that the killer could have disappeared before Rodriguez got here, I started scanning the crowd in earnest. He was nowhere to be found.

One of Bruce and Scott's part-timers, Leslie, called me over from behind the auxiliary bar. "Are you looking for a man in a blue hat?" she asked.

My heart sunk to my feet. Had I been that obvious?

Too busy to notice my reaction, she dug into her pocket. "He was looking for you. I told him I didn't know where you were, so he left this note." She handed me a folded piece of paper. I recognized it instantly as one of ours. Amethyst Cellars provided logo-stamped notes and pens for customers to use to jot down their impressions of wines as they tasted them.

Fingerprints, I thought. Maybe they can't easily be lifted from fabric, but I knew they could from paper. I took it from her gingerly, using my fingers as pincers. Leslie gave me the weirdest look. "What are you doing?"

I didn't answer as I dropped the paper onto the bar and used a pen to unfold it.

"Was there something wrong with the guy?" she asked. "Does he have a medical condition?" Her voice grew ever more desperate. "He isn't contagious, is he?"

She was drawing the attention of the nearby wine tasters. "It's okay," I lied. "I need to see what this says."

"I think there was something wrong with him," she said. "Why else would a guy wear gloves in weather like this?"

"Gloves?"

"Yeah. That's why I wanted to know if he was contagious. He didn't do any tastings, did he?"

My shoulders slumped. "Gloves," I said again. I hadn't noticed him wearing them. Of course I hadn't. I'd been too intent on capturing his photo. Thank goodness that part had gone smoothly. I pushed the folded sheet open, still using the back of the pen. When the message was finally visible, I took a sharp breath.

You're dead. You just don't know it yet.

I WAITED FOR RODRIGUEZ INSIDE THE FRONT door of the shop, telling myself that there was no need for him to cause a ruckus inside Amethyst Cellars when the killer had already left the building. Truth was, I was shaking hard and wanted to scream. Staying indoors, swarmed by warm bodies, should have appealed to me, but all of a sudden I felt trapped. The spacious room had closed in around me, making me feel tight and constricted. I wanted fresh air, but had to settle for whatever wafted in when a new customer entered the shop.

Scott kept me company even though they were still very busy. He insisted I stand behind him in case the guy decided to take a shot at me.

"There are too many people outside," I said, looking at the note again. "He got his message across. He's long gone."

Scott stared out into the night, scanning faces of the evening's revelers as they meandered by. "I hope you're right."

Rodriguez arrived moments later. I showed him and his officers the note, which they quickly bagged as evidence.

"Gloves," Rodriguez said in much the same tone I had when I explained what had happened. "Where's the girl he spoke to?"

I pointed out Leslie then gave Scott a gentle push. "You need to get back in there. The officers here will watch over me. I'm fine."

Reluctantly, Scott returned to his post behind the auxiliary bar and helped the next group in line. The presence of the police at the front of the store was clearly making some folks uncomfortable, so Bruce announced an impromptu ten percent off sale for anyone currently in the store. That got their attention, and the two uniformed officers and I were, if not forgotten, at least diminished in importance.

One officer was stationed outside the doors, the other inside, next to me. "Can I make a phone call?" I asked him.

"Why not? You're not under arrest."

I pulled up my cell phone again, intent on dialing Mark, but stopped myself in the nick of time. He was probably still with Bennett and I wouldn't want to disturb them. I took a deep, impatient breath, and waited for Rodriguez to finish.

*   *   *

WE ALL AGREED MY SHIFT AT AMETHYST CEL-
lars was over. Rodriguez and company accompanied me
back to my home. Joy of joys—Flynn met us there. I was
spared any scathing remarks this time because after a quick
discussion, both detectives insisted on making a thorough
search of the house to ensure no one was lying in wait for
me. "You do have a reputation for getting into trouble, you
know," Rodriguez said solemnly.

I went to unlock the back door for them, but it swung
open at Rodriguez's touch. He eased his gun out of his hol-
ster and motioned Flynn and one of the other officers to
join him. "The door doesn't always lock all the way," I
whispered. "We've been meaning to get that fixed."

Flynn shot me a furious look as though I should have
anticipated being stalked by a murderous bald man. I pretended not to notice. "Don't let my cat get out, please."

I held my breath, worried for Bootsie while the cops
took what felt like an interminably long time to get clear-
ance. When the place was finally pronounced safe, I was
allowed back inside. The two detectives stood inside my
kitchen. All the lights were on in the house and I felt a
welcome sense of comfort as I scooped Bootsie into my
arms.

Rodriguez said, "Nice cat. What's her name?"

I told him as I nuzzled her face. "I'm glad she's okay."

Flynn surprised me by reaching over to scratch under
Bootsie's chin. She raised her little head in an effort to request even more attention. "You don't let her out?" he
asked.

"She hasn't been spayed yet," I said. "Too young. But
even once she is, I think I'd rather keep her indoors all the
time. It's a dangerous world out there."

Flynn's face, which had relaxed slightly as he petted the
cat, hardened again. "It would be smart if you remembered
that yourself."

Rodriguez and I discussed the night's events a little longer, with Flynn interspersing commentary every so often. The younger detective was far less quick to snap today, I noticed, and both seemed genuinely concerned about my well-being.

Flynn surprised me again by saying, "I'll keep an eye on your place tonight. You have any problems, you call for help immediately. You got that?"

"You're going to stay?" I repeated disbelievingly. "Are you sure that's necessary?"

"Like my partner said: You do have a reputation. But this time, at least, you did the right thing by calling us before you got into trouble. I'll circle around and keep an eye on the place for as long as I can." As he and Rodriguez left for the night, he tapped my back-door lock. "Get that fixed first thing in the morning."

I promised I would.

Chapter 19

I WOKE UP AT SEVEN WITH BOOTSIE STILL snuggled behind my knees. She stretched, then gave a giant yawn and started in on some serious mattress kneading while I dressed and brushed my teeth. It was too early to call Mark to ask about how his dinner with Bennett had gone. Truth be told, I was reluctant to tell him about what had happened last night. Especially over the phone.

Instead I went out to the driveway to pick up the morning newspaper, surprised to see a familiar car parked out front. I walked down to the sidewalk and leaned in through Flynn's open passenger-side window. "Were you here all night?"

He'd been hunched down in his seat, eyes closed, until I interrupted him. Blinking and sitting up, he rubbed his face. "A few hours last night and then a few more this morning," he said, his voice gravelly from lack of use.

"Thank you. I didn't expect you to do that."

"Something is wrong with this guy. The killer," he added as though I didn't understand who he'd meant. "He's brazen and cocky. I wouldn't put it past him to come right up to your door and try to kill you in cold blood."

Wasn't that a pleasant thought to start a Saturday with. "This is all because I might have seen him?"

"Seems like." Flynn faced me, one arm draped on his steering wheel. Wide awake now, he'd gone from zero to sixty in half that many seconds. "What I don't understand is why he hasn't attempted anything yet. He would have had ample opportunity yesterday when you left the wine shop. He could have even gotten you before you went in."

"Geez, Flynn, you sure know how to cheer a girl up."

He ignored that. "We're missing a part of the puzzle. That's my point."

He'd echoed Tooney's cogitations almost word for word. "How do we figure out what it is?"

He shook his head. "You got that lock fixed yet?"

"I called Larry this morning," I said, gesturing toward town where Larry Langdon the locksmith had a shop. His alliterative name and occupation made him very easy to remember. "He wasn't open yet, but I left a message."

Flynn scowled. "His answering service could rouse him. You should have said it was an emergency."

"I'll be home all morning. Shouldn't be a problem."

My assertion didn't help Flynn's mood, but then again, nothing much did. "I have to shove off," he said. "I don't think he's going to bug you. Not just because it's daylight, but because I think we're dealing with something bigger here. I wish I knew what it was. Either way, you keep us updated. You see anything, hear anything, you let us know, pronto."

"Got it," I said. "By the way, do you know if that photo I sent Detective Rodriguez has gotten any hits?"

"What, you think there's some Bat-computer out there where we can slide in a photo and the criminal's identity pops out?"

"I was just asking."

After he'd vented further about my lack of forensic expertise, he said, "Rodriguez is getting in touch with John Kitts,
the tour guide, to see if he recognizes the man, but even if he
does, so what? We're already pretty sure the guy is the killer.
If Kitts and the other victim, Ellroy, recognize him, that will
help when we make the case. What we need is to find out
who he is, and—more important—*where* he is right now."

I was about to ask him a question, but he anticipated and
answered before I could get one word out. "Yes, Miss Nosy.
We've gotten all we can from the Oak Tree Hotel. If he was
staying there, he's long gone."

"I'm sorry to hear that."

"We got a photo from your security staff, though."

"Of the killer?"

"The guy with the briefcase. Remember him?"

I did. He'd claimed to have been at Marshfield on business but Bennett hadn't invited him. "What did you find
out?"

"We talked again to the guard who'd stopped him and
he verified it was the same guy. We're sending that picture
to Kitts, too, but I don't think it will amount to anything."

"Why not?"

"Murderers don't walk around with gift-wrapped bottles
of wine."

"Come again?"

Flynn shifted. "That's one of the things he had in his
briefcase. The picture that security captured of him was
when he'd pulled his stuff out for the guard. One of the
items he was carrying was a fancy bottle of wine."

"Hillary," I said.

He looked confused.

"I don't think he's your killer, either. I have a feeling he
was at Marshfield to visit Hillary."

"The stepdaughter?"

I nodded. "It's just a hunch. Let me check with her and
get back to you."

"You and your hunches."

I patted the top of the passenger-side door with both hands. "Thank you very much, Detective. I really appreciate all you're doing."

With a nod of acknowledgment, he started the car and pulled away.

LARRY THE LOCKSMITH SHOWED UP AT MY front door about thirty minutes later. An affable man of about sixty, he told me he'd made my visit a priority this morning because of all the business Marshfield had provided over the years.

He and I made our way through the house, with him commenting about how pretty the inside was. He sounded surprised and I couldn't blame him. Although the boys and I, with Bennett's help, had grandiose plans for renovation, we hadn't had the chance to really get started yet. "My son has a big house like this in Georgia," he said. "Not exactly like yours, mind you, but roomy and good for the kids. I've got three grandkids, you know." He proceeded to pull out his wallet and show me pictures of the little ones. "Look like their dad. And everybody says he looks like me. But look at these cuties. I don't think there's any resemblance, do you?"

I oohed and ahhed and assured him that all three cherubs looked just like their grandpa. They did have his chubby cheeks and turned-up nose. Larry beamed.

I made sure to lock Bootsie in the basement so that she couldn't escape during the repair.

"So what have we got here?" Larry said when I showed him the back door.

"The lock doesn't always catch," I said. "We can jiggle to make sure, but sometimes . . ."

He'd tuned me out, already crouching to view the mechanism at eye level. He played with it at length, while Bootsie meowed pitifully from behind the basement door. "She wants out where all the action is, huh?" Larry asked.

So deep was the man's concentration, I hadn't realized he'd even noticed. "She's a real people cat."

He began to disassemble the lock onto the floor. "Give me a few minutes here."

I did. First things first, I called Mark. I wasn't disappointed when his phone went to voicemail. I was still considering how to broach the subject of last night's excitement. "Hey, Mark," I said at the tone. "I've got a few things going this morning, but I'd love to get together later, like we talked about. Let me know what's up."

I frowned as I hung up thinking that was an awkward message, but he would understand. After that, I wandered around the house, taking care of small tasks that I'd let pile up. I sorted through old magazines, cleared the dishes from the sink, and even traipsed upstairs to make my bed. When I returned, the lock was put back together.

"Fixed already?" I asked.

Larry had gotten to his feet and shut the door. "Not yet, but you can let the cat out." The kitten scampered into the kitchen and hugged the far wall, watching Larry with sharp suspicion. "This is one old mechanism," he said. "You can put a brand-new lock in, easy, but this door looks like an antique—a real beauty—and I don't think you want to mess with drilling new holes into it. Your decision, of course."

I tried to pick Bootsie up, but she wouldn't have anything to do with that. "I worry about her getting out if the lock doesn't catch."

He made coaxing noises, but Bootsie arched her back and hissed at him. Larry laughed. "Cats don't like me," he said, then sobered. "Does she try to get out?"

I thought about it. "Not really. She seems curious about the outdoors though. She loves to sit in the window and stare out the screen." I thought about it. "So, what are my options?"

"I can order replacement parts. They'll be expensive, but not much more than doing a full install. You've got a good lock, well made. Problem is you have a lot of wear and tear on it right now. If I were you, I'd try to maintain the door's integrity and repair the lock you've got instead of replacing it with one that's substandard."

I thought about how happy Flynn would be at this turn of events. "How long will it take to get the parts?"

He made a so-so motion with his head. "I've got a supplier I've worked with for years, mostly for Marshfield's locks. He's good at rush orders. If I need it fast, they do their best. I can probably have it within a couple of days."

"That's not bad."

"Business days, I mean," he said. "I'll get in touch with them first thing Monday morning. I bet I'll have it in hand by Wednesday at the latest."

I wasn't thrilled. "Is there anything we can do to keep the back secure until then?"

"Keep doing what you've been doing. Wiggle it a little until it takes. Once the lock's engaged, you're good."

I thanked him and told him to let me know the minute the new parts arrived.

I called Bennett to see if he had time to meet. He seemed less surprised than I'd expected to hear that I'd be coming in on a Saturday. He also sounded concerned. "I'll have Theo set lunch for two, is that all right?"

Bennett often invited me to dine with him. I supposed it got boring, having every meal to yourself with only a few butlers for company. Most people envied his wealth and longed for his lifestyle. Over time, I'd come to realize how lonely he really was. "I would love that."

"Excellent. I'll see you shortly."

"YOU LIKE THIS ROOM SO MUCH, I DECIDED we'd eat in here today," Bennett said when I met him in the

Sword Room. Theo had set up a linen-covered table for two right in front of the fireplace between the two tall columns of crisscrossed swords. "I have to tell you that neither of my wives cared overmuch for the décor in here, so I'm surprised to find that you do."

With the faint memory of cigar smoke, burled wood furnishings, and reminders of wars gone by, this was a room that didn't get much traffic. "I know this place is special to you," I said. "That's why I like it here."

He chuckled. "The best part is that Hillary thinks of it much the way her mother did—boring, old, and devoid of treasures." He glanced at the cherry wood chest across the room. "Little does she know."

"It bothers me that you keep an item of such great value out in the open like that," I said.

"The only people in this wing are employees I trust with my life. You. Frances." He said her name with a trace of amusement. "Lois and the rest of the administrative staff. Most everyone has been with me for decades. You're the new girl on the block." He sat back. "Should I start suspecting you'll break in here and steal the tiara? You do have access afterhours."

I laughed.

He tapped a finger to his lips and squinted at me. "It would look good on you." Sitting up again, he rang a bell to let the butler know we were ready to eat. "Let's let Theo feed us before he has a coronary about the food getting cold. I have a great deal to discuss with you, my dear, and it will all be better on a full stomach."

I had a lot to discuss with Bennett as well, but I decided to hold my tongue until after Theo had served lunch, poured coffee to enjoy along with our raspberry sorbet, and excused himself from the room.

Bennett took a final sip from his rose-covered coffee cup and returned it to its saucer with a delicate clink. "So, my girl, it seems you've been busy."

I didn't understand.

"Do you think word doesn't reach the old man? I heard all about the killer visiting your friends' store last night." His silver brows came together, deep vertical creases running between them. Bennett rarely raised his voice to me, but his concern this time was tinged with anger. "You could have been killed. Have we not had this conversation before?"

"I haven't gone looking for trouble, I swear," I said. "This time it seems to have come looking for me."

His expression softened ever so slightly. "That's what has me worried most of all. It's as though you're a magnet. Worse, you're always caught in the crosshairs while doing your best to protect me."

"The police are on top of this."

He made an impolite noise. "It's about time," he said, then asked, "You have another reason for wanting to see me today, don't you? You want to know what I thought of your young man."

I felt my face redden. "Well, of course I'd like to know about that, but the real reason I wanted to meet was because I promised I'd talk with you about the investigation. But it seems you're already completely up to speed."

Fingers knotted across his middle, he settled himself as though to talk, but I detected a shrewd glint in his eyes. "For the record, I don't believe he intends to sue. That's unusual these days. Everyone looks for an excuse to demand a windfall, and frankly, I'm surprised." I was digesting that when he asked, "Have you ever been to Colorado?"

"Except to change planes once, no."

"Your Mark Ellroy seems like a very earnest fellow. Handsome, successful, and—although he took pains not to admit it to me—smitten with you."

"I wouldn't say smitten . . ." I protested, though inwardly I cheered.

Bennett grew serious. "You know I will never stand in

the way of your happiness. Even if it comes at the expense of my own."

I leaned forward to touch his arm. "Bennett—"

He clasped a hand over mine. "All I ask is that you slow it down. You have plenty of time to make decisions that could affect the rest of your life."

"We've only gone out once."

"And look at how you blush when we talk about him," Bennett pointed out. "The few times we've discussed Jack, you've never had such a strong reaction."

"That's because Jack . . ." I stopped myself. I'd been about to say that my relationship with Jack had had a very slow start and had suffered delays, distractions, and detours.

"Because a relationship with Jack could be difficult and this new shiny attraction to Mark is easy?" he asked.

I didn't answer.

"Your young man and I met in this very room."

"Why here?"

"I don't care to invite strangers into my personal living space. I don't care for the assumptions people make, nor do I enjoy having my private rooms invaded." He waved the air. "Call it a phobia, call it whatever you will, but I prefer to visit with new acquaintances elsewhere."

"Why didn't you have him to your office?" I asked.

"Too cold. I wanted the man to let his guard down. I wanted to see who you were attracted to, and why."

"You liked him?" I asked, believing I was reading between the lines.

"I 'like' anyone who makes you happy. Mark Ellroy makes a good first impression. Let's see how he holds up over time."

Chapter 20

MARK HAD LEFT A MESSAGE ON MY CELL phone while I was meeting with Bennett. He told me that his arm was much better now. So much so that he'd jettisoned the sling and rented a car. He intended to pick me up tonight like a real gentleman ought to. He assured me he remembered where I lived, but promised to call in the event he got lost. Listening to his enthusiasm, I realized how much I was looking forward to tonight.

I thought about what Bennett had said about taking things slowly. I knew he worried that I'd follow Mark out West and that he'd never see me again. What Bennett didn't realize was that he was as important to me as I was to him. That I loved my life here. That Emberstowne was home. I'd considered telling Bennett about how Mark confessed he was considering a career change. That maybe he wanted out of Colorado. But to share that would have been to admit that I was in deeper than I'd let on.

It was nice to have a man courting me, I thought as I

prepared for our evening. I donned my favorite sleeveless dress and spent extra time with my makeup.

As I was getting ready, I couldn't help but think about the case. I felt certain that the photo I'd taken would help in identifying the killer. Flynn's Bat-computer comment notwithstanding, I'd called Rodriguez to find out if he'd heard anything from John the tour guide. The news hadn't been encouraging. Whether it was because he was viewing in an e-mail a photo taken with a phone, John couldn't say for sure if my bald and threatening visitor was the guy he'd seen that day at Marshfield.

Flynn's point that it didn't really matter until they determined his identity crowed in my brain, but I'd wanted to hear John say yes, certainly, absolutely that was the guy. I felt as though it would bring us that much closer to a solution to the problem.

I was in the middle of twisting a lock of blonde hair around my curling iron when a thought occurred to me. "Tooney!" I said aloud.

Bootsie had taken up a position outside the bathroom and had fallen asleep. Her eyes opened again, pupils huge. I turned to her. "Why didn't I think of this before?"

I ran over to my purse, grabbed my phone, and dialed Tooney's number. Briefly, I explained.

"Say this again," he said. "You're sending me a photo of the possible killer? How did you get it?"

I didn't have time to explain. "I happened to run into him yesterday," I said. "I'll tell you about it later."

"I don't like the sound of that."

"Everything is fine. I've sent the photo to Rodriguez and Flynn, but it dawned on me that if you had it, you could use it when you ask about the blazers at the secondhand stores. Maybe seeing the guy's face will jog their memory."

"Good thinking," he said.

"I wanted to get this to you so you could talk to them bright and early tomorrow."

He hesitated. "Most of the secondhand shops are closed on Sundays."

I made a noise of impatience.

"Don't worry," he said, "I'll hit them first thing Monday morning and I'll let you know what they say."

"Sounds good." It would have to do. "As soon as we hang up, I'll send the photo to you. Text me back when you get it."

"Yes, ma'am."

Two minutes later we were all set. Knowing I'd taken my amateur sleuthing about as far as I could for the day, I went back to curling my hair and thinking about the evening ahead.

Mark arrived right on time in a four-door Ford Taurus. I'd been ready for fifteen minutes and kept checking the front window, so when he pulled up in the driveway, I opened the front door to welcome him. "You look wonderful," I said as he got out of the car. The sling was gone, and if I hadn't known better, I never would have guessed this handsome guy with the bold stride and wide smile had ever suffered a gunshot wound.

"You look pretty wonderful yourself," he said as he took the front steps two at a time. When he reached the porch he pulled me into a hug. "It's so great to see you. I feel as though it's been a lot longer than one day." As he squeezed tight, he said, "God, it feels good to have the use of both arms again."

"It still hurts though, doesn't it?"

"Doesn't matter. This is worth it."

I held him close for a breathless moment, taking in his strength, his warmth, his smell. "I like your aftershave," I said when we broke apart.

"I'll buy a case of it."

I considered inviting him in to meet Bootsie, but decided that move might play better later this evening. "Let me get my purse." I rushed in, said good-bye to the cat, and then met him on the porch again.

"You have a lot of land here," he said on the way to the car. "It's nice that you and your neighbors aren't on top of one another. In my suburb outside Denver, the homes are much closer together." He patted his chest with both hands. "Here you can breathe."

"I'm lucky," I said. "I couldn't afford this house if I wanted to buy it today. These old beauties are very expensive. Even run-down ones."

He pointed to a house farther down the street where the FOR SALE sign had been covered with a bright red banner that read: SOLD. "Looks like someone was able to buy onto your block. Getting new neighbors?"

I thought about it. "That house has been vacant for a couple of months. The owner got transferred," I said, repeating what I'd heard. "I didn't really know them, so it'll be nice to meet whoever moves in."

"This neighborhood suits you," he said. "I can't explain why, but it does."

"I love it here," I said as he held the door open for me. "It would take a lot to get me to move away now that I've finally put down roots."

"I wanted to talk with you about that," he said with an odd look, "but it can wait until we're at dinner."

He shut the door and came around as I pondered his words. He'd broached the subject of a long-distance relationship last time we'd gone out. I'd had time to think and I couldn't see any reason why not to give this the best chance we could. I was looking forward to talking about that, too.

"Would you mind if we went to Bailey's again?" he asked. "I know I'll lose points for originality, but I liked the seclusion."

"The food was spectacular," I said. "It's fine with me."

We had a different waiter this time, but sat at the same table overlooking the pond. Like déjà vu. What was different this time was Mark. Where last time he'd been attentive and in high spirits, today he was thoughtful and much quieter.

"What's wrong?" I asked after the waiter poured our wine and left with our dinner orders. "Something is bothering you."

He swirled his glass, watching the ruby liquid as though mesmerized. "Bennett," he said. "Have you talked with him since he and I met?"

"A little," I said, reluctant to share Bennett's confidence. "He said it went very well. Why do you look like you're in pain?"

He laughed and put his glass down. "Just the opposite," he said. "Bennett was gracious, interesting, and the evening was enjoyable."

"Then why the pensive look?"

"He worries about you."

I smiled and sipped my wine, thinking that Mark would continue. When he didn't, I said, "He worries about all of us."

Mark leaned forward, his eyes intense. He leaned his elbows on the table edge and held up a finger. "No, there's more there. He looks at you the way a father would a daughter."

"What's wrong with that?"

"Nothing, if you're never planning to leave Emberstowne."

My stomach knotted. "I don't have any immediate plans to leave."

"Not now," he said, "but what if . . ." He stopped himself. "I can't do this to you. I can't ask you to think that far into the future. Not when we're only on our second date."

I didn't want to go there, either. Not so soon. Not when such topics held the potential to ruin the evening. "Let's talk about something else," I said. "Other than discussing me, how did the rest of the evening go?"

Mark leaned back, stretching his hands out. "The room we were in: Wow. It's gorgeous. I mean, after having taken the tour I should have expected it, but all that history in one amazing room. The space felt more personal to him, somehow."

"Bennett loves to collect." I thought about telling him about the tiara, but decided against it. The cursed object and lost love seemed like a bad tangent to follow. "You were a few steps away from my office there."

"Really? So close? I'd love to see where you work every day."

"I'm not so sure that's a good idea. That means you'd have to meet Frances. She's a real hoot." I explained, giving him a few Frances highlights.

"I'd love to meet her."

Maybe it was the wine speaking, but I said, "You know, I believe you'd charm her socks off."

"Not sure I want to do that."

After dinner, and after we'd declined dessert and decided to relax with coffee, I broached a tougher subject. "I had a visitor last night," I said cryptically.

Obviously assuming I was about to share a humorous anecdote, he smiled. "Go on."

I told him about seeing the killer at Amethyst Cellars the night before. Mark's face took on an expression I'd never seen before—it was a combination of concern and panic. He sat forward, hands on the table, looking ready to leap into action. "You could have been hurt. Did he see you? Did you call the police? What happened?"

"Everything is fine," I assured him. I waited for him to settle down again before I resumed the story. I told him about taking the guy's picture.

Mark raised his hands to his head. "What were you thinking?"

"He didn't see me." Mark looked so upset I decided not to tell him about the warning note. No sense in making things worse. "I sent the picture to Rodriguez and he talked to John Kitts about it."

"And?"

"No luck," I said, dragging my phone out of my purse. "Do you want to take a look and see if he's familiar at all?"

"Of course I do," he said, reaching across the table. I sorted through the menu until I pulled up the shot I'd taken, then handed it to him.

He studied it, squinted, then held it at arm's length. "I don't know," he said at last. "It could be." With a hopeful look on his face he asked, "Do you think that maybe you were mistaken and that you took a photo of a complete stranger?"

I hesitated. There was no way to insist I was right without spilling the beans about the note. "I'm pretty sure this was the same guy I saw at the Oak Tree Hotel when I was waiting for you."

Mark looked at the photo again. "It could be the guy who shot me, but I can't say for sure." He handed my phone back. "Let's hope you just took a random photo of a fellow and you don't get into any trouble."

"Yeah," I said with resignation. An idea popped into my head and I sat up. "Hey . . ."

"Uh-oh."

"What?"

"For half a minute there you seemed to relax. Now all of a sudden, you're all riled up again."

I leaned forward, elbows on the table, excited by the thought that had occurred to me. "I've got a great idea."

He mimicked my movement, smiling. "And what is that?"

"I don't remember if I told you, but I have a friend who works at the Kane Estate in California."

He leaned back. "A male friend?"

I laughed. "*She* is a former teacher of mine, working out there in much the same position I have here. I guess the estate suffered a significant theft recently."

"You think that's tied to what's going on at Marshfield?"

"It may be; worth asking, at least. She doesn't have a cell phone, otherwise I'd text the photo to her now. I'll wait until Monday when I can call her at the office and then send an e-mail. Nothing may come of it, but I'd really like her to have a look at this guy. With all the people working on her case, it may trigger a memory." I silently berated myself for not thinking of doing so sooner, but, like me, Nadia didn't work weekends, so it probably didn't matter.

Mark smiled at me from across the table as I slipped my phone back into my purse. I'd been about to mention that Tooney would be taking the photo around as he checked with the secondhand stores, but all thoughts of continuing that thread of conversation ceased when I caught the look on Mark's face.

"What?" I asked.

"You're different than any woman I've ever met. Amazing. Fearless."

I laughed out loud at that. "Are you kidding? I was shaking in my shoes when I took this."

"I can't wait until the police catch this killer and close the case. Only then will I feel you're completely safe." He reached across the table and held my hand. "Because I want you around for a long, long time."

THE RIDE BACK TO MY HOUSE WAS CHARGED with delicious tension. I wasn't sure what kept Mark from conversing but I knew I was imagining how the evening might unfold. We drove through the busy part of Emberstowne, past a bustling Amethyst Cellars. "They look busy tonight," Mark said.

I glanced at the dashboard clock. "They'll be there another hour at least."

Mark glanced over at me. "That's not very long."

My stomach gave an excited flip-flop. I didn't really have an answer for that so I kept silent, and willed myself not to blush.

We took the turns that led us to my house. As though

he'd read my mind, he said, "I hate that I have to leave Wednesday."

"I've been trying not to think about that," I said. "It isn't working."

He shot me a wide smile. Deep dimples, dazzling teeth. I sighed with blissful pleasure as he pulled onto the driveway. "Is it okay if I park here?" he asked. "Or would it be better on the street?"

"The driveway, definitely." I wanted Bruce and Scott to know I had a visitor tonight. That could prevent any accidental embarrassing moments. "Why don't you pull up next to my car? My roommates will know to pull in behind me."

"You got it."

We took the few steps to the back door, my heart fluttering, pulse pounding. I knew my cheeks were bright pink, but I loved it all. This evening was developing into a dream and I didn't want it to end. "The locksmith said the new parts should be in any day," I said in an inane attempt to keep up conversation.

But tension was thick in this humid night. Before I could unlock the back door, Mark took my shoulders and turned me around. "Are you sure you want this, Grace?" he said, his eyes searching mine.

Something deep within me responded, and I melted against him, our lips meeting in a slow, gentle caress. His hands came up around my back, drawing me closer, tighter. We kissed slowly, longingly, until neither could take the breathtaking pressure another moment. "Let's go inside," I said hoarsely.

As was my habit, I snapped on the kitchen light as we entered, mostly to ensure that Bootsie didn't run out. But she wasn't in the kitchen.

"I don't think so," Mark said. He shut the door behind us and turned the lights off again. "I like it much better like this, don't you?"

He took me into his arms again, and for the first time in

a very long time I felt what it was to be needed, desired, cared for. Mark took his time kissing, trailing warm lips along my neck, running his hands down along the inside of my upturned arms to settle on my waist. He pulled away and we were both out of breath.

"Do you have any idea how long I've wanted to do that?" he asked.

I rested my head against his chest as I curled a finger around his neck. "Me too."

"Is there . . ." He broke away slightly. "Somewhere more comfortable?"

"My room is upstairs."

I took his hand and led him through the dining room into the parlor, planning to make a quick right toward the steps. The two tall windows flanking the fireplace sent eerie tree-branch shadows across the floor. Even though I could make out the furniture with all the lights off, I walked gingerly. "I don't want to trip over Bootsie," I said in a whisper.

He whispered back, "I'm hoping to meet your little rascal, you know." He waited a beat. "But not right this minute."

"No, not right this minute."

I turned around to smile . . . and screamed.

Chapter 21

"WHAT? WHAT?" MARK ASKED.

I grabbed his arm, pointing. "There, in the window. He's here."

Mark ran over to the window to the left of the fireplace. He cupped his hands around his eyes and stared out into the night. "I don't see anything."

"It was him," I said, words spilling out so fast my breath caught. "The guy from the hotel. From Amethyst Cellars. The one I took a picture of. He was staring in."

Mark turned, looking worried. "There are a lot of tree branches overhead. Do you think you may have seen a shadow?"

"I saw his face."

"Okay," he said, starting for the door. "Let me take a look."

"Don't go outside," I shouted. "I'm calling the police."

Mark took both my hands. "What kind of a man would I be if I didn't at least go out and check?"

I pulled my hands away, knowing seconds counted. I ran

for the house phone—the one I knew would give the 911 operators my address the moment the phone made contact—and begged him not to go outside. "He's the killer, Mark. Don't. Please don't." I pulled up the cordless handset and hoped to heaven the line hadn't been cut. A dial tone. Thank goodness.

I flicked on the lights and shouted for Bootsie.

The dispatcher's unemotional greeting helped calm me. "The Marshfield killer is outside my house," I said, doing my best to keep my voice steady. I gripped the phone with both hands and spoke as slowly as I could manage. "The killer is here. He's trying to get in."

Bootsie meandered upstairs from the basement and wound between my legs, arching as though to scratch an itch. I picked her up and held her tight.

Mark had opened the front door and stepped outside. Watching him disappear through the gaping maw into the night terrified me more than I could say. I wanted to run out there after him, yet at the same time I wanted to stay on the phone with the dispatcher until help arrived. "Tell Detective Rodriguez," I said, "and Detective Flynn."

Her monotone voice and unruffled demeanor continued to soothe me more than anything could, but all I could do was stare at the open front door and listen to my heart speed beat.

"We have a car in the area," she said. "They should be there very soon."

"Please hurry." I hung up.

I ran for the front door as Mark came back in. His mouth was set in a grim line. "Are you okay?" He looked as though he wanted to take me into his arms, but I held Bootsie for dear life and he gave a sad smile. "I'm glad she's safe."

"What did you see? The police are on their way."

He nodded. "I didn't see anything, or anyone. Whoever might have been out there is long gone."

Even though that meant the killer had eluded our grasp, I was glad. "Thank God you weren't hurt," I said. "He knows you can recognize him."

Mark wrapped an arm around me, careful to not squeeze Bootsie. "Are you sure you're all right?"

I broke away and tried to smile up at him. "I'm fine." I took a deep breath, willing my pulse to slow, my heart to stop racing. I scratched Bootsie's neck and behind her ears but I could tell she was getting antsy.

Sirens sounded in the distance, and moments later heavy treads landed on my front porch. "Police," they called.

Two uniformed officers introduced themselves, listened to what I had to say, and then questioned Mark about what he might have seen outside. "You should not have gone after the intruder," they told him.

He shrugged it off. "I had to."

The two officers made a circuit of the house, searching outside first and then returning indoors, as Rodriguez and Flynn pulled up. They were surprised to see Mark with me. I excused myself to put Bootsie in the basement again. "I'm sorry, honey," I said as I shut the door, "but I can't risk you running out." She gave me a disdainful look, a silent rebuke for taking her away from the excitement, but it couldn't be helped. Her safety was the most important consideration right now. Rodriguez came up beside me as I made sure the door closed all the way.

He lifted deep-set eyes to indicate Mark, who was talking with Flynn, across the room. "Are the two of you seeing each other socially?"

I admitted we were. "It's still pretty new."

"I imagine," he said dryly.

"He and I had just gotten back from dinner, but Mark didn't see the guy's face. I did," I said. "It was the same man from the hotel and from the wine shop. I recognized him right away."

"By your own account, you said your glance was fleeting."

Was he doubting me? "So?"

"Do you think it's possible that your fears are making you skittish? That you may have only thought you saw the man in the window?"

"Why don't you believe me?"

Rodriguez rubbed his chin. "Ms. Wheaton, with your history, we can't help but believe you. The thing is, Flynn and I were out front here minutes before you allegedly saw the man. We were watching your house."

"You were?"

He nodded. "Nothing amiss. Nobody walking by. Complete quiet. We must have taken off a minute before you got home. We'd decided to take a break and get some food when the call came in."

"How can that be?"

"He's either very good at avoiding detection or you didn't see anything after all." Before I could protest, he added, "No one is blaming you. If I were in your shoes I'd be scared out of my mind, too."

Bruce and Scott arrived home to chaos. "What's going on?" Scott asked. "Where's Bootsie?"

"She's fine," I said, tapping the basement door, "but I know she'd love it if you picked her up and gave her some attention. I'm sure she's confused right now. All these people."

Before they could rescue the kitten, Mark approached. Flynn had turned his attention to another matter, thereby freeing Mark to return to my side. He extended a hand to Bruce first, then Scott, introducing himself. "What a shame to meet under these circumstances," Bruce said.

As we explained everything that had happened, Scott grabbed Bootsie from the basement. "She's a little rambunctious tonight," I said. "She doesn't want to be carried around."

"No problem," he said and pulled out her harness and leash. We'd tried taking her outside on the leash, once. Ears flattened, she'd belly crawled along the driveway, as though looking for a place to hide. She wasn't terribly fond of being tethered, or of being controlled via the harness, so we'd never tried it again. But tonight I was glad we had the option.

Flynn pulled me into the adjacent dining room, where he and Rodriguez asked me a few more questions. "One thing doesn't ring true with your story," Flynn said, adopting that condescending tone he was so fond of. "There's no illumination in that part of your property." He gestured toward the windows in the next room, where Mark was retelling the sequence of events to Bruce and Scott. "I put one of our guys out there and I stood right where you said you were standing."

He walked into the parlor and turned sideways. "When I look out I see nothing. I even told my guy to cup his hands around his eyes and press up against the glass. At that point I could make out that he was there, but there was no way to recognize his face."

I waited for him to finish. "Were the lights on in this room?"

"Of course."

"They weren't when we were in here," I said, "maybe you should try your experiment again."

"Why were the lights off?" Flynn asked angrily. He must have answered his own question because he flushed bright red and stormed away, calling for assistance.

While Flynn re-created his little experiment, Mark, the boys, and I took up a position in the kitchen to wait. "Can I get anyone anything?"

Bruce made me sit. "We're the ones who should be waiting on you," he said.

Mark didn't want to sit. He paced. "I don't like this," he said. "I want to get out there and find this guy. Rip his head off."

Scott and Bruce exchanged a look that Mark didn't see, but which I read as approval.

"Listen, Mark, I think the police are finished talking with you. Why don't you head back? There's not much else either of us can do," I said.

He stopped pacing long enough to look at me. Rubbing both hands up his face and into his hair, he said, "You're probably right. Walk me to the car?"

The place was teeming with police inside and out so I didn't worry about the killer jumping into the fray to have another go at me. "Sure."

We made it to the driver's side of Mark's rental car. "I'm really sorry about all this."

"Not your fault," he said. He pulled me into a hug. "But I do want to ask you something. It's hard for me to put it into words . . ." I tried to pull back to see his face, but he kept me close to his chest. "Do you think we were rushing things?"

I didn't answer immediately. "Maybe."

"Don't get mad at me, Grace."

"For what?"

"What I'm about to say." He breathed in deeply, then said, "I think it's possible that you *thought* you saw the killer. I turned the minute you screamed and I didn't see anyone there."

I tried pulling back again, but he held tight.

"Just listen," he said. "Maybe, just maybe, you didn't want to take that next step and your subconscious invented a distraction."

This time I pulled away hard enough to make him let go. "Absolutely not."

His eyes were sad. "Okay, I believe you." But I could tell he didn't. He got into his car and rolled down the window. "I'll call you tomorrow."

Chapter 22

AFTER REPLAYING OUR LAST CONVERSATION
in my head all night, I wasn't quite ready to talk to Mark
Sunday morning, so I wandered around the house, ner-
vously checking the front and back doors and every single
window to ensure I wasn't being watched.

Scott and Bruce had already gone in to Amethyst Cellars, but only after they'd argued at length about one of
them staying home with me. I knew their income was tied
directly to how much business they brought in and that every minute at the store counted. As did every customer.
Both of them needed to be there, so I shooed them out with
the promise that I'd stay safe.

Bootsie followed me around from room to room until
even she grew bored of my impatience and promptly fell
asleep on the couch.

I decided enough was enough and pulled up the phone
book to look up Larry the locksmith's number again. He
wasn't thrilled with my Sunday-morning phone call.

"I'm so sorry," he said. "I've got my grandkid's first

birthday party this afternoon. Besides, I haven't even been able to order the parts yet. Nothing I can do until they arrive. Remember, as long as you make sure the door is secure, you're fine. It's when it doesn't catch that you might have a problem."

The logical part of my brain that didn't lend weight to the scary noises I heard every five minutes, reminded me that I had plenty of work to do. But Tooney's and Flynn's words haunted me. There was a missing piece to this puzzle. A big one.

Why did the killer appear to be targeting me? Why had he followed me to the wine shop, and why had he spied on me here at home? It didn't make sense. He had gotten into Marshfield, stolen a few items, and gotten away with it. Whether he'd intended to kill Lenore and Mark was beside the point. He was wanted for murder and attempted murder. There was no good reason for him to stay in town.

Unless his job wasn't finished.

The thought popped into my brain again. I paced, mulling it over. What could be left for him to do? And how on earth did I figure into it? I remembered Nadia telling me that there had been a series of smaller robberies before the big one. Our early robberies had triggered the decision to reschedule the DVD filming to hours when the mansion was closed. If, by making that change I'd thwarted the killer's plan for a bigger haul, he could be seeking vengeance. Still, getting away with murder ought to trump any aspirations for doing me harm. At least it would in my world. But then again, I didn't think like a criminal.

I stopped pacing, heart in my throat. Would Lenore still be alive if I hadn't changed the schedule? The thought that I may have played an unintentional role in her murder made it difficult for me to swallow. Even more, it made me determined to do whatever I could to bring the killer to justice.

Pacing again, I remembered the idea I'd come up with at dinner last night and decided not to wait until Monday to send Nadia the photo. Who knows, maybe she occasionally came into her offices at the Kane Estate on weekends, the way I did. No matter, I could at least get things moving on my end. I had to. Maybe then I'd feel as though I was doing something worthwhile.

"Duh," I said aloud as a new thought occurred to me. I'd texted the photo to Rodriguez and to Tooney, but I hadn't sent it to my home or work computers where it would be easy to pop it into an e-mail.

Bootsie was lying on her back in one of the parlor's wing chairs, her rear white paws braced up against one arm, her body curled outward toward the seat, one paw over her nose. She opened her eyes for a moment to see if I'd been talking to her. Assured I wasn't, she closed them again.

I raced over to my purse and pulled it up from its spot hanging over the back of one of our kitchen chairs. All I needed to do was send the photo to myself, either to my computer here at home or to the one at work. Then I'd be able to forward.

I opened the Velcro strap that kept my phone in place, so engrossed in thinking about this new possibility that I didn't look down until my fingers came up empty. The phone was gone. I straightened, remaining in place as I scanned the room, trying to remember when I'd used it last.

I looked under the table, on the countertop. I checked every horizontal surface in the room and in the dining room. Nothing.

I thought about having dialed 911 last night, but I'd done that from the house phone. The boys and I had made the decision to maintain a landline despite the added expense. This morning I'd called Larry the locksmith. Again from the house phone.

Why not use it again? I picked up the kitchen receiver and dialed my cell, walking into the parlor to listen for its ring. But the house was completely quiet.

Wait. I snapped my fingers. Yesterday I'd e-mailed the

photo to Tooney while I was getting ready to go out. I might not be able to hear it from here. I bolted up the stairs to look for it, getting halfway up before I remembered pulling it out at dinner to show the photo to Mark. I also distinctly remembered returning the device to my purse. But I'd done so without looking. Could I have dropped it instead?

I immediately looked up the phone number for Bailey's and called. Their recording informed me that they wouldn't open until three o'clock. "Great," I said aloud.

The only other possibility was that I might have lost it in Mark's car. It had to have fallen out at some point, and I closed my eyes trying to remember. When I'd gotten into the passenger seat on the way back from Bailey's I'd put my purse down by my feet. When I'd grabbed it again at home, it had been upside down. I'd righted it immediately, but had never thought to double check for my phone.

I growled my displeasure and started for the house phone to call Mark.

That's when I realized I didn't know his cell phone number. I'd programmed it into my own cell but had never made the effort to memorize it.

This was turning out to be one of *those* mornings, wasn't it?

"Fine," I said to no one.

I lugged the phone book up again, thinking about how Bruce, Scott, and I had debated even keeping the thing, but I'd won out. This time I turned to the residential pages; I was certain I'd find a landline for the listing I sought. Scanning down the page with my fingers I read . . . yes, there!

Tooney, Ronald, and his phone number.

He picked up after one ring, saying, "Grace?" with puzzlement in his voice. "Is anything wrong?"

I explained about my lost cell phone and the fact that I didn't have Mark's number memorized. He asked, "Why don't you call him at the Marshfield Hotel? He's still staying there, isn't he?"

I could have smacked myself in the head. "Good idea. In the meantime, do you remember that photo I sent you? The one I took at Amethyst Cellars?"

He didn't need me to explain. "What do you need me to do?"

Wanting to get off the phone in a hurry so I could reach Mark at the hotel, I decided not to tell Tooney the story of my visitor last night. "Could you send me the photo?" I rattled off my e-mail address even though I knew he already had it.

"Sure," he said and I heard clacking in the background. "Doing it right now."

"Thanks, Tooney. I owe ya."

"Done. Hey, don't forget I'll be going around to the secondhand stores first thing tomorrow," he said. "The minute I hear anything I'll let you know."

"I appreciate that."

After we hung up I opened Tooney's e-mail. I was about to send it to Nadia at Kane, when I had another idea. I could ask Corbin to take a look at the photo, too. With all the filming they'd been doing at the manor—including the day of the murder—one of his team may have caught the culprit on film. It was a long shot but worth pursuing.

Why hadn't I thought of that sooner? Yesterday's fright had left me more frazzled and scatterbrained than I'd realized. Unfortunately, I didn't have Corbin's number here at home. It was, again, on my cell phone.

I stood, clenching my fists for a long moment to try to regain control.

I dialed the Marshfield Hotel and asked for Mark's room. No answer, but our hotel offered a high-tech messaging system so I left a voicemail asking him to call me at home. "I may have lost my phone in your car last night. Would you mind taking a look? Here's my home phone number. I'll be here all . . ." I thought quickly and changed my mind. "I'll be here for a little while longer, then I'm heading into Marshfield for a bit. Here's my number there."

I hung up, blew my bangs out of my face, and decided to head out.

Flynn appeared on the driveway as I pulled my back door closed. "You get that lock fixed yet?"

"I'll spare you the boring details, but Larry the locksmith can't get to it for a few more days."

He rolled his eyes. "You'd think a town this size could afford more than one locksmith."

"He said it requires special parts."

Flynn made a noise of disgust. "An excuse to overcharge, I'm sure." He watched me secure the back door and walked me to my car. "Where are you going now?"

"Marshfield. I thought of a few more people I want to show that photo to."

"Stay out of trouble."

"Yes, sir."

WHEN I SAT BEHIND MY DESK AT MARSHFIELD I finally relaxed. I felt safe here, safer than I did at home. I doubted the killer would skulk around my house during daylight hours, but as a precaution, I'd set up a soft bed for Bootsie in the basement with her litter box, food, and water all handy. The house would be vacant until I got home tonight and I didn't want to take any chances.

Within moments of my arrival, I'd located Nadia's contact information, sent off a concise, clear e-mail explaining what had gone on, and asked her to take a look at the attached photo. I decided to do the same with Corbin. I checked my files, pulled up his phone number, and was delighted when he answered on the second ring.

"I hope I'm not bothering you, Corbin," I began.

"On the contrary, you're just the person I wanted to talk to."

"What about?"

"You first," he said.

I explained about the photo I'd taken and asked if he wouldn't mind having a look. "You never know. He may have shown up in some of the guest footage you shot before we changed schedules."

"Tell you what," he said. "I'll get my guys to take a look at that picture of yours on one condition."

Warily I asked, "Condition?"

"I've got a free afternoon and I still need to film you and Bennett." He hesitated. "And Hillary, if you two don't mind. The shutdown last week screwed up our schedule and time is so tight it's squeaking. If I can get you three together today I can cross at least one big task off my list."

"I don't really think I belong in the Marshfield video—"

"Not my decision. Not yours either, from what I gather. I'll get back to you. Stay put."

The phone rang seconds after I'd returned the receiver to its cradle. It couldn't be Corbin. A glance at the caller ID let me know it came from within the Marshfield property. "Grace Wheaton," I answered.

"Grace," Mark said. "I got your message. I am so sorry. I've been on the phone all morning."

"Everything okay?"

"No," he said, making my heart sink. "Problems back home. One of my employees called. I may have been the victim of identity theft."

This was too much of a coincidence. "You don't think it's tied to what's going on here, do you?"

"I don't know what to think. All I know is that I have to get this squared away. I can't reach my bank today because they're closed. I can't access my accounts online because I'm blocked. It's like someone changed all my passwords."

"Oh my gosh, Mark. I'm so sorry."

"I promise to check for your phone as soon as I can," he said.

"Do *not* make that a priority. Take care of yourself first, okay?"

"My head is swimming," he said. "I'll keep you updated."

When we hung up I felt worse than I had before. How could so much bad luck happen like this all at once?

I wasn't able to ponder long. The phone rang again. Corbin. "Bennett and Hillary can't make it until tomorrow. We're meeting at eleven. Can I count on you?"

"Yeah," I said. "Sure."

Chapter 23

CORBIN CALLED ME AGAIN LATER THAT EVE-
ning. I'd given him my home number just in case. "You're
still coming in tomorrow for filming?" he asked again.
"You promised."

"I didn't forget," I said.

"I know you aren't thrilled about it—"

My patience was at an all-time low. I hadn't heard from
Mark in hours, the boys were at the shop until ten tonight,
and Bootsie seemed to sense my unease because she
squirmed out of my arms whenever I picked her up, prefer-
ring to spend the day batting her pink felt mouse all over
the wood floor.

"You aren't calling me to confirm, are you?" I asked
Corbin.

"No, I'm not." His tone was much more gleeful than my
mood could tolerate. I wished he would get to the point. "I
was going to wait until morning to tell you but I thought
you might appreciate a heads-up tonight."

"What is it?"

"You know those two men from my crew? Donald Lee Runge and Harry Hinton?"

"Yes." My tone was clipped.

"I put Harry in charge of looking to see if that photo you gave me matched up with anyone we might have caught on tape."

He had my attention now. I sat up. "And?"

"I told you those guys were friends, right?"

"Did they recognize him?"

"That's the funny thing," Corbin said, driving me bonkers with the pace of this revelation. "Harry was running through the dailies, checking out the background people for you when Donald Lee came in and asked what he was doing."

I willed myself to remain silent.

"When Harry showed him the picture you sent, Donald Lee recognized the guy."

"He knows who he is?"

"No, no, sorry," Corbin said quickly. "He doesn't know the guy, but he remembered seeing him during the filming on one of the days we had access to the grounds during open hours."

"And?" The word came out high-pitched and impatient.

"Your guy looks just like Donald Lee's uncle Robert. Donald Lee noticed him walking around the gardens, staring up at the south wall during one of the days we were filming."

"Okay, so?"

"So then Harry knew which day's filming to check. And we found him. You were right: He's got a full head of hair, but it's the same man."

I nearly yelped, I was so excited. "Is there any way to send me a still shot of the guy?"

"In this digital age? You bet."

I asked him to send it to me both at my home and office e-mail addresses. "Thank you, Corbin, you're a doll."

"Remember that tomorrow," he said and hung up.

As soon as the file arrived, I dashed off another e-mail to Nadia at the Kane Estate with another request for her to see if she recognized the guy. I sent an update to Rodriguez, too. Then I crossed my fingers.

MONDAY MORNING DAWNED BRIGHT AND warm, but there was little sunshine in my heart, despite the phone call from Corbin the day before. I decided to wait to reach Mark until I was in my office at Marshfield.

"I'm not so worried about the credit card fraud," he said when we finally connected. "That's how they caught this originally. I'm worried about what's going on in my investment accounts. They aren't huge, but they're all I've got."

"Will you be heading home then?" I asked.

"As soon as I can get a flight out. That's tough to do without a valid credit card, but the card companies have been great. With any luck, I'll get out later this morning. This afternoon, at the latest."

"I'm so sorry."

"I meant to tell you, I found your phone," he said. "I was so worked up last night I couldn't sleep so I went outside for a walk. Took me about two miles of circling before I remembered. I've got it here. Do you need me to drop it off?"

"Don't worry about it right now," I said. "Worry about getting things fixed for yourself. We'll figure that out later. I'm surviving without it."

"Thanks for understanding," he said. "I'll make it up to you."

"Nothing to make up. Just keep me informed if you can, all right?"

"I promise."

"What was that all about?" Frances asked when I hung up.

Even though it was only ten-thirty in the morning, I was

spent. Call it weakness, call it a lapse in judgment given my assistant's propensity for gossip, but I brought her up to date on everything.

Frances took a seat across from me and let me talk. I'd bottled up all my frustration, and once I started, it poured and I found myself unable to stop. Even as I talked, I realized the anger and irritation I was experiencing was probably small in comparison to what Mark was dealing with right now.

"Your problem is that you're too empathetic," she said when I finished. "You make everyone else's problems your problems. And that's a problem."

I smiled, realizing she'd been attempting—lamely—to compliment me. "In some ways, it's good that Mark's getting away from here for a while. With the killer on the loose, you never know if he'll target Mark next."

I told her about sending the photo to the Kane Estate and about Corbin's guys finding a match in the footage they took. "I don't know what I expect to come from this, but it's better than doing nothing at all. And then . . ." I rolled my eyes. "Bennett insists I participate in the filming for the DVD." I glanced up at the clock across the room. "I'd better get down there. It's almost eleven."

HILLARY AND BENNETT WERE WAITING WITH Corbin inside Marshfield's giant front doors. "It's about time," Hillary said, making a show of checking her watch. She was decked out in pink today. Not pastel, but not hot pink either, it was a color that brightened her complexion and brought out her eyes.

She and I waited on the sidelines while Corbin worked with Bennett, who bristled at taking direction.

"You look great," I said to Hillary in a low voice.

"Thanks. I consulted a friend who's spent a *lot* of time on the big screen. Nothing like relying on expert advice.

She told me exactly what color to wear." I couldn't miss the up-and-down glance she tossed my way. "You're not supposed to wear white or off-white. I'm surprised you didn't know that," she said, not unkindly.

I shrugged. "With any luck, I won't even have to be on the tape at all and it won't matter."

Hillary grimaced. "Papa Bennett insists. I swear, I don't know what hold you have over him."

"Hillary," I said changing the subject, "remember that bottle of wine I brought to you?"

Her cheeks turned a deeper shade of pink. "What about it?"

"Who did you give it to?"

"That's none of your business."

Why was every conversation with this woman such an ordeal? "You're right, it's not. But the police are looking for him."

"Whatever for?"

"He was caught on tape leaving the mansion right after the murder."

"They think Frederick is the killer? Oh, for heaven's sake." She laughed more sincerely than I'd ever seen. "What was he doing on the tape that made them so suspicious?"

I explained why a person carrying a briefcase was cause for concern and I mentioned the bottle of wine he had with him—the clue that led me to her.

"He's not a killer," she said. "That should be good enough."

"So his claim that he was here on business is valid?"

"It is."

"What's his full name? I'll give it to the police so they can verify his story."

Her brows came together. "Is that really necessary?"

One of the crew shouted, "Quiet on the set."

Properly chastised, I whispered, "We'll talk later."

She shook her head in disbelief and we watched as Bennett, following Corbin's direction, took a step toward the camera and welcomed visitors to his home.

BENNETT SPENT A LOT OF TIME IN FRONT OF the camera. I could tell he was tiring—not so much physically as temperamentally. Although Corbin was patient to the breaking point with him, Bennett was uncomfortable following orders. He argued everything—word choices, where he was told to stand, how to manage his inflections. But even I could tell that once the edits were done, Bennett's role as patriarch here at Marshfield was solid, his scenes golden.

I knew Hillary concurred because she said, "Nice," very quietly after Bennett's final take. It had been decided that Hillary would talk about tourism and how to plan a visit to Marshfield. Her portion was filmed immediately inside the front doors, where, behind her, visitors checked in and received brochures, maps, and radio headsets. She delivered her lines flawlessly, as though she was born to perform. I was impressed.

My turn. As curator and manager of the estate, it fell to me to talk about the mansion's history and restoration projects we'd completed and those that were currently under way. Bennett and Hillary stuck around to watch. I wished they would leave. I felt incredibly uncomfortable.

"Just relax," Hillary said, once Corbin called "Cut" after the fourth time I'd blown my lines.

"I'm sorry," I said. "I'm not good at this."

Hillary strode forward, telling Corbin to wait for a moment. She brought her face close to mine, keeping me from asking what was up with a stern look of warning. She whispered softly so that no one nearby could hear, but there was an edge to her voice. "Why Papa Bennett wants you up here is a mystery to me. But this is important to him."

"I know."

"Then do this. Forget about being shy in front of the camera. Forget everything that makes you nervous. It's not about you. It's about him. What he wants."

Hillary lecturing me about loyalty to Bennett? Dumb-founded, I nodded.

"Okay," I said. Suddenly it was. Hillary was right. Once I started doing this for Bennett, I stopped worrying. I put all thoughts of Mark, the killer, and my concerns about how I might look on camera out of my head. I stole a glance over to where Bennett and Hillary stood. He gave me a nod of encouragement.

"Let's try this again," Corbin said.

I relaxed. Even more surprising, I enjoyed myself.

I DIDN'T GET BACK TO THE OFFICE UNTIL AF-ter three. "Did Mark call?" I asked Frances, not even both-ering to disguise my eagerness.

"He stopped by," she said, opening her side drawer, "to drop this off." She held up my phone.

I started to take it but she moved it out of my reach.

I wasn't in the mood for antics.

"Before I give it to you, I have some bad news."

"Go ahead."

"Your friend Mark is on his way to Colorado. He wanted to tell you in person and I offered to accompany him down-stairs so he could see you, but he was in a hurry to make his flight. He offered his apologies for taking off without a proper good-bye."

That was a blow.

Frances placed the phone on her desk in front of me and pushed it forward with the tips of her fingers. "You can't trust men. When are you going to learn that?"

I bit the insides of my lips hard not to make a snippy retort. "I'm sure he'll be in touch when he gets things straightened out at home," I said. Before she could reply, I turned and headed into my office.

I wasn't fast enough.

"I wouldn't hold my breath."

CELL PHONE IN HAND, I SHUT THE DOOR BE-tween our offices and dialed Mark immediately. His phone went directly to voicemail, meaning it was probably turned off. I hadn't asked Frances if she knew what time his flight was scheduled, and I wasn't about to go back in there and ask her now. For all I knew, he was in the sky this very moment. He would call me when he landed. I had no doubt.

I had a pile of paperwork in front of me, representing projects I'd let slide since Lenore's murder. I'd tried my darnedest to catch up, but there was always a greater influx of things to do than an outflow of missions accomplished.

Buried deep in necessary minutiae—the kinds of tasks that kept Marshfield running smoothly—I didn't realize there was a knock at my door until it sounded a second time.

I glanced up. "Come in."

Frances appeared in the doorway. "You have a visitor," she said. "Can I show him in or are you busy?"

My heart surged. Mark. I stood. "Show him in, by all means."

When Jack walked through the door, I felt my mood deflate. Frances shot me a look that I couldn't parse—sympathy or "I told you so," I wasn't sure—it was hard to tell from across the room. She said, "I'll be right here," and shut the door behind her.

"Hey, Grace," Jack said, taking a couple of steps forward. "You have a minute?"

I'd just said that I did, so it would be ridiculous to tell him I was busy now. "Sure," I said, gesturing to the chair across from me. "Make yourself comfortable."

He wandered to the windows and looked out. "It's better over here."

We stayed that way for more than a minute: me next to my desk, Jack at the window. I resisted the urge to stand next to him. As usual, he projected a vibe that discouraged closeness.

"Did you ever hear that old song?" he asked, not looking at me. Rather, his gaze wandered over the expansive grounds and garden as though he were seeing them for the first time.

"Which one?"

" 'Too Much, Too Little, Too Late'?"

"I've heard it."

He finally turned to face me. "I'm sorry, Grace. I haven't been fair to you. And I'm sorry it's taken me this long to realize it."

His face was tight with emotion. This was difficult for him.

Oddly enough, it was difficult for me to hear.

He'd taken two strides toward my desk when I broke eye contact. "It's okay. Let's just put everything behind us," I said.

Stopping short, he said, "You're shutting me out. Because I shut you out."

"I'm not," I lied.

"I hurt you."

"You didn't." Another lie.

"Now you want to hurt me."

I did.

I looked over at him again. "Why are we even talking about this? We're both adults. Let's agree to be friends and move on."

He worked his jaw. "I messed up. Badly. For that I apologize. I know you'll tell me it wasn't all my fault, and you'd be right. It wasn't all my fault." He focused on the ceiling. "I wish I could go back thirteen years and prevent it from happening but I can't." Looking at me again, he said, "I can't start over, but I can start anew."

I was confused. "Start what?"

"Putting my life together. I've let circumstances dictate my direction for too long." He got a wistful look on his face. "Far too long."

I didn't know what to say. What came out was a very lame, "I wish you the best of luck."

Still at least six feet from my desk, he raised his chin. "How is the relationship with Mark going?"

"Very well. And how is yours with Becke?"

He closed the distance all the way now, and perched his fingertips on my desk. "There is no relationship with Becke."

"I've heard differently."

"Then you've heard that we've gone out a couple of times. I've been polite. Much like you would be in the same situation. She wanted to get together, so we did. For old times' sake, she said. In the interest of honesty, I'll admit she's made it clear she would like to pursue a romantic relationship." He stared with a penetrating gaze. "But I don't. Becke abandoned me when I needed her most. That doesn't bode well for a long-term relationship, does it?"

"No," I admitted, "it doesn't."

"You, on the other hand, stuck with me, stuck with Davey, stuck with my family, throughout the entire ordeal."

"An ordeal I inadvertently set into motion."

"No, you didn't." He said it with such vehemence I leaned back. "It was a ticking bomb. All it needed was a spark to light the fuse. You had nothing to do with that."

If Jack's little speech had come a week earlier, I might not have even given Mark a second look. "Thank you for saying that," I said, sincerely. "It means a lot."

He rubbed his hands down the sides of his khaki shorts. "There's one more thing. I told you that business has picked up, right?" He waited for me to nod. "I'm now doing well enough on my own to be able to give up my work here at Marshfield."

"What? We depend on you." He couldn't do this, could he? "Why? Aren't we a major client? Won't that hurt you?"

"Marshfield *is* a major client. My biggest client, in fact, and yes, losing your business will make things difficult for a while. But for years I've known that the only reason Bennett kept me on was because he wanted to give me a hand when I was down. I will be grateful to him forever, but it's time I let him choose a landscaper who better serves the mansion's needs."

"No, no," I said. "It's not like you're a charity case. You've done amazing things here at Marshfield."

"And I've learned a lot while I was at it. Truth is, I'd like to go back to school. Finish that degree like I always planned. Take hold of my life in a way I never believed I could. I know you, of all people, must understand that."

I nodded.

"Consider this my two weeks' notice. I'll be happy to come up with a list of qualified landscape consultants you may want to consider."

"That would be nice," I said dumbly. Bennett was going to be horribly disappointed.

He turned to leave. Before he opened the door, he turned. "Giving up the Marshfield account will hurt. But it'll hurt a lot less than watching you in a relationship with someone else."

Chapter 24

WHEN THE DOOR CLOSED BEHIND HIM, I SAT and dropped my head into my hands. I'd worked hard to repress my feelings for Jack and I'd been successful enough to almost believe I was over him. This apology or confession or whatever it was set me off my axis and I needed to get my head together before it burst.

I reminded myself that work was the greatest panacea for heartbreak, so I pulled up last week's timesheets, vowing to bury myself in my to-do list and not come up for air until I heard from Mark again.

Instead I stared down at the numbers and names in front of me, unable to figure out what anything meant. "Thanks a lot, Jack," I said to myself.

As I did so, there was another knock at my door.

This time Frances didn't enter, Bennett did. Behind him, Jack's younger brother, Davey, followed, carrying a sheaf of papers.

I stood. Judging from the twin looks of sorrow on both

their faces, they'd heard the news. "Jack just left," I said. "He told me."

They exchanged a look of puzzlement. "Told you what?" Bennett asked.

I gestured for them both to sit, but neither did. What was up with that today?

"He told me that he's giving up Marshfield. His business is booming and he thinks we would be better off with another landscape architect."

Davey's head dropped back, as if in defeat. "I'd like to wring his neck."

Bennett's expression hadn't changed. "I'm sorry to hear that," he said without emotion. I would have expected more of a reaction. "But that's not why we're here."

I was at the breaking point, yet I could tell that I was in for another blow. "Just tell me. Whatever it is. I can handle it. I've handled enough already."

Bennett looked almost as grim as he had when Abe died. Davey shuffled in place, his gaze flicking between me, Bennett, and the papers in his hands, looking like he'd rather be anywhere but here.

"Have a seat, Grace," Bennett said. It worried me that he didn't call me Gracie.

"I'd rather stand."

Bennett held a hand out toward the younger man. "As you know, Davey has been helping me with my technical needs. I've come late to the information age, and he's been a willing and able mentor."

"I know." All I could think was that I'd done something terribly, horribly wrong.

Bennett lifted his chin. "I won't blame you if you're angry—"

"Bennett, please. Tell me."

Finally, his eyes softened. "I'm very sorry. Very sorry."

He turned to Davey, who had been shifting his papers from one hand to the other. "Go ahead."

Davey swallowed. "Mr. Marshfield asked me to run a background check on Mark Ellroy."

I looked to Bennett, who refused to meet my gaze. Suddenly light-headed, I sat. "This isn't good news, is it?"

Davey shuffled in place again. "Mark Ellroy told you the truth about a lot of things. He's a jeweler in Denver, and his parents died a few years ago, but he lied about one important fact."

I stared down at the blotter on my desk, knowing exactly what was coming next.

"His wife didn't die. She's . . . still alive."

The deep breath I tried to take came in with a shudder. I didn't look up. I swallowed past a lump of sandpaper several times before I managed to say, "Thank you for telling me."

"Gracie?" Bennett asked.

"I'd like to be alone now, if you don't mind."

Bennett hedged.

"Please," I said.

"Very well. I'm here if you need me."

He and Davey started to leave, but as they reached the door, I called, "Wait." They turned. "Have you shared this with anyone else? Anyone at all?"

They said they hadn't.

I looked at Davey. "Not even Jack?"

"Not even Jack," he said.

I blew out a pained breath. "Thank you for that. Please don't mention this to anyone. Not yet, at least."

The door closed behind them with a sad, final, click.

Mark, for all his declarations of truthfulness, was a liar after all.

My head hurt. My heart hurt. I felt stupid and used and ready to explode.

I wanted to vent, wanted to scream at Davey and Bennett for delivering the news. Even more for pitying me. I knew deep down that these two people were part of my life and—despite their unsolicited involvement—had done me a favor I couldn't yet appreciate. The logical part of my brain recognized that they'd saved me from bigger mistakes ahead. But the pain was unbearable.

I thought about Eric and now about Mark. What was wrong with me? What drew me consistently toward losers? I was angry, full of rage so profound it took up residence in every inch of my being. I didn't trust myself to talk to anyone right now, so I picked up the phone and waited for Frances to answer.

"Please hold all calls and all visits," I said, adding, "no matter who it is."

Frances didn't question me. She probably knew why I was asking, knew the whole sordid mess. "Sure thing."

I stared out the window.

Could this day get any worse?

FRANCES KNOCKED AT MY DOOR AN HOUR later. "I'm sorry to disturb you," she said.

I looked up at the clock surprised to see that it was already after five. I'd lost the entire afternoon feeling sorry for myself. "Shouldn't you be heading home?"

"Soon."

She watched me carefully as she crossed the room. "I took care of all your calls, like you asked. No visitors."

"Thank you." Politeness came automatically.

"I decided to intercept your e-mails," she said, fingers fidgeting in front of her waist. I often asked Frances to handle my e-mails for me. What about it was making her nervous this time?

"Something important?"

"I think you need to read one of them," she said, indicating my monitor with her eyes. "From your friend at the Kane Estate. Nadia. She thinks she has a match."

I wouldn't say I was elated—how could I be after such a day?—but the idea that Nadia might have recognized the killer from the photos I'd sent was truly the only good news I'd received recently. "Thank you," I said sincerely.

But Frances was shaking her head.

"What's wrong?" I asked as I accessed my inbox.

"She said they didn't know for certain that he was their thief. Not until you sent the photo."

I clicked the e-mail and it opened on my screen. "You mean I might have helped them?"

"The photo that matched ours was taken several days before their biggest loss. It's security footage of visitors entering the grounds."

"Still," I said, eagerly scanning the message. It read precisely as Frances was describing. "This will be a huge help to the investigators."

"She included copies of the photos from their security cameras."

"Even better," I said as I scrolled down the page, thinking about how quickly I could get Nadia's information into Rodriguez's hands. "That way I'll be able to see for myself that he's—"

There he was. The killer I'd photographed. The one I'd run into at the Oak Tree Hotel. In this photo he had a full head of hair, just like he did in Corbin's footage. There was no doubt this was the same man. No doubt at all.

Just as there was no doubt that the man next to him in every single shot was Mark Ellroy.

Chapter 25

I HAD NO AWARENESS. I HAD NO FEELINGS. MY world spun as sparkles danced in front of my eyes.

Frances's words drifted toward me but it took forever for them to register. "I'm sorry," she said. "But you needed to know."

"I think I may throw up," I said.

"No you won't." Frances took a seat. "You're stronger than that."

Even my ingrained politeness was no match for this. I couldn't speak. All I could do was stare at the screen. He'd manipulated me. Made me believe he cared about me. Lied. Worse, he'd stolen from Bennett and been involved in Lenore's murder.

"Why don't you go home?" she said. "Nothing much good can happen here tonight."

I didn't answer. I wasn't finished putting all this together in my overworked brain. Mark was working with the killer. What other explanation could there be? He'd had himself shot and gotten involved in the investigation. Why? He'd maneuvered me into a very vulnerable position. He'd worked hard to get me to care about him.

"To what end?" I asked, finally facing Frances. "Why?"

Her eyes were clouded. "I don't know."

"We must have been getting close. Otherwise why run now?" I stopped, remembering. "Of course." I said as I pulled up my recently returned phone. "I told him I was going to send the photo of the killer to the Kane Estate. He had to have known there was a risk of our discovering this." I flung a hand toward the screen. "That's why he's gone. I had the photo . . ." I sorted through my options, trying to pull up the shot I'd taken of the killer at Amethyst Cellars. After two tries, I looked up. "It's gone. He deleted it. He stole my phone and then returned it after he made sure to delete the picture."

"He didn't know you'd sent it?"

"No." I barked a laugh. "I told him I was going to do that today. But I wound up sending it yesterday instead."

I tossed the phone onto the desk, disgusted with him. Disgusted with myself. Was I that easy of a target?

"It's a good thing you did," she said. "It's a good thing you found out about him now. Before you got hurt."

Anger thundered in my chest. "I'm calling Rodriguez right now," I said, grabbing for the desk phone.

Frances shook her head. "Already done."

"When?"

Frances gave a helpless shrug. "Nadia's e-mail came in right after Davey and the Mister left. I didn't think you'd want to see it right then. You needed a little time."

So Frances knew all of it. For once, her nosiness didn't bother me. "Now what?" I asked.

"Rodriguez and Flynn said they would be in touch. And they have been."

As she talked, I wondered how it was I could remain upright when my soul had taken so many personal hits in such a short period of time. I listened, distancing myself from the emotion, telling myself I'd sort it out later, but that now I needed to focus on the crime, not my defeated-and-left-to-die ego.

"They found Mark Ellroy's rental car. He'd returned it at the airport. They assume he and the killer hopped a flight, but they don't know their destination."

A question began to form in my brain but Frances answered it before I could put the words together.

"They can't track where he went because he was using an alias. Mark Ellroy isn't his real name. He lifted that from a real jeweler in Colorado, a guy whose story fits what he told you—except for the dead wife."

At least Mark Ellroy—the real one—wasn't a philanderer. Oddly enough, I was happy to know it. There was hope for the world. "Does Bennett know?"

"He said for you to come upstairs if you need to talk."

"I think I need to handle this alone for a while." I shot another glance at the clock. "The boys will be out until at least ten tonight. If I leave now I can have the house to myself for a few hours."

Frances stood. "Will you be all right driving?"

"Yeah," I said, standing, "I'll be fine."

THE DRIVE TOOK LONGER THAN USUAL. AT least that's the way it felt to me. I couldn't wait to get home. Couldn't wait to climb into my T-shirt and sleep shorts, grab Bootsie, and drown my sorrows in a glass of red wine and mindless TV. It wouldn't fix anything, wouldn't even make me feel better, but it had the potential to quiet my turbulent emotions.

Nothing I'd ever been through before compared to today. I kept the radio off as I drove through the forested area, aware of little more than clanging criticism in my head. Was I forever destined to fall under the spell of despicable men? I thought about my sister, Liza, now married to my former fiancé. Was this some sort of genetic defect? Did I have any hope? My parents' marriage had been a good one—a great one, really—but I knew my maternal grandmother's had not. Her husband had been a bon vivant, a philandering boor. And when my grandmother had finally found love, it had been in the arms of Bennett's father. Add adultery to the list of my bloodline's sins.

Get a grip, I told myself. But could I?

I was surprised and disappointed to see the boys' car parked in the driveway. The shop didn't close for another several hours so their car being home did not bode well. Two possible scenarios: one of them had taken ill, or there had been an emergency at the store and they'd shut it down for the day.

Either way, I didn't feel like facing Scott and Bruce. They would know at a glance that something was horribly wrong and I dreaded having to revisit my hurt so soon. There hadn't been enough time to develop a sufficient scab and here I'd be, ripping it off to expose it again.

Maybe, I thought, I could sneak in, feign weariness, and disappear into my room. Whether they would buy it or not was immaterial. They'd give me privacy if I made it clear that's what I needed.

Plastering on as neutral a face as I could muster given the circumstances, I headed up the back steps. When I saw that the back door hadn't closed all the way, my anger resurfaced bright and hard. I was instantly furious at Bruce, at Scott, at the locksmith for taking forever to get this small project done. Did no one realize how important it was to keep Bootsie safe?

I swung open the door and stepped inside, ready to explode at whomever I happened to encounter first.

"Welcome home, Grace." Mark sat at my kitchen table, wearing a navy nylon jacket and a smug smile. He had a newspaper spread out before him and the coffee mug I'd bought on my last trip to Boston next to his hand. He would have looked like the picture of domesticity if it weren't for Bruce tied to the chair opposite him, his mouth duct-taped shut. "It's about time you finally showed up."

Before I could spin and run for help, I was shoved deeper into the room from behind. The man I'd photographed, the killer, Mark's cohort, had been waiting behind the door. Before I could exclaim or scream, he shoved the barrel of a gun into my cheek and said, *"Shh."*

He shut the door behind me and pushed me into one of the unoccupied kitchen chairs.

Next to me, Bruce's eyes were wild. "Are you okay?" I asked. Stupid question. Of course he wasn't. He tried to speak but his efforts were futile and sad.

All thoughts of personal misery were gone in a snap. "What did you do to him?" I shouted, reaching over to grab an edge of the silver tape.

"Don't touch him," Mark said, "or my good friend Lank will have to stop you. And that will make a very big mess."

Bruce made noises that sounded as though he were trying to tell me he was okay. But the sweat dripping down his face and the veins popping out from his arms, stretched tight and tied behind his back, told a different story.

"Where's Bootsie?" I asked, looking around in panic. "Where is she?"

I looked over to Bruce, who shrugged, then pointed to the open basement door with his eyes. I hoped to God she was upstairs. I started to rise, but Lank pushed me back down. He was wearing gloves. I glanced over. So was Mark. My heart sank.

"Why?" I asked Mark. "What can you possibly hope to gain? Why didn't you get away while you could? Nobody even suspected you."

He smiled and the dimples were back. Rather than thrill me the way they had, they made me want to reach across the table, haul off, and slap his face.

Lank stood behind my chair, humming as he ran the

cold metal of the gun alongside my neck. Bile rose up the back of my throat as hatred like I'd never known before filled my heart.

"Can't you guess what happens now?" Mark asked.

"How about we call the police and they cart you two sorry idiots away?"

Mark leaned forward. "Grace," he said softly, reaching a finger up to caress my cheek. I jerked back. "You used to like it when I said your name. You should have seen the way your face lit up every single time I said it." He smiled again. "Do you have any idea how easy you are to manipulate?"

"I'll have to remember to work on that." Assuming I survive this. "What do you want, anyway?"

"You're a little spitfire, aren't you?" Mark stood and crossed to the counter, where he poured himself more coffee. "Where was that spark when you and I were together?"

"We were never together."

Behind me, Lank gave a short laugh. "Only because you spotted me in the window that night." He clucked his tongue. "Mark's never going to forgive me for spoiling the fun we had planned for you."

Mark gave me a baleful stare. "You do have a way of screwing up plans."

Lank laughed again. The noise set my teeth on edge.

Bruce was breathing so hard through his nose I was afraid he'd hyperventilate. "Please," I said, "take off the tape on his mouth."

Mark gave a brief nod and Lank came around me, ripping the duct tape from Bruce's face with a sound that made me gag. Tiny beads of blood instantly appeared around Bruce's lips as his shocked skin paled and flushed in the span of two seconds. "You won't have to shave for a week," Mark said, then adopted a more serious tone as he addressed me. "*If* he ever shaves again. That, my darling, is up to you."

"Bruce," I said, choking up at my friend's pain. "What happened? Why are you home?"

He worked his mouth, and when he spoke, his voice was hoarse. "A text. From your phone. Said Bootsie had gotten out and to come home to help you find her."

I spun in my seat. "You used my phone to bring Bruce here?"

Mark took a sip of coffee. "Can you think of a better way?"

"What do you want?"

"You really don't know, do you?" Mark held the mug with both hands, elbows on the table. He smiled up at Lank, who was still behind me. "If you had any idea how much trouble you've caused us so far . . ." He shook his head. "But I digress."

"I'm sorry, Grace," Bruce said. "When I saw Mark I thought he was here to help look for Bootsie, too. It wasn't until—"

"Shut up," Lank said. Now that I was able to face him fully, I hated what I saw. His bald head was sickly pale compared to his suntanned face. He had small, cruel eyes, which stared back with what I could only characterize as triumph. He was enjoying himself and making no attempt to disguise it. The mark on his neck wasn't a tattoo after all—it was a thick, scabbed lesion that hadn't yet healed. I wondered if he'd gotten it during his escape from the Kane Estate.

"What I want from you, Grace," Mark said, as though there had been no interruption in the conversation, "is simple. Get me into and out of Marshfield Manor without raising any alarms. There's an item we've been hired to obtain: a certain tiara."

I sucked in a breath.

"Ah, you know the one I mean. Our employer was dismayed when Bennett Marshfield acquired it. In fact, I would say he was quite miffed. That was our primary reason for visiting your lovely attraction." He smiled at me. "You turned out to be bonus."

"If he wanted it so badly, why didn't he outbid Bennett?"

"Our collector friend is a man of considerable means, but he's nowhere in the same league as your boss. While our services are expensive, our price comes in significantly below the auction price Bennett paid. See? This way, everybody wins."

"Except us."

He ignored that. "Once the mansion is clear for the evening—yes, we're aware of your protocols and we know that only a skeleton crew works the night shift—you will take me back to Marshfield. Together we'll pick up the tiara and bring it back here. I have no doubt you know exactly where Bennett keeps it." He looked to me, but I didn't respond. "If I learned anything during my dinner with Bennett it's that he trusts you implicitly and that you have full control over the entire estate." Mark's eyebrows came together briefly. "That man is certainly crazy about you. In his eyes, you can do no wrong."

"I won't steal the tiara for you."

Behind me, Lank chuckled again.

"Really, do I have to spell everything out?" Mark used the mug to gesture toward Bruce. "You refuse, we kill him. You refuse again, we kill you." He held out a supplicating hand then double-gripped the mug again. "Look how easy we've made the decision for you."

As though to emphasize Mark's words, Lank stood next to Bruce and tapped the top of his head with the butt of the gun.

There was no way for me to overpower Mark, no way for me to wrestle the gun away from Lank. I couldn't fight two men alone with my only ally tied tight to a chair.

"Fine," I said, "let's get this over with."

Chapter 26

WHEN THE SUN BEGAN TO GO DOWN OVER the distant mountains, Mark declared it was time to move out. "We'll take your car," he said, accompanying me outside and holding the door open as I took my spot behind the wheel. He kept a tight grip on the keys until he was settled into the passenger seat. "My colleague isn't the only one with a weapon, so don't try anything." He pulled his nylon jacket to the side to reveal a silver revolver tucked into his waistband.

Don't try anything? Was he kidding? My mind was so jumbled with fear I could barely remember to breathe. All I could do was to follow what Mark told me to do and hope an opportunity presented itself.

I pulled out of the driveway and turned the car toward Marshfield. "That's it," he said, "nice and easy. We aren't going to break any speed limits, all right?"

I didn't answer. I just drove.

"What's your real name?" I finally asked.

"Found out about that, did you? I was wondering why you were less than shocked when you discovered me in your kitchen." He seemed to be waiting for me to respond. When I didn't, he shrugged. "It's the same. Mark. Taking on a new identity is always easier when there isn't a new first name to get used to." He leaned over close enough for our shoulders to touch, whispering, "But I'm not going to tell you my real surname. I'm sure you understand."

I stared straight ahead.

"Here's the deal," he said when we'd cleared the main part of town. "You have only until nine-thirty to get us in and out with the tiara."

"What happens then?"

"First of all, you won't have to check in with your guard if we're in and out before ten. Second, as soon as I'm free with treasure in hand, I will text Lank. If nine-thirty arrives and he hasn't heard from me, he'll assume that you've mucked up the works again, the way you've so brilliantly done thus far. At that point, it's bye-bye Bruce. Well before his partner returns home."

"Bruce hasn't done anything to you."

"He's important to you. That makes him important to us."

"I hate you," I said.

"There's a fine line between hate and love . . ." he said, reaching over to brush a strand of hair from my face. "Or haven't you heard?"

We got through the front gate without a problem. Joe, in the booth, waved hello and smiled as we passed. I bit my tongue, remembering having shared that ten o'clock tidbit with Mark the night I drove him back here after our date.

I turned left toward the mansion.

Our date? Dates. Ashamed of myself, and angrier than I'd ever been, I wanted to hit the accelerator and ram the car into the nearest tree. But that would do little to help Bruce.

As though he'd read my mind, Mark said, "My cell phone has a security lock. Even if you overpower me, you can't text Lank. The phone won't let you."

"Seems you thought of everything."

He gave a brittle laugh. "Not everything. Lenore is dead because of you, you know."

Instinctively, I glanced over at him.

He was watching me. "You heard me. The original plan was to take advantage of the film crew being on premises, but you messed that up for us by changing their schedule."

I thought about Lenore. The poor thing. Such a short, sad life. "No," I said, "that wasn't my fault. I'll bet you encouraged her to walk away from the group. You knew she had a problem with those voices in her head, didn't you? That's why you targeted her."

He made a so-so motion. "That was kind of fun. And it's all working out now, isn't it? It would have worked the other night if you hadn't screwed things up by calling the police so quickly."

"Yeah, this is all *my* mistake."

"You really do have spirit, don't you, Grace?" he said, shaking his head. "A lot more than I gave you credit for. You seemed so eager to jump into a romantic relationship. So willing to believe me."

"Just shut up."

"I may have misjudged you," he said. "It doesn't matter now, though. We're going to finally get this done. Tonight."

I was putting pieces together in my head. "Why did you have to kill Lenore? I'm sure she had no idea what was going on. What did she ever do to either of you?"

"She was easy to manipulate—easier even than you proved to be. She dropped into our laps. And what more compelling distraction can there be than murder?"

"Lank shot you on purpose, then. Why?"

"Victims are above reproach."

I didn't understand. Nothing made sense until Mark added, "Even better, victims are irresistible to trusting women. Like you."

The pieces fell into place with a suddenness that took my breath away. "I was always your target?"

"Not bad for a plan cobbled together in a hurry, is it?" he asked.

We were close to the mansion now and I took the drive that led to the underground parking garage. "No," he said. "Park outside up front. Fewer guards that way."

I realized I'd talked too much. I'd chattered about life at Marshfield, never imagining that his eager questions about things as mundane as where I parked each morning would come back to bite me now.

"We'll go in through the administrative entrance." He smiled at me and tapped his temple. "I pay attention."

I parked the car as close as we could to the front doors, hoping one of the guards would wonder what I could be doing here at this time of night, but I knew better. I'd been here this late plenty of times and everyone knew my little car.

Our footsteps crunched the gravel walkway that led to the side entrance, where I swiped my laminated card and got a green light to enter. Poor Terrence. He'd recently overseen the installation of this new security measure and now I was abusing it.

"Hang on," I said once the door closed behind us.

"What are you doing?"

I typed a code into the system. "I have to verify that I got in safely after the door closes," I said. "It resets the alarms."

"You really needed to do that?"

"If you want this tiara, yeah," I said. "If I don't reset the alarms within thirty seconds, security will be down here to find out what's wrong."

I released the alarms and reset them again once we'd passed through doors on the second and third floors. Each time, I felt a little bit better, a little more hopeful. I tried to keep my face averted so Mark wouldn't be able to read my mind, as he seemed so capable of doing.

We made it to the corridor outside my office without encountering a guard. "Why are we here?" Mark asked with suspicion. "I told you not to try anything."

Emboldened by anger, I faced him. "You want this thing? Then follow me and quit asking questions."

He hesitated, but I didn't. I walked past my office and strode with purpose toward the Sword Room at the end of the hall. Outside its ornate doors, I stopped.

"This is where Bennett and I had dinner," he said.

"This is where the tiara is."

"I was this close?"

I didn't answer.

I opened the door to the dark room. "You first," he said.

"Yes, sir, Mr. Brave Man," I said deadpan, as I turned on the lights.

He made that *tsk*ing sound again. "Where does this steel reserve of yours come from?" he asked as I led him over to the cherry wood cabinet. "I was sure you'd be shaking in your shoes."

I ignored him.

"No really, I want to know. You come across so sweet and gentle. Look at you, all tough and sassy."

"Take it," I said, pointing. "Then text your friend."

He tucked his gun into his waistband and used both hand to lift the lid with reverence. As the tiara came into view, his breath caught. "This is better than I'd imagined." He drew the tiara up out of its cradle and held it to the light, mesmerized by the gems' gleam. "Incredible." He smiled broadly, and again all I wanted to do was rip his face open.

"Text," I said. "Now."

He looked at me quizzically.

"You have your prize. Now tell your friend to let Bruce go."

He shook his head. "No . . ." he said slowly. "That's not quite how it works."

He had both hands busy handling the tiara, his gun forgotten in his excitement. I hadn't forgotten, but it was clearly out of reach.

"How are you going to get it out?" I asked. "You plan to wear it on your head?"

"Such a sense of humor. No, my dear, you will carry it for me. And, then, only if you're a good girl, I'll text Lank once we're outside your front gate."

When he grinned, I recognized the deception at once. Like a bright, brass bell had dispelled the fog with its clear clang, everything suddenly became obvious. Why had it taken me so long to be able to read him? Had I been so blinded by his charm?

"You're lying," I said. "You have no intention of letting Bruce go."

He shrugged. "Bruce's fate is out of my hands. Lank gets to decide what happens next with him, just as I get to decide what happens next with you."

"Lank's going to kill him because he can identify both of you. As can I."

I backed away from him and could tell from his expression he thought it was because I was afraid. I was—utterly—but I knew I had to do something and I might not get another chance. I needed to save myself and I needed to find a way to save Bruce, too.

His amused, cocky expression broadened. "Grace, let's not make this difficult. You can't deny you're still attracted to me. I can see it in your face. You can't understand it though, can you? You're repulsed yet drawn. The man, the mask. You want us both. Even now."

"In your dreams."

"Don't deny it. I'm strong, virile, I've bended you to my will. This is what you wanted all along, isn't it? A man to take control. I've done that and you can't resist, can you?"

If I'd wanted to retch before, the feeling was a thousand times stronger now. Mark was here to steal from Bennett, ready to kill one of my best friends, and he believed I found him attractive.

"You make me sick."

"Enough foreplay," he said, tilting his head toward the door. "Come here and take the tiara so I can keep you covered and make sure you don't run off."

"I refuse. You want it so badly, you take it," I said, inching ever closer to the fireplace. "Good luck with that."

"And leave you here so you can call for help the moment I walk out the door? Give me a little more credit than that." He removed his nylon jacket and tied the tiara into it, using the sleeves to make a wide knot. This he slung it over one arm as he drew his gun up again, pointing it at me. "There, you happy? Let's go."

"I'm not going," I said as I backed into the wall next to the fireplace. "And neither are you."

"How do you plan to keep me here?"

I held up my laminated ID card, the one that had allowed us inside. Before he could react—before he could comprehend what was happening—I slid it through the brass fitting on the floor, sending it on its merry way down to the trash. "You need the card and the code to get in. You need one of them to get out. You don't have the card and I'm not giving up the code."

Mark rushed past me, diving to the floor in an attempt to retrieve the placard. He shouted obscenities as he shoved his right arm into the former cigar disposal. He yanked off his gloves and tried again, sweating, positioning himself like a three-legged stool. One hand, still holding the gun, and his two knees formed support, and he dug as far down the chute as he could.

Intent on getting the card back, which I knew was long gone, Mark didn't notice my movements. I backed away, reaching above the fireplace, grabbing the Japanese sword displayed above. Heavier than the ones I'd used in my college fencing classes, it felt like I'd hefted a sledgehammer.

I grabbed the hilt with both hands. With the blade in a high vertical line above me, I stomped down on the hand with the gun as I slammed the hilt onto the back of Mark's head with every ounce of strength I had.

I'd expected him to go down, to be rendered unconscious. Isn't that how it happened in the movies? He yelped, dragging his arm out of the chute as he rolled away and onto his side, the gun skittering between us. Before I knew it, he'd scrambled to his feet, his nylon jacket holding the tiara now hanging from his elbow. In his face I saw a new ferocity and I knew this man was prepared to kill.

He lunged for the gun and I lunged for him. Because the sword was unwieldy I caught him with it broadside against his injured left arm. He recoiled; I'd stung him badly but hadn't accomplished much else. I whacked again. A welt sprang up immediately where I'd hit him in the face, but he didn't let go of the weapon he'd managed to reclaim, and I knew that when he turned to point it at me, he was not going to take time to talk.

I lunged again, determined to take him down, but this wasn't a long and elegant rapier like those I was used to. Wielding it like a club, I batted him across the head, not giving him time to aim before he tried to shoot. As I pulled it back to strike again, I sliced a hot line of red across his cheekbone and he screamed in pain.

As his hand grabbed at his ripped face, the gun tumbled once again to the floor. I kicked it to the side then stood over the weapon like a sentry.

Bent in half, with blood running through fingers that tried in vain to staunch the flow, he stared at me with wild eyes.

"What is wrong with you, woman?"

"I wouldn't worry. You survived a gunshot, after all."

At the word *gun*, he glanced at the weapon between my feet.

"Don't," I said, waving the blade.

"How long do you think you can you keep me at bay?" he asked, breathing hard.

"As long as I need to."

He held one hand up to his cheek, the other out in a plea. "You didn't mean to hurt me. This was an accident," he said. "You don't have the guts to use that against me."

"Are you trying to convince me, or yourself?"

"What are you going to do?" he asked with a furtive glance at the gun. I could see him working out calculations as to how to get to the pistol without getting stabbed. And as he winced with pain and tried hard to stem the blood gushing from his cheek, I knew one thing above all else: He was counting on me watching him and gauging his moves. He was anticipating my reaction. Even now, his scheme was to manipulate me.

Not this time, buddy.

"Speaking of guts," I said, in as calm a tone as I could muster, "did I ever tell you I shot a man?" I'd been reluctant to share the specifics of my involvement with the last murder, but now seemed the best possible time to own up. "Yep," I added brightly. "I forgot to mention that, didn't I? Didn't want to scare you off."

I worried that my sweating palms would cause me to lose my grip, but whoever had created this sword had seen fit to add texture to the hilt. I thanked him now, wherever he was, for the friction required to hold tight.

Speaking with fervor and bravery I didn't actually possess, I continued my manic soliloquy. "He came at me with a knife, can you believe it? Smaller than this, of course. I shot him."

I could tell I'd confused him. Good. Keep him guessing.

"He survived only because my aim was off. It was dark. Not like this." I forced a laugh, and I watched him jerk in surprise at my apparent madness. He started inching toward the door, his eyes beginning to tear. From pain, I hoped. I pretended not to notice, pretended to be caught up in my story while my heart beat like a feral animal caught in my chest. "I hadn't ever taken shooting lessons." I tilted my chin toward the gun without ever taking my eyes off Mark. "I've since rectified that."

That wasn't true, but he didn't know it.

"You ought to know I was a fencing champion in college." Another lie, but what did I have to lose? I shot him a crazed smile. "So which is it going to be? Do you prefer to be stabbed or shot?"

"Grace . . ." He held out his hands and shuffled sideways, closer to the door.

"You've heard the saying about women scorned."

Relief flooded his features. "I understand," he said, "I'm sorry. You know I am." He ran a nervous tongue over his bottom lip. "I never meant to hurt you. Listen," he said, "what I felt for you was real. Grace," this said so softly and with such sincerity that I wanted to run him through with the sword that moment. Instead, I worked up an insipid, hopeful expression and trusted he'd buy it. The man was supremely confident of his allure. "Let me go," he whispered. "I need this." He held up the nylon jacket and I could see the outline where the tiara had settled inside. "Give me a head start, that's all I ask. Please, Grace. For what might have been."

Pretty speech. I swallowed hard, blinking. "On one condition."

I caught the wariness in his glance, suspicious of my agreeing so quickly.

"Promise me," I squeezed a crack into my voice. "Promise you'll let Bruce go. Promise me he'll be safe."

His relief was nearly palpable. "For you, anything." He swallowed, then asked, "The code, Grace?"

I pretended to ponder. "Warren, senior's birth year. Eighteen seventy-one."

He started for the door again, then stopped. "I need my gun."

"No you don't."

"But what if . . ."

"I won't let you hurt anyone else. Go now before I change my mind."

"Give me a half-hour head start, all right? I should be gone by then."

"You promise you'll save Bruce?"

"I promise."

I widened my eyes and nodded.

He hoisted the nylon jacket back up to his shoulder and went to the door, questioning me with his eyes. "No guards in the administrative wing overnight," I whispered. He nodded, looked back over his shoulder, and smiled. "I won't forget this."

It sickened me to return his lovesick smile. "I know."

The minute he reached for the doorknob, I hauled back and smacked him sideways across his head.

This time he went down for good.

Chapter 27

THE SECOND HE CRUMPLED TO THE FLOOR, I rushed to the phone to dial security. Seconds later, sooner than should have been possible, alarms rang out all over Marshfield and I waited for the troops to storm in. I picked up the gun and placed it atop the fireplace mantel, within easy reach. I wanted to stay as well armed and as far away from Mark's prone form as possible. You never knew when the killer would get up again.

I then called Rodriguez, talking so quickly, trying to get him to understand that Bruce needed help, that it took me several seconds and Rodriguez several tries before I realized he was trying to tell *me* something.

"Bruce is fine. He's fine."

"He is?"

"Sit tight. More later." He hung up.

I heard the noise outside the Sword Room as security barged in and took control. I explained what had happened, as Mark began to stir.

Within minutes, he was again facedown on the floor, but

this time his arms were cuffed tightly behind his back, and six tall guards surrounded him, just itching for him to make a move. I was surprised to see Terrence among them. Our head of security wasn't in uniform.

"Why are you here at this time of night?" I asked, pointing. "In workout clothes?"

"No time to change. Rodriguez called when they found your roommate tied up."

"How did they know to go to my house?"

Terrence shook his head. "That I don't know yet. What I do know is that Rodriguez called here immediately and my guys called me. We mounted a rescue operation and were ready to storm in." He glanced down at Mark, who stared away. "Looks like you didn't need us."

"I'm glad you were here," I said, feeling weak in the knees all of a sudden. "And I'm glad Rodriguez got to my house. I was so afraid. Where's Bennett?" I asked.

"I sent a team up there immediately to protect him. Weren't sure if that's where the crown they wanted was stored, or what. He set us straight. We might have been here sooner if I'd known . . ."

"The tiara!" I said. Mark's nylon jacket was still tied around his elbow. I tiptoed around him and crouched next to his face. I couldn't stop myself from saying, "You don't mind, do you, darling?" as I untied the arms of the jacket and pulled the gleaming treasure from its hiding place.

Mark didn't answer. He had a giant bump growing on his head, but the look in his eyes told me he'd heard me just fine.

I stood up and handed the tiara to Terrence. "That's what they were after?" he asked.

"All along. They knew Bennett had acquired it and they set their sights on stealing it for some collector . . ." I rubbed my eyes, thinking about what other treasures this collector might have acquired. "I suppose the police will want to investigate his involvement, too."

Suddenly overcome with weariness, I wanted nothing more than to go home. I knew I needed to talk with Bennett, but right now I believed Bruce needed me more. "Can you tell Bennett I'll be back later?"

"You need a ride?" he asked.

My body and brain had been working in sync for such an extended, pressure-filled period of time that driving myself, alone, would be a thoroughly terrible idea right now. "I'd like that."

FOUR POLICE CARS FORMED A BARRICADE IN front of my house, rendering the entire block impassable. The squads' red and blue lights rippled high through the dark canopy of trees and sliced across my neighbors' windows in madcap repetition. Dozens of nosy onlookers, enticed from their homes by the promise of excitement, formed a bustling perimeter. They stared toward the house, talking among themselves, oblivious to us pulling up behind them.

I opened my door when the guard stopped at the corner.

"My job was to see you home safely," he said.

I got out. "I'm safe. Go back. You're needed at Marshfield."

"But . . ."

"Go back," I said, but I'd already slammed the door and was running into the crowd toward my house. "Excuse me," I said, pushing past neighbors I didn't take time to recognize. "Let me through."

Every light in my home was on, the front door wide open. Even though Rodriguez had assured me Bruce was all right, he'd said nothing about Bootsie. Terror gripped my heart again and I ran like a crazy woman up my front lawn. Uniformed officers policing the outside appeared eager to stop trespassers. They must have recognized me, however, because they allowed me by without a word. I raced through the front door. "Bruce," I called. "Bootsie."

Everyone was in the kitchen. I heard Scott call, "In here."

I'd made it through the parlor, heading into the dining room, when Rodriguez stepped out to meet me.

"What happened?" I asked.

"Why don't you sit down?"

"Bootsie? Where is she?"

"Your cat?" Rodriguez blinked slowly. "Oh, yes. She got out."

Oh, please, no.

"She's fine," he said quickly when he saw my expression, but I didn't calm down until Bruce came through the kitchen doorway a second later with the little black-and-white bundle sleeping in his arms. He edged around Rodriguez's wide frame and handed her to me. "She's had a big night."

"So have you," I said to Bruce as Bootsie opened her eyes long enough to see who was holding her. "Thank heavens," I said with relief. "How did you—"

"Your cat got out," Rodriguez said again, and this time I waited for him to continue. "Flynn was checking to see if your locks had gotten fixed yet and saw the kitten outside the back door. He picked her up to bring her in and walked in on the crime scene in progress."

Behind him, Bruce nodded. "Couldn't have come at a better time. Lank was about to have me drive who-knows-where when Flynn barged in. It was like a perfectly scripted TV show with the bad guy who never saw it coming. Flynn dropped Bootsie, then managed to take the guy down in three seconds flat."

I held a hand to my head. "That's probably the first time I'm glad Flynn acted first and asked questions later."

Rodriguez gave a low chuckle. "Me, too."

"Is he here?"

"He's getting ready to take Lank, or whatever this guy's name is, down to the station to book him. I should get down there, too, since we have your friend Mark to process as soon as Terrence brings him in."

"I'm sure he's there now."

Rodriguez nodded then pointed out front. "I'll get my team out of your way so you can relax."

"Relax?" I asked.

Rodriguez patted me on the shoulder. "You did good, kid. Again."

I finally made it into the kitchen, in time to see Flynn making his way out the back door, accompanied by two uniformed officers who walked a handcuffed Lank between them. I was thrilled not to have to face that man's evil face again, but I had something I had to do. "Flynn, wait."

He turned and instructed his guys to hold up on the driveway. As always, the young detective's tone was brusque with me. "What do you need?"

"Thank you," I said simply. "You saved Bruce, you saved Bootsie."

Flynn grimaced. "Got lucky," he said.

"Not luck. You saved them and I won't forget that. If it weren't for you, this night could have had a terrible ending." Still cradling Bootsie with my left arm, I touched his hand. "Thank you, Flynn."

"Ethan." He worked his jaw. "I have a first name, you know."

"Thank you, Ethan."

He reached over and scratched Bootsie behind the ears. "I'm glad everyone is okay." With that, he turned and rejoined the group, taking Lank out to one of the waiting squads.

Scott had provided coffee and soft drinks for everyone and now started to clean up. "Well, wasn't this a party?" he said when he, Bruce, and I were alone.

Suddenly remembering something, I made a beeline for the sink. "There you are," I said, dragging my souvenir

Boston mug from the bottom of the pile. Scott looked puzzled, but when I glanced over to Bruce, he nodded. I knew that I would forever picture Mark calmly drinking from it at my kitchen table while Bruce's and Bootsie's lives hung in the balance.

I marched over to the wastebasket and threw the mug in. "Good riddance to bad rubbish," I said.

Bruce applauded.

The house was ours again, the street dark and quiet, with only the murmurs of neighbors' conversations and sounds of them shuffling to their own homes keeping us company.

Bruce closed the front door. "Are you okay?" he asked.

"Yeah," I said, and explained what had happened after Mark and I had left the house. As I talked, I noticed that the pinpricks of blood around Bruce's mouth had worsened while I'd been gone. I pointed. "Does it hurt?"

"Not as bad as being dead would have. Thank goodness Flynn was on the ball."

Scott was looking from me to Bruce and back to me again, his eyes filling with tears. "I could have lost you both tonight."

I didn't want to think about that. I pulled Bootsie close to my face and nuzzled her neck. "We're here and we're safe. That's all that really matters."

OVER BRUCE'S AND SCOTT'S VOCIFEROUS OB-jections, I returned to Marshfield the next morning. I knew Bennett would want to talk with me. Not only that, I needed to present a calm, confident front for all Marshfield employees. I needed to appear strong if I planned to continue guiding them in the future. We'd been duped—all of us—and I'd been the worst offender. If we were to move forward, we needed to learn from this experience, to work together to ensure nothing like this ever happened again.

"Hi, Frances," I said as I walked in.

She'd been sitting behind her desk. Wordlessly, she leapt to her feet, flung her glasses from their perch on her nose, and let them hang from her neck as she pierced me with a glare. "What now?"

"You heard?"

"Everyone heard. Why didn't you call me?"

"Last night, you mean?"

She jammed her fists into her wide waist and waggled her head. "Yes, I mean last night."

I hadn't thought to call her, but that didn't seem to be the best answer right now. "I had to give a statement. Walk the police through every step. Multiple times. It was late by the time we finished."

By the way her eyes narrowed, I knew she didn't buy it. "The Mister wants to see you."

"That's my first order of business today."

"Good. He's waiting in your office."

I pointed. "Now?"

She nodded with vigor. "And if you think I'm riled because you didn't call me last night, just wait until you deal with the Mister."

He must have heard us talking because he appeared in the doorway seconds later. "Gracie," he said, opening his arms.

I stepped into them, allowing myself to be comforted by this man who, no matter what any test might say, was family to me. "Oh, Bennett," I said into his chest as he hugged me tight. "I'm so sorry. It's all my fault."

He grasped me by both shoulders and pushed me to arm's length, his face creased with both worry and relief. "Your fault? No, he fooled all of us. *They* did. There was no way to anticipate any of this."

I closed my eyes, knowing Bennett sought to console, but knowing that it had been I who had messed up so terrifically. "I was too eager to believe him," I said. "I fell for every word."

He shook me gently, making me open my eyes again. "As did I. But you had the will to fight him and look at the result. You're stronger now, aren't you?"

That question had plagued me all through a night of restless sleep, but I'd come to believe that I *would* be stronger now. Although he hadn't sought to do it, Mark had given me a gift. It was one I wasn't happy to accept, but one I could never return. Not if I lived to be a hundred.

From this day forward, I knew I'd be more cynical, more jaded. I'd had blinders on, failing to catch his manipulation because he'd cloaked it in kindness and warmth. Never again. I'd believed him to be strong, compassionate, and honest. All that baloney about never lying. Yes, I was tougher now, but I was a little less optimistic, too.

"I am stronger," I said.

Bennett held me tight again. "I am so proud of you."

Frances cleared her throat. "Some of us have jobs to do around here," she said when we broke apart and looked over. Making shoo-shoo actions with her hands, she said, "You know we'll have our hands full trying to hold off the reporters. No time for this emotional stuff. Everybody back to work."

"Yes, Frances," I said, grinning at Bennett.

Frances rolled her eyes and blew raspberries as she returned to her seat. The phone rang and we waited while she answered it. I had to give Frances credit. Her one-word responses didn't let on to the caller's identity even one little bit. "Yes, I'll tell her," she said finally and hung up.

"Good news," she said to both of us, although you couldn't read it from her expression. "They were able to recover all the items stolen from Marshfield, including the golden horn and the picture frame."

I took a step toward her desk. "Was the photo of Bennett still in it?"

She nodded. "Yes, indeedy. All items will be returned once the police are finished with them."

"That is excellent news," I said, feeling a lightness of being stir within me again. "I'm beyond happy." I turned to Bennett. "You know what's best of all? It wasn't Hillary who took anything."

"With the way she treats you, I'm surprised to hear you defending her," he said.

"I may not be particularly fond of Hillary," I said, "but I didn't want to see her falsely accused."

Frances snorted as the door to her office opened. She said, "Speak of the devil."

"Nice to see you, too," Hillary said to my assistant, belatedly noticing Bennett and me in the room. "Oh, hello. I was looking for you, Papa Bennett." Hillary was wearing blue jeans and a casual shirt. That in itself was unusual, but the accessory that completed her ensemble, a rolling suitcase, was what caught my attention most.

Bennett spotted it, too. I watched an expression of surprise cross his features. "Let me guess. Now that the filming is complete, you're leaving us?"

"Even better," she said with gusto. She turned to me. "I told you that the man I met with—the one with the bottle of wine—had nothing to do with the murders, didn't I?"

"You did."

"See! I wouldn't lie to you."

That was a lie right there, but I didn't call her out.

She jabbered on. "You wanted to know who he was. Well, now I can tell you."

"A new boyfriend?" Frances asked.

Hillary shot her a withering look. "No . . ." she said stringing the word out. "Frederick is my new business partner." Hillary let go of her suitcase handle long enough to hold her hands out in triumph. "I'm an interior designer," she said with a radiant smile. "Frederick is putting up the money and I'm putting up the talent." She winked at me. "The wine was one of the gifts I gave him to grease the wheels. And it worked!"

I tried to wrap my head around what she was saying, but the only question I could come up with was, "Why didn't you tell us this earlier?"

"It was no one's business but my own."

"Do you have any idea how much police manpower it took to look for this guy? You should have said something. You cost the taxpayers of Emberstowne."

She gave a "who cares?" shrug. "Well then, I guess I cost myself."

My ebullience crashed and I thought I heard Bennett growl. "What do you mean?"

"You know that house a couple of doors away from yours that just got sold?" she asked me.

My stomach turned to stone. "No . . ."

"Turns out I couldn't afford my place near the coast, after all. But I can afford to live here. Especially now that I have a real job." She tapped a happy finger on my arm. "You and I are going to be neighbors," she said. "Can you believe it?"

Bennett said nothing.

Frances said nothing.

"I can't believe it," I croaked.

"I have to run. Frederick is waiting. We're looking at locations for our offices and I'm moving into my new home. See you all later."

The door closed behind her and we three stared at one another, utterly dumbfounded.

Bennett finally broke the silence. "Gracie, do remember that acquisition trip I mentioned last week?"

I nodded.

"What do you say to taking that trip sooner, rather than later?"

Frances wagged a thick finger at us. "If you think I'm going to stay back here and face all the drama"—she pointed to the door where Hillary had exited—"that's about to erupt around here, you two are asking a lot." She looked from Bennett to me, back to him, then picked up the phone. "Fine," she said, "which travel agent do you want to use?"

"Whoever you think best, Frances." He turned to me. "What do you say, Gracie?"

I closed my eyes for a moment thinking about Mark's cruelty, Jack's abrupt resignation, and Hillary's unexpected news. Life had been crazy around here, and it wasn't going to get better anytime soon.

I opened my eyes. "How soon can we leave?"